MILES APART

WILLOW ASTER

To the friendships that stand the test of time and get stronger through every adversity: you are worth it.

Miles Apart
formerly titled *5,331 Miles*, same book
Copyright © 2019 by Willow Aster

ISBN-13: 978-1-7373619-4-7

All rights reserved.

Without limiting the rights under copyright reserved above, no part of this publication may be reproduced, stored in or introduced into a retrieval system, or transmitted, in any form, or by any means (electronic, mechanical, photocopying, recording, or otherwise) without the prior written permission of both the copyright owner and the above publisher of this book.
This is a work of fiction. Names, characters, places, brands, media, and incidents are either the product of the author's imagination or are used fictitiously. The author acknowledges the trade-marked status and trademark owners of various products, bands, and/or restaurants referenced in this work of fiction, which have been used without permission. The publication/use of these trade-marks is not authorized, associated with, or sponsored by the trademark owners.

License Notes
This ebook is licensed for your personal enjoyment only. This ebook may not be re-sold or given away to other people. If you would like to share this book with another person, please purchase an additional copy for each recipient. If you're reading this book and did not purchase it, or it was not purchased for your use only, then please return to your favorite ebook retailer and purchase your own copy. Thank you for respecting the hard work of this author.

1

PRESENT

END OF MAY **2019**

If you could crawl out of the pages and help me manage not to embarrass myself this weekend, I would greatly appreciate it. I've done enough of that for a lifetime.
My sincerest appreciation, Mira

I'VE LOVED Jaxson Marshall most of my life. Before you assume I'm exaggerating, just listen. Our mums are best friends. There are pictures of Jaxson and me in the tub together when we're like, one and two. The story goes (and goes and goes—I swear it's been told every time our families are together) that we were happily playing in there until *someone* pooped in the tub. Okay, it was me. I know, so embarrassing. But it gets worse.

When I was in year 8 and Jaxson was in year 9, his family moved from England to California. His mum and mine couldn't stand being apart and we followed six months later.

We were best friends too, until he moved to the States. That's when everything got weird. There have been snapshots of "us" over the years, but every time we've started to get close again, something happens to ruin it.

He was my first kiss...I'll have to get to that later. It's hard for me to think about it without dying a little more inside. He became the slut of high school, while I was the one hiding behind my glasses, book, and a donut. It was just as pitiful as it sounds.

After an extremely humiliating experience at prom, in which I came to the conclusion that I will never love, or even *like*, Jaxson again, I've tried to disappear whenever he comes home from school. At first it didn't work, but I've managed not to see him for a few years now.

But now he's graduated from Berklee in Boston and is apparently home for good.

And my mum is forcing me to see him...tonight, at his welcome home party.

The old me would have hidden and said, "I hate my life!" but the new me is ready to show Jaxson what he's been missing. Not that I *want* him or anything. Just...aw, bloody hell, I hate my life.

———

MY MUM STANDS in the doorway, watching me finish my makeup. "You look so pretty, babe."

"I'm thinking about changing into jeans..."

"No! Your dress is perfect for the beach. Please don't change—your legs go on for miles. Jaxson won't know what hit him."

"I'm not dressing for Jaxson, Mum." I roll my eyes.

Okay, maybe I'm kinda dressing for Jaxson. But, not in *that* way. I just want to look my best. That's all.

"I know. Just...don't forget a light jacket," she says.

I grin. She says that every single time I go out the door. "You ready? Dave is waiting on us."

"Oh, I thought I told you—Chad's picking me up." I turn to look at her and see the disappointment on her face.

Until I am pronounced someone else's wife, she will be plotting for me to end up with Jaxson. My mum and I used to plot together, and she can't understand why I ever stopped. I shake my head. I have to stop thinking about all that. Jaxson does not have any control over me anymore.

"You're bringing Chad?" Her face scrunches up. "This seems like a—I don't know—more of a family thing, I guess..."

"Chad's my boyfriend, Mum. I wish you'd at least *try* to like him."

"He's fine, he's just not..."

"Don't say it," I warn her.

"I only wish things were different with you and Jaxson," she says. "It's such a shame. The two of you were..." Her eyes well up with tears and I panic. If she cries, I'll cry.

"Please don't cry. I just finished. Look," I point to my eyes, "perfect smokey eye, please don't let me mess it up." I pat her on the shoulder and walk to the closet to get a light jacket. I hold it up for her and she smiles. And sniffles.

I kiss her cheek. "You better go, Dave's waiting."

She sighs. "Okay, but don't be too late. Anne's bringing the food out right away. You won't want to miss the shrimp," she says on her way out the door.

I USED to have an issue with food. As in, I ate it whenever I felt sad, mad, depressed, lonely, or embarrassed. So, in other words, all the time. That pretty much describes my high school experience.

My dad left not long after we got to California, so with him leaving and the huge culture shock, I was a mess. Thankfully, I had a late growth spurt at sixteen and shot up six inches. At 5'1" there hadn't been much room for the tons of junk food I ingested. Those extra six inches helped a *lot*. But it wasn't until I met my best friend and roomie at UCSD, Maddie, that I started trying to get fit. She's a yoga instructor and hopelessly optimistic. It's hard to be sad around her. I've forced myself to exercise until I finally like it. I try to go to the healthy stuff when I'm down, instead of Reese's peanut butter cups or salt & vinegar potato chips. I still indulge *plenty*, but I'm way more balanced than I used to be.

When my stomach feels the way it does tonight, though, all nervous and jumpy and nauseated, the last thing I want to think about is shrimp.

The doorbell rings and Chad is smiling when I open the door. He whistles when he sees me, taking my hand and twirling me around to see every angle.

"You look hot."

He's a man of few words, but he looks so good, it doesn't matter. I take in his sun-kissed face and biceps and thank God for surfers. He fits the profile perfectly.

"You do too." I step outside and walk to his Jeep.

Is it okay to admit that I really hate his Jeep? It's falling apart. Everyone and their brother can hear us coming. He keeps it all open, so my hair never stands a chance. I try to hold as much of it down as I can, but my hair is long and thick, so it still flies everywhere.

"Who's this party for again?" he yells.

"Jaxson. We grew up together." I look out the window and swipe my sweaty palms on the seats. My hands pick up some crumbs, so I spend the rest of the ride trying to get that off.

I wish I'd gone with my mum and Dave.

When we finally stop in front of Jaxson's house, I hop out and stand in front of a tree (that Jaxson and I used to always climb) and try to salvage my hair.

Chad puts his arm around my waist and nuzzles into my neck. Mmm, never mind, I'm glad I rode with Chad.

"How long are we staying?" he whispers in my ear and then kisses back down my neck.

I shiver. "Not long," I promise.

"Good." He pulls me against him and puts his hands on my bum. I'm about to reach back to pull them up before someone sees us, when I hear my name. Or, rather, the name *he* calls me.

"Bells?"

I jump back from Chad and turn around. Jaxson is leaning against the gate, arms folded, and looking me up and down. And back up. And down again. You get the point. It's a long pause and awkward. I can't tell if he's pleased with what he sees or angry with me.

"Hi," I say quietly.

He stands tall. "You gonna feel each other up out here all night or you comin' to my party, *Mirabelle*?"

My heart drops out and I'm pretty sure I go red.

He walks until he's standing right in front of me.

"Well, when you put it that way, we might be out here a while, *Jaxson*," I say, standing as tall as I can. I've never been so glad to be wearing three-inch heels. It annoys me that I still have to look up a bit.

At first he just stares at me, jaw ticking. And then he wraps me up in a huge bear hug.

"I've been waiting—I heard you were coming." He leans back and pushes my hair off one shoulder. "I was afraid you'd talk yourself out of coming in..."

I forget how well he knows me.

"You look *so* beautiful," he whispers.

My heart skips a few beats ahead and I step back.

"This is my boyfriend, Chad." I move my hands back and forth. "Jaxson, Chad. Chad, Jaxson."

Jaxson nods and stretches out his hand. "Hey, man." They do a guy shake.

"Hey," Chad says.

This might be the first time I've wished for Chad to be... talkative. Or something just...*more*. Jaxson stands an inch or two taller than Chad, but besides their similar height, they couldn't look more different from each other. Jaxson has curly, dark hair with green eyes and a constant smile. Chad has straight, blond hair with brown eyes and it takes a lot to make him smile.

Jaxson holds his hand out to me. "You don't mind if I walk her in, do you, man?" He threads his fingers through mine and I think my ovaries just melted. "I haven't seen her in so long."

Chad shrugs. "Sure."

I'm so gonna let him have it later.

Jaxson holds my hand up to his chest and smiles down at me. "Boyfriend, huh?"

I glare at him and try to take my hand away, but he grips it tighter.

"I've got you now, Bells, you're not escaping this time." He laughs his charming, perfect laugh, and I grit my teeth.

We walk along the sand to the back of the house, tiki

lamps leading the way. We go down a few steps and then reach the gorgeous beachfront. Their backyard has always been my favorite view. The party is underway.

"Quite the party," I tell him.

"You know my mum. She goes all out," he groans.

It feels as if everyone sees us at once and freezes. Then my mum and Anne rush toward us, excited, but trying not to act *too* excited so they don't jinx it. Anne is just as guilty as my mum in their "Mira & Jaxson forever" fantasies. They've plotted our wedding since their pregnancies, when they found out what they were having.

"Oh, you look gorgeous, Mira. Doesn't she look absolutely gorgeous, Jaxson?" Anne never takes her eyes off me.

"Her boyfriend and I have both told her how gorgeous she is, in our own way," Jaxson says. He then has the nerve to kiss the back of my hand.

I want to pop the smirk off his face.

Anne's smile widens and then drops a little when she sees Chad. She quickly props the smile back on. "Hi, you must be Chad. Vanessa was just telling me all about you." She looks at my mum and back to Chad. "Why don't you come with me and I'll introduce you to everyone?"

I know what she's up to and I'm sick of it. I let go of Jaxson's hand and grab Chad's arm. "That's okay, I'll make sure he gets around."

I walk a few feet away with Chad and hear Jaxson behind me.

"I'm sure he already does," he mutters.

I turn around so fast, my hair flies into my eyes. I toss it back and walk toward him, so close that only he can hear.

"Just because *you've* slept with the entire state of California by now does not mean my *boyfriend* has. Take your opinions and shove them up your ass."

"That's *arse* to you, Bells!" He laughs his stupid adorable laugh.

I walk without even thinking about where I'm going and end up in front of Chad's Jeep. I don't hate it so much at the moment.

"Mira? We're leaving?" Chad looks confused.

"Yes, please." I get in, shut the door, and try to figure out how to avoid seeing Jaxson the rest of the summer.

2

PAST
SEPT 23, 2008

MIRA, **10**

I think it's safe to write my wish here. You won't tell anyone, right? My grandma sent a birthday box and I opened it last night. I've been wanting a journal just like this one. Some days I think all my thoughts are going to burst out of my head and I will give away the only secret that my best friend, Juxson, doesn't already know.
I will write it as much as I want in here: I love him. I love him. I love him.
Like, love him, love him. I love Jaxson.

MY CHOCOLATE CAKE had ten flickering candles. I looked around the table, laughing at all my favorite people singing, "Happy Birthday."

Jaxson sang the loudest.

"Make a wish, Bells!" he yelled. He stood on my left

side, ready to help me blow out the candles if I didn't hurry up already.

"Done," I said, blowing all the candles out.

Wishes. I wished that Jaxson and I would stay best friends forever and that we'd get married and have three babies. Two girls, one boy. And even though I was going over the maximum limit on wishes, I wished he'd kiss me before I turned twelve. That seemed like enough time to get ready. I'd probably need to practice on a pillow or something lots before then.

Jaxson's sister, Gemma, hugged me. Sometimes she was too cool for Jaxson and me, but tonight she was being sweet.

"Hurry, I want you to open our present," she said.

"What is it?" I looked at her and then Jaxson.

He wouldn't look at me—he knew I'd get it out of him. He was terrible with surprises.

Gemma snorted. "Oh Jaxson, you're all mouth and no trousers." She jabbed me in the arm. "He's the one who bought your present. You should have heard him goin' on about it."

Jaxson turned bright red. "I know what she likes!"

I couldn't wait after all this. "Can I open it, please?"

"Jaxson, go get it." She leaned over and whispered, "He even wrapped it himself."

Jaxson's embarrassment surprised me, but I was too excited to see the gift to worry about it. I stuffed the rest of the cake into my mouth just as Jaxson got back. First he told me to close my eyes and hold out my hand. Little balls dropped into my hand. They smelled so good I knew right away what they were.

"Maltesers!" I didn't even open my eyes; I just popped them in my mouth and crunched. My very most favorite candy. He did know what I liked.

Then he put a box in my hand and told me to open my eyes. I looked at him before I looked at the present. He shifted from foot to foot. Shy.

"Go on, open it," he said softly.

It was a small box wrapped in orange paper, our favorite color.

"Pretty," I whispered.

Inside the box was a silver necklace with a heart.

"Jaxson, I love it!" I said in shock.

"It's from Gemma too," he said. "But I knew you liked hearts a lot, because you're always drawing them on everything." He finally looked at me and smiled.

"Thank you, Jaxson." I stood up and gave him a hug, nearly knocking him over. He was used to my powerful hugs and tolerated them.

He gave my back a few pats and stepped away, still red.

"Thanks, Gemma," I said.

I went in for a hug, but she laughed. "Save the hugs for Jaxson," she said. "I've already handed out my hug for the day. Happy Birthday, kid."

I stuck my tongue out at her and made her help me with the necklace.

As soon as the necklace was on, Jaxson took my hand and dragged me outside.

"I have one more present for you." We were almost to the rose garden and he pulled me behind a tree and pointed to the ground.

A little box sat in a dug-up hole.

"Is that our collection box?" I bent down to pick up the box.

"Yes, I thought we better move it someplace safer. And no one will mess with it here, right?"

"Good idea, Jaxson."

We'd been working on this box for months. It had our favorite rocks, a few books, candy, pictures of our favorite football players, and a CD of our favorite songs. We'd decided to only open it every couple of years to add new favorite things.

He gave me a playful nudge and pulled something out of his pocket.

"I just have to add this one thing," he said. He held up a folded piece of paper.

"I want to see!" I held out my hand.

He held the paper just out of my reach as I tried to grab it. "I don't know. I think I'd like you to read it later. Much later. Like, when we're fourteen and fifteen or something…"

"C'mon, let me read it! It's my birthday." I fluttered my eyelashes and he laughed.

"Stop it. Here, read it." He gave me the paper and stuck his hands in his pockets, looking shy again.

I wasn't used to him being the timid one.

"You're being so weird today." I shook my head at him.

"I should have just put it in the box before I showed you. But now, I can't have you beggin' me forever." He rolled his eyes.

I flicked his arm and he laughed, rubbing his arm.

"I have to see it if it's in *our* box!"

I unfolded the paper and it was a list in Jaxson's writing.

The Life List for Jaxson & Bells

1) Be together forever.
2) Go to America and eat peanut butter every day.
3) Go to the top of the Eiffel Tower.

4) And the Empire State Building.
5) Make enough money to eat out all the time.
(Unless Bells learns to cook.)
6) Read every single book at the library. (Bells)
7) Go swimming with dolphins.
8) Visit all the zoos in the world.
9) Always have a dog.
10) Live on the beach.
11)

I read it a few times, nodding as I thought about each one. Finally I looked at him. "You need to read the books with me."

"We'll see," he teased.

"What was number eleven going to be?"

"I-it was, uh, about kids."

"What kids?"

"Um, our kids?" he said.

"Oh. *Our* kids?" I smoothed out the paper and tried to see if anything was written in that he'd erased. "You mean, yours and mine?"

"Yeah."

"That we have together."

He sighed. "Yes, Bells. See why I didn't want you to read it yet?"

"Oh. Okay." I nodded again. And couldn't stop smiling. "Just making sure. We should write that in then—got a pen?"

He reached in his pocket and pulled out a pencil. "Just this."

He handed the pencil to me, but I gave it back to him. "It should be in your writing, since you made the list."

He took the pencil back and the paper and leaned against the tree to write: *Have kids.* (*At least two.*)

When he was done, he looked at me and lifted an eyebrow. "Is that good?"

"Two's good. Three's better."

He nodded, erased the two, and added a three.

"So...we're doing *all* of these things together?" I just had to make sure I was *fully* understanding what he meant with this very beautiful and important document.

"Yeah!" He pointed to number one. "See? It says right there."

I had to press my lips together to keep the grin from cracking my chapped lips.

"I like it," I said.

"Good. Now, let's sign it and bury it."

We both signed our names, and he put the list in the box and locked it. We both spread the dirt over the box and patted it until there was no sign that anything was there.

He held up his pinky finger and I latched mine around it.

"Okay, it's official," he said.

Best day of my life.

3

PRESENT

I never knew I was a violent person until tonight. Is it okay to be both proud and horrified? You don't have to answer that, Diary, but I think it's fair to say I'm a disaster.
Yours truly, Mira Hart

WHEN WE GET to the house, Chad follows me to the door and steps inside. I turn around and put a hand on his chest, wanting to push him right back out the door. He doesn't get the hint. He walks me into the wall and kisses me. I dodge under his arms and put my hands on my hips.

"I'm not feeling it tonight, Chad. Sorry. I'm...just not."

"We have the house to ourselves!" He glares at me.

"I don't care! I didn't leave the party to come have sex in my mum's house!" I lean against the back of the couch, suddenly exhausted.

"Why did we leave then? We haven't been together in weeks, and the last time was trying to be quick before

Maddie got back to the dorm. What's going on, Mira?" he asks.

I look out the window as images of Jaxson float through my mind. Us running through the woods as kids. Dreaming up new adventures every day. The smile he'd get when I tried to sing and sounded so terrible. The way he took care of me every time I was sick, even more than my mum did.

The last few years I've only been able to think about the negative. The horrible way things turned upside down with us.

But tonight...seeing him again...I can't seem to stop thinking about all the good. There was so much good.

I shake my head and try to clear Jaxson out. I can't afford to get sentimental now. He wrecked me, and there is no way I'm going to allow him to do it again.

"It's nothing big. I'm tired. Not feeling too well. Let's talk tomorrow, okay?"

Chad walks over and puts his arms around me.

"Okay. But I want to spend time with you this summer. I'm tired of the long-distance thing."

I roll my eyes. "I've been twenty minutes away, Chad. Hardly qualifies as long distance."

"You know what I mean. You're finally home for the summer. I'm tired of missing you when you're not right here." He puts his hands on my bum and pulls me in tighter. "I don't want to have to miss you when you *are* here too."

I think this is the most Chad has ever said in one conversation.

"I hear you—we've been busy with work and school. But it's going to be a great summer," I tell him.

And I try to really mean it.

CHAD IS GONE FIVE MINUTES, tops, when my phone starts blowing up. Unknown number.

DID **you really have to leave?**

I've wanted to see you for so long. A few minutes wasn't enough.

You took my breath away, Bells.

Remember that time we nearly set my mum's kitchen on fire baking cookies? The way my heart pounded that day…that's how it felt tonight when I saw you.

Bells?

Me: Jaxson?

Yep, it's me.

Me: Lose my number.

C'mon. How long can this go on?

SOMETHING TAPS MY WINDOW. It happens again. And again. No way.

I look out and Jaxson is in the tree outside my window. He gives a cheeky grin when he sees me.

I groan and open the window. "You've got to be kidding me."

"Let me in," he says.

"No."

He looks over his shoulder. "I'd forgotten what a view you have up here." He lifts an eyebrow. "I can stay out here all night, you know."

I stand back and hold out my hand, giving him permission to climb inside. I know he's stubborn enough to stay out there all night and bug me. It wouldn't be the first time.

Once he stumbles inside, he looks me over and lifts both eyebrows. "This outfit is even better."

I suddenly feel self-conscious in my tank and short shorts. I try to pull the shorts down a little, but it's hopeless.

His green eyes are all lit up, making it hard to look away. His dimple is out in full force, and I think for probably the zillionth time in my life that Jaxson is the most gorgeous guy I've ever seen.

I force myself to stop staring at him and sit on my bed. Determined to not let him get to me, I lean against the headboard and pick up a book. He sits beside me and puts his chin on my shoulder. I jump up and he falls over.

"Why now, Jaxson? You're acting as if no time has passed at all! You don't get to march in here and act like... like everything is just as it was!" I'm pacing and waving my arms around like a crazy person. "It isn't. We're not friends anymore. You don't know me anymore. I don't know you. Our friendship," I point back and forth between us, "was a very long time ago and it's over now. Nothing is the same, Jaxson. Nothing." My voice warbles at the end and I look at the ceiling, willing my eyes to stop watering.

He stands up and puts his hand on my arm, stopping me in my tracks. "Mirabelle," he says softly, "it's still you and me and it always will be. You can't just forget all that we mean to one another."

"You did," I whisper.

"Never. I *never* forgot, I promise you that."

He pulls me closer, brushing his fingers against my shoulder. I shiver and then get embarrassed that he's able to see how much he affects me. His eyes are locked on mine, pulling me in. His hands clutch either side of my face and he moves closer. My eyes shut just as his lips touch mine.

For a minute, I lose myself in him. He groans and deepens the kiss. I grab his hair and kiss him the way I've dreamed of kissing him for so long. It feels even better than I remembered. His soft lips and tongue make my heart fall into my feet. I haven't kissed him like this since…

———

The brakes screech for me. I pull away and punch him in the face.

4

PRESENT

Finally something in my life worth writing about: I'm going to be famous.
Sincerely, THE Blue-Eyed Shadow

JAXSON PULLS AWAY, holding his nose. "What the bloody hell?" he yells. He's nearly lost all of his accent, but when he says that, he almost sounds like we used to. Blood gushes out of his nose and onto the floor. "I think you broke my nose."

"You're fine. It's just a little blood." I grab a towel from the bathroom and hold it up to his nose. "You had it coming."

I scowl at him while putting pressure on the towel and then nearly bite a hole in my lip. When it seems the bleeding is letting up, I sit back down on the bed.

"I'm sorry I hit you, okay?" I mumble. "I shouldn't have done that. You just...you need to leave." I glance at him and then walk to the window. "I've changed, Jaxson. I'm not the little gullible fool I was growing up. I'm not the girl you can just use whenever someone else isn't available."

I feel his hand on my back and close my eyes. Every time he touches me, my skin jumps to attention. His breath is hot against my neck.

"I know I've made mistakes, Bells," he leans close and whispers in my ear, "but you were never one of them. Every moment we were together, I knew I was right where I was supposed to be. It's all the time apart that has been hell." He tugs on my arm and gently turns me around. "I've changed too. I know I messed up. Please let me back in. Give me another chance. We made promises to each other —remember?"

He lifts my chin and tries to get me to look at him, but I don't.

"You are the best friend I've ever had, Mirabelle. Ever. I know a lot of time has passed, but...my heart is still yours. We have things to do." He laughs. "Come on, look at me!"

I finally do and he smiles the cheesiest grin and shakes my shoulders. "We have a list we still need to check off! And you're not getting out of it." He quickly kisses my cheek and climbs out the window before I can even digest what just happened.

I watch him jump out of the tree once he gets low enough. I put my elbows on the windowsill and lean out. "I don't know when you think you gave your heart to me, Jaxson. I must have missed that."

He looks up and puts his hands on his hips. "Looks like I'm going to have to remind you that you love me."

"That was never in question," I mutter under my breath. Thankfully, he doesn't hear. What I say loud enough for him to hear is: "Forget the list. There's no way I'm having your babies."

He shrugs. "I'm up for the challenge. Tell Channing to watch his back."

"It's Chad, and you know it."

"Whatever."

I slam my window down before either of us can say another word. And then I pace.

I've never doubted that Jaxson probably regretted not having a friend like me anymore, but I thought the "Will Jaxson and Mira be a couple" question had been put to rest long ago. We shut that door, and I can't believe he'd try to reopen it.

———

OVER THE NEXT FEW DAYS, I hide out in my room. I blame exhaustion when my mum tries to get me out of the house. I tell Chad I need to spend time with my mum. And I try to pretend Jaxson doesn't exist.

He texts for three days and I ignore every single one. The last text is a picture of us photoshopped, swimming with dolphins. It makes me laugh, but I quickly get a little twinge in my gut. I stare at Jaxson's face in the picture for the longest time and wonder if it will ever stop hurting to look at him.

———

MADDIE DRIVES over from Santa Barbara for the weekend. We catch up quickly, talking about everything and nothing. My mum comes in while we're getting dressed to go out.

"Looks like it took Maddie coming to get you out of the house," Mum says with a smirk.

I bite my tongue. I just don't want to talk with her about Jaxson and that's all she wants to talk about. Later, Maddie and I meet up with Chad and his friends, Chance and Bobby, at Beaumont's. It's one of our favorite places—good food, live music. As we're looking at the dessert menu, the band comes out and starts tuning their instruments. I hear it in the background but don't pay attention until they start playing.

"Who is this?" Maddie asks. "They're amazing!"

"I love that guy's voice," I say and turn around to see who it is.

My breath catches in my throat. Jaxson is standing in front of a band, singing his heart out. I've heard him sing before, but never like this. The other guys in the band are singing now too, but Jaxson is the only one I see.

Chad mutters something, but I can't even pretend to be interested. In fact, when the guys try to get us to leave and go to a movie, I tell them to all go without me. Maddie holds onto my arm.

"I wanna stay with Mira," she says. "Maybe we can catch up with you guys later."

Chad glares at me before stalking off.

"Somebody's not happy." Maddie laughs. "Are you and Chad fighting?"

I shrug. "We haven't been. He's annoying me right now though," I admit. I lean over and yell in her ear, since the music is getting louder. "That guy singing ... remember me telling you about Jaxson?"

She nods.

"That's him."

Her mouth drops and she looks between Jaxson and me with huge eyes.

"No wonder Chad is annoying you." She lifts an eyebrow. And then she mouths: *"Oh my god!"*

I roll my eyes. "No. I know. I mean, I don't know. I-I just can't let him see me here, but I want to stay and listen. It's been so long since I've heard him and he never sounded quite like this. He's been texting me nonstop since his party the other night, and I—"

"Wait, hold up. You've talked to him?"

I nod and put my finger up to my lips, shushing her. She puts her hands on her hips and I laugh. I know I'll have to fess up soon enough, but for now, I just want to stare at my beautiful boy who is now a stranger.

A few songs later, I know the moment he sees me. He smiles a heart-stopping smile and doesn't look away. Between songs, he says something to one of the guys, straps on an acoustic guitar, and sits on a stool. The other guys step back and listen as Jaxson plays.

His eyes find mine once again and Maddie squeezes my arm.

"He's completely into you!" she squeals.

I swat her hand away and listen to every word Jaxson sings.

I CAN'T BELIEVE *I let you walk away*
   I didn't know you meant forever
   We spent a lifetime chasing firefly dreams
   Now it seems you have forgotten

BLUE-EYED SHADOW
   Black-haired beauty
   Remember me

Come home
Blue-eyed shadow
Black-haired beauty
Remember me
Come home

I TOOK *a detour along the way*
 I didn't know what I had until you were gone
 All the promises and memories
 Now it's up to me to remind you

BLUE-EYED SHADOW
 Black-haired beauty
 Remember me
 Come home
 Blue-eyed shadow
 Black-haired beauty
 Remember me
 Come home

WHEN HE'S DONE, he stares at me before giving the guitar back to his friend. A tear runs down my cheek and I turn away. Maddie puts her arm around me and we walk out.

"Mira! I didn't realize," she says. "The two of you…"

I shake my head. "It doesn't matter. He didn't mean it."

5

PAST

2010

You never write me back, but I feel like you have more to say than Jaxson's measly letters. Give me some meat to those bones, boy! UGH. I guess you'll have to do, Diary. Sigh.
Love, Mira

THE NIGHT BEFORE JAXSON MOVED, we lay on the floor in his room, looking at the ceiling and not saying much. We'd spent the day together packing up his room and moping. We took a brief time-out to ride our bikes to our favorite chippy place then came back full and lethargic.

"I already know I'll hate it there without you," he muttered. His head turned toward me and I kept my eyes on the ceiling, afraid I'd cry.

"We've always wanted to go to America. You're going to love it there and forget all about me," my voice trailed off.

Jaxson's hand found mine and he squeezed it. "Stop with the crazy talk, Bells. Like I'd ever forget you. I'm gonna write every day," he promised.

At nearly twelve and thirteen, we were about the same height, which annoyed Jaxson daily. We measured once a week to prove he was getting taller—his idea—but he was as lanky and short as ever. I was glad—my boobs hadn't come in yet either. He already had a year on me, so in most everything else I was usually behind. At least in this, we were both playing catch-up. He motioned to the wall of our measurements and said, "Maybe I'll have finally passed you by the next time I see you."

I didn't dare comment. Stupid baby tears still clogged my throat and I didn't know when or even *if* I'd ever see him again. He hated when I talked like that, so I'd stopped saying it. Our mums would make sure we saw each other, he always said. But I wasn't so sure. My dad's job had been unpredictable for a while and we had to live a lot tighter than Jaxson's family. I heard my mum call my dad a skinflint at least weekly and would try to hide after that because it set off one of his rants every time.

"I've already got some saved." Jaxson propped his head on his elbow and turned my chin to face him. "I'll get a job when I get there...find a way to make some money. Don't worry."

He could usually tell what I was thinking without me saying a word. I wondered if that would change when we lived an entire world away from one another.

"Come here." He pulled my hand and we stood up. He opened his laptop and typed in my address and his new address in La Jolla, California. When the directions came up, he tapped the screen. "Look at that," he said, his arm looping over my shoulder. "Only 5,331 miles...that's not so bad. It would really suck if you lived in Sydney, Australia. Look..." He typed Sydney where Holmes Chapel had been and 7,506 miles came up. "See?"

I couldn't hold it in any longer. A sob burst out and I covered my mouth with both hands. I looked at him in panic and ran out of the room. I made it to the front door and made it a few feet down the sidewalk before he caught up.

Neither of us said a word as we ran to my house. When I reached my steps, I turned to him and put my hand out.

"I don't think I can tell you goodbye," I said, no longer bothering to wipe the tears that weren't going to stop.

Jaxson put his hands on my cheeks and looked from one eye to the next. We were so close I worried I might look cross-eyed to him. I closed my eyes and his thumbs smoothed away my tears. And the next thing I knew, his soft lips were on my chapped ones. My eyes flew open and his were scrunched closed as he kissed me. I held onto his arms and kissed him back. After a few perfect moments, he pulled away and I wasn't even disappointed he hadn't tried a "real" kiss. I sighed and he rested his forehead on mine.

"We won't say goodbye. Not now and not ever. Okay?" he whispered.

I nodded and more tears came. He hugged me tighter than he ever had and then took off running down the street. He looked back once more before rounding the corner.

"I'll see you soon," he yelled, waving and grinning.

―――

HE DID WRITE A FEW LETTERS. The first one was disappointingly short.

HEY BELLS,

I've never seen sunshine so many days in a row. It's pretty sweet. That's what they say here...sweet.

Speaking of that, EVERYONE makes fun of my accent. Everyone. Most of them can't even understand me half the time. I feel like I have to say everything extra S-L-O-W. But two weeks down with school, the people aren't so bad. Get this—year 9 is eighth grade here. Weird, eh?

How's school going there? I hope you manage to avoid Ms. Rafferty.

I heard my mum telling yours to get here quick. I'm counting on that.

Missing you.

Jax

I SCRUNCHED MY FOREHEAD. Jax? Since when did he go by Jax? And I couldn't help but wish he'd mentioned *something* about our kiss. I hadn't been able to stop thinking about it, but maybe for him it had just been an alternative to saying goodbye.

I put the letter in the drawer by my bed and took it out each night to read it. Some days it made me feel better, and other days it made me even more miserable. I *had* gotten stuck with Ms. Rafferty and she was worse than the rumors about her. Mum and Dad were fighting constantly it seemed, and there was no escaping to Jaxson's house to ease the sadness. The days felt long and hollow. I wished I were in the land of sunshine. I didn't have anything exciting to write about, but I did write him back a week later.

His letter came three weeks after I mailed his letter. I knew because I'd counted the days and checked the post relentlessly. When it finally came, I clutched it to my chest and ran to my bedroom before carefully ripping it open.

. . .

HEY BELLS!

Still sunny. Can you believe it? It's like freakin' paradise here. You've gotta come. I'm sorry I haven't written more often. I got a job mowing lawns in my neighborhood. It's a sweet neighborhood too—I couldn't believe anyone would trust me with their flawless grass! But the man next door told me I did a good job on ours and asked if I'd help him out. Now I'm mowing ten yards every other week. I'll have money to come see you in no time...or I've been thinking, would your parents let you come here to see me? Think about it.

Anyway...I've gotta go. My friend Derek is coming over in a few minutes to play basketball.

Oh, one more thing. You better sit down for it. My mum is dating someone. Shocking, right? And I think she might really like him because she said she wants me to meet him soon. Hopefully I like the dude.

Missing you.

Jax

YES, very shocking. I wondered how much my mum knew about it. She hadn't said anything. Anne had never dated anyone that I knew of. Jaxson's dad left before he was born and between raising him and her job as a court reporter, she claimed she didn't have time for anything extra.

Her extra was hanging out with my mum, I thought. Now that they were also divided by an ocean, I guessed she'd found time after all. I hoped her son wouldn't find a new best friend too.

———

MONTHS WENT by with no word. Desperate, bleak months where I cried myself to sleep and often in the bathroom at school. Before, I had been okay without many friends because I had Jaxson to look forward to at lunch and after school. Without him, the days felt endless.

My dad lost his job. The fighting was now the norm. I couldn't fit into any of my clothes and we didn't have money to get new ones. It felt like the worst time in my life and Jaxson was nowhere to be found.

And then this letter came...

HEY BELLS!

Has your mother told you yet? I'm positive you've heard the news that my mum is getting married! It's fast, but I actually feel good about the whole thing. Charles is great. He's nice and—get this—he's quite well-off. I'm laughing when I write this because...wait until you see the place I'm moving into, Bells. "Well-off" is an understatement. It's far swankier than The Vicarage, I'll say that much. And it's on the beach, Bells! Can you believe it?

I can't wait for you to get here. Mum says your mum is her matron of honor, so that means I'll see you soon! It's been way too long.

Missing you.
Jax

I IMMEDIATELY WENT to find my mum, bouncing on the balls of my feet with excitement. I couldn't believe she hadn't told me this news—it would've made all the difference in the world to know I had this to look forward to. Maybe she'd been planning to surprise me...

I knocked on her bedroom door and stepped in when I heard her blow her nose. She was sitting on the edge of the bed, crying.

"Mum, what's wrong?" I rushed to her side and sat down.

"Things are just complicated right now," she said. "Your dad...his job...and now Anne is getting married. She wants us to come, which is wonderful, but I don't see how we'll be able to..."

I gasped. "We have to go. We can't miss it!"

She wiped her face and gave me a sharp look. "Believe me, I want to be there as badly as you do."

"Well, we have to find a way. When is the wedding?"

"Next month."

We sat there in silence for half an hour, both trying to come up with ways to make quick money and becoming more and more hopeless as the seconds ticked by.

The next morning, my mum screamed and I went running to find her. She was laughing and crying, jumping up and down and screeching on the phone. "No way!" she cried. "I should tell him absolutely not, but I can't afford to be too proud at this moment." She put her hands over her mouth and her shoulders shook as she cried. She saw me then and pulled me close. "Jaxson gave Anne money for our tickets last night. When Charles heard what he'd done, he refused to let Jaxson pay for it. Actually...we're flying on his private plane." I'd started jumping up and down while she was telling me and we had Anne on speakerphone, yelling and cheering with us.

Before we hung up, Anne said, "Jaxson's been working tirelessly since we got here, even with school...so he could see his Mirabelle again."

I went to bed smiling and it didn't wear off that entire month…until we got to the States.

6

PRESENT

What does love have to do with anything? That's what I want to ask him. But instead I will pose the question to you, in hopes that you will talk some sense into me.

ON THE WAY home from the restaurant, I pull over at a scenic overlook and stare at the ocean until my emotions are somewhat under control. But when I pull in front of the house, Jaxson is there and all that peace I'd found vanishes.

He opens my car door and holds his hand out to help me. I ignore it and step out of the car. Instead of backing up to give me space as a normal human being would, he stays perfectly still and I have nowhere to go but into his chest.

"Did you like your song?" he asks, moving my hair away from my eye.

"It's been so long since I've heard you sing. You've... improved," I tell him.

His face falls slightly and I step around him, feeling some satisfaction in not giving him the answer he wanted. It fades when he falls into step next to me, walking to the house.

"Did you meet the guys in Boston? Are they your band?" I ask.

"One is from here too, but yeah, we all met at Berklee. We're going to see if we can get some work out here. Give it a shot."

We move inside the house and I throw my keys on the kitchen counter.

"Good for you," I say. "Well, I'm beat. Make yourself at home. I'm going to bed."

"Wait...can we talk? Or just hear me out?"

I put my hand on my hip and look at the ceiling, exhaling a long rush of air. "Three minutes," I say.

"That's hardly anything!" he says.

I wave my hand. "Better hurry then."

"Okay."

His eyes narrow and he presses his lips together, the look he gets when he's frustrated. I grin.

"The line in the song I wrote for *you*—'I didn't know what I had until you were gone'—it's the truth. But now I live with that every day and I can't stand it anymore. I need to at least have you as a friend, Bells. Please." He holds his hands together and gives me pleading eyes.

I chew the inside of my cheek until it feels all rippley inside.

"I propose we go to the San Diego Zoo as a step in bringing our friendship back. What do you say?" he asks. When I don't say anything right away, he adds, "Remember we signed on it..."

"That piece of paper became null and void when we went our separate ways. You're gonna have to do better than that," I tell him.

"No, it didn't. It was just paused...until we could pick up where we left off. And now we have a responsibility to each other to keep the promises we made." He grins and steps closer to me.

"No," I reply.

He holds up a hand and drops it, stunned that I won't cave in the way I always used to when he wanted me to agree to something. He crosses his arms and his eyes smile as he assesses me.

"You really think it's as simple as you giving me your best charming smile and telling me what we're going to do, and I'll jump." I shake my head. "You should know by now that those days are over."

"When are you going to forgive me, Bells?"

I go still when I hear the tone of his voice. He sounds grave and all the lighthearted teasing that I'm used to hearing from him is stripped bare. I can't look at him when he sounds this raw. I shake my head, willing the tears to stay down.

"I will regret losing you for the rest of my life," he whispers.

I jump when his hand touches my shoulder.

"Please tell me there's hope. That you'll give me another chance. I was young and stupid. I'm *still* young and stupid, but I know that I can't live without you in my life. In any way you'll have me." He leans closer, his breath wispy against my ear. "Please say you'll at least think about it."

A tear drops on my hand and I nod slowly, still not trusting myself to speak.

He leans his forehead against the back of my head for a moment and then backs away, clearing his throat. "Okay, I'll see myself out."

His steps are slow on the way out of the kitchen. When

he's near the back door, I turn and he looks at me at the same time, his eyes hopeful.

"Why now?" I ask. "You've been quiet for a while. Why is my friendship suddenly so important to you?"

"I've never given up hope that you'd come back to me. But I know I blew it. In every way." He takes steps toward me and I back into the kitchen cabinet. He reaches me and takes my hand in his. My heart threatens to pound out of my chest. "It wasn't until I saw the way you looked at me the other day at the party...I felt hopeful then that you still feel the same way I do." He pulls my hand up to his lips and kisses my palm. "Do you still love me?"

I reluctantly tug my hand away from him, looking at my hand as if it's betrayed me. My hand shakes and I quickly put it in my pocket.

"I'll always *love* you. We grew up together. We were important to each other...once," I tell him. "But that doesn't really make a difference as far as I'm concerned. I've moved on. I finally learned about self-preservation, thanks to you."

He looks so heartbreakingly sad that I almost feel bad for what I've said. But then his mouth tightens, and his jaw clenches. "How can you say it doesn't make a difference? It's *everything*. And that's not the kind of love I meant and you know it...although it should count for something." His voice cracks at the end of his words and I swallow hard, fighting the urge to wrap my arms around him and hold him the way my heart wants to.

That self-preservation kicks in and squelches the feelings, moving around him and opening the door. I wave my hand for him to walk through. "Why don't you stop trying to tell me what I feel and worry about taking care of your own feelings."

His Adam's apple bobs twice and his eyes are glassy

when he slowly walks to the door. When he reaches me, he stops and puts his hand on my cheek. "I should have told you then how much I loved you. How much I cared about your opinion of me. How I was going to work hard to win back your trust and prove that I was the person you knew me to be. I'll always love you. I'm *in love* with you, Bells. That's what I discovered in losing you...what I knew as a boy but somehow lost sight of for a while there...that you are the love of my life and you always will be. I'm sorry I'm too late," he says softly. His hand drops and he walks out the door.

I stare after him, stunned. It takes everything in me to not run after him. He's just said everything I've always longed to hear but that he never, not once in our lifetime of back and forth, has ever said.

7

PAST

2010

I know a secret, Diary. All those ads of the beautiful people frolicking in the Pacific Ocean like they are in paradise—
LIES. All lies.
THAT OCEAN IS BLOODY FREEZING!
That is all for now.
Yours, Mira

MY MUM and I were exhausted as we stepped off the plane and walked through LAX. She hadn't slept at all on our flight over and I barely had either, too excited to be flying for the first time. I could hardly believe I would be seeing Jaxson soon...in America. It was the culmination of all of our dreams finally coming to pass. I lugged the stuffed panda Jaxson had given me a few years before, feeling slightly childish but also still not comfortable with the idea of smooshing a panda in a suitcase due to lack of air quality.

We walked toward baggage claim and when we got

through customs and security, Anne was standing with a bouquet of flowers. We beamed at each other as she walked toward us, but I quickly looked behind her and all around... even behind myself...but I couldn't spot Jaxson. Maybe he was in the loo. Anne hugged my mum and me at the same time, the two of them laughing and crying.

"Where's Jaxson?" I asked when we pulled away.

"He had to stay after school for football practice," she said.

My shoulders sagged with disappointment, but Anne put her arm around my shoulder. "Don't worry, he'll be home by the time we get there."

We were only going to be there for a week, so I'd hoped between our limited time and the preparations for the wedding, he wouldn't have to worry about school.

Anne saw my expression. "He's had to work really hard to get caught up at school...I barely see him between homework, his jobs doing yard work, and sports." She scrunched up her nose. "They don't allow them to miss any practices unless there's an emergency." She rolled her eyes. "Believe me, it's killing him to not be here."

That soothed me a bit.

"And I'm so sorry," she added. "Charles is mortified that you had to fly in here instead of closer to home. When you leave, you'll fly out of San Diego, and it will be much closer!"

We didn't care; we were just happy to be on the ground. When we reached her car and I saw the steering wheel on the wrong side and the beautiful sunshine with the most perfect puffy white clouds, I got excited all over again. America. I was finally there! Where they made movies! It was too much. I wished Jaxson was by my side when we passed the ocean, which was love at first sight. Jaxson and I had talked about learning to surf, thinking it would come in handy when we swam with the dolphins. Maybe we could try it out that week. The traffic made me a nervous wreck, but there was too much to see and the stretches of moving at a snail's pace gave me time to take it all in.

It took a couple of hours to get to the house. I thought the anticipation would kill me if we didn't get there soon. By the time we finally pulled into the driveway of a mansion, I figured we were making another stop before home and I couldn't take anymore. I flounced back against the seat and groaned just as my mum gasped.

"You're kidding me," she yelled. "Is this your place?"

I leaned up, sticking my head between the two of them. "What? This is where you live? How is that possible? Jaxson said *swanky*, but this is beyond! This is outrageous!" I clamped my hand over my mouth because my voice was getting too loud for the car, but I was in shock.

Anne laughed. "I'm still in shock about it myself. Wait until you see the view from the back. It's a dream. I'm—well, I assure you I had no idea Charles had…anything like this…when I met him. Honestly, I think he was scared to show me at first. And he was right to be. I nearly did a runner." She laughed again and I took a good long look at her, noticing for the first time how happy she seemed, how peaceful.

"I'm so happy for you, Anne," Mum said and burst into tears.

Anne looked at her sharply and put her hand on Mum's arm. Mum shook her head and opened the car door.

"Don't pay me any mind. I'm tired and overly sentimental. I can't wait to meet Charles. And if anyone deserves this lavish lifestyle, it's you," she said.

Anne didn't look like she quite believed my mother's

explanation and I didn't either, even though I knew she meant what she said about Anne. But she'd been crying more than ever lately and had tried to no avail to get my dad to come with us on this trip. I thought maybe she was depressed and as I stepped out of the car, I hoped being here would help her feel better. Anne came around the car and hugged my mum. I leaned over on my mum's back and hugged both of them. And then we were nearly barreled over by someone huge who joined the hug. His hair was wet and I pulled away to avoid getting wet too.

I looked up and up and there stood Jaxson.

"What happened?" I asked dumbly.

Jaxson just stood there smiling proudly while Anne answered, "I can't keep this guy in pants and shoes! All of a sudden, he's outgrowing everything. Six inches taller since we got here and some days I swear he's growing right before my eyes."

My mum gave him another hug while I swallowed hard and looked over his face, which had a few zits that weren't there before either, but other than that, he looked like my Jaxson. Just lots bigger. It was unsettling, but then he put his arm around my shoulder and turned me toward the house. I could see the ocean waves just past the house.

"As soon as we get your things inside, Mum said I could take you down to the beach. You're gonna love it here," he said.

Anne started to say something, but Jaxson jumped in. "Yes, I finished my homework," he said, smirking.

My shoulders loosened when he smiled down at me. I couldn't believe how different he looked. While I'd stayed the same short, slightly tubby girl, my best friend had grown into a humongous teenager. I always thought he was beautiful, and now he really was, hormonal skin and all. His newly tanned shade helped conceal the imperfections. A pang sharpened in my chest. It felt like he was passing me by, in more ways than one. He even sounded a wee bit different...deeper, and like the California was weaving its way into every part of him.

"Come on, Bells. I've been waiting forever to show you everything." He picked up Mum's luggage and I took mine, leaving our mothers behind as we hurried into the house.

He didn't give me time to gawk at the stunning high ceilings and enormous chandelier in front of the winding staircase. He loped up the stairs and I followed, wishing I hadn't packed so many outfits. When I reached the guest room, he had the suitcase sitting on a luggage rack and took mine and placed it on the one next to it.

"It's like a grand hotel," I told him, excitedly. "This place would fit like, twelve of our houses from home."

He motioned for me to follow him and when he reached the door, he turned and looked at me. My cheeks bloomed with shyness, which was just crazy. It was Jaxson, for crying out loud.

"I'm so glad you're here," he said. He reached down and hugged me.

My world suddenly righted—we were together again. When we pulled away from each other, I beamed up at him. "Me too. I can't believe how tall you are." He puffed his chest out, looking even taller, and I rolled my eyes at him as he laughed. "Let's see that beach."

I LOVED the feel of the sand on my feet. Jaxson ran straight to the water and motioned for me to follow him. When the water hit my feet, I yelped and backed up.

"It's bloody freezin'!" I yelled.

That cracked him up. He tried to pull me in and I tried with all my might to stay on dry ground.

"How are all these people in the water?" I looked around in shock.

"You get used to it," he said. "Come on. You have to try it if you're ever going to learn to surf."

He looked behind him and pointed at the surfers coming in. A couple of them rode the waves all the way in. When they got closer, one of them waved at Jaxson. He flushed and waved back. When I got a better look, I realized it was a girl. She picked up her board and walked toward us, sending sprays of water flying when she shook her hair. It was hard to ignore the fact that her curves were perfectly accentuated in a wet suit. She smiled up at Jaxson, and against her tanned skin, her teeth gleamed bright. I waited for him to introduce us, but he stood still, looking transfixed by her beauty.

I wished I could burrow into the sand like a crab, but then Jaxson spoke.

"Heather, this is the friend I was telling you about... Mirabelle Hart. She's a year younger than us but cool."

My hackles rose at that, but he smiled so charmingly, I shoved those feelings down and smiled at Heather. "Hi." I held my hand up into a tiny wave and awkwardly dropped it when she didn't say anything.

She moved closer and threw me completely off guard when she put her arm around my shoulder. "Aren't you adorable!" she said, squeezing my shoulder. "Jaxson has told me all about you and how you're like his sister. He's missed you so much." She gazed at me fondly, but I was stuck on the "sister" part and couldn't quite formulate words.

"You must be thinking of Gemma," I muttered.

"No, no. You're Bells, right?"

Glumly, I nodded. I looked at Jaxson then, hoping he'd say something—anything—to set her straight. *Like his sister?* But he just looked at us with such contentment on his face, I realized I was the one who needed to be set straight.

8

PAST

2010

Life is really hard sometimes, D.
Is it wrong that I don't want to be an adult? I already feel
like the oldest person in the room most of the time...like
gnarly-grey-and-veiny old, not cool, I-know-the-wisdom-of-
life old. What's it going to be like when I really am the adult?
I don't think my heart can take the sadness.

OUR WEEK in California was amazing. After we got over the initial adjustment of being around each other again, Jaxson and I got back to normal. We spent quite a bit of time with Jaxson's friend Derek, who was almost as good-looking as Jaxson, and Heather, who I liked more than I had expected to. The time flew by and at the wedding, when I was crying over how beautiful everything was, I realized I never, ever wanted to go home. When my mum and I said our goodbyes at the airport, there were a lot of tears between us. Jaxson stood there stoically, but even he looked devastated.

"Please come back soon," Anne said, clasping my mum's hand.

Charles patted Anne's back and passed each of us a tissue. I liked him. He didn't talk much, but it was clear by the way he looked at Anne and Jaxson that he adored them.

Anne and Charles were waiting until we left to take their honeymoon but hadn't acted like they minded whatsoever, despite my mother's protests that they should go on their wedding night.

"Come back for Thanksgiving," Charles added. "We'll take care of everything. Just hurry back."

My mum smiled, but we both knew it would be a long time before we'd be able to do this again. She couldn't afford to miss work, and even though it had worked out for us to fly on Charles' plane, we didn't want to assume that would happen again.

"I'll text you," Jaxson promised. "Now that we both have phones," he grinned at Charles, "it'll be a lot easier."

I still couldn't believe Charles had given me a phone. *"So you and Jaxson don't have to wait so long to hear from one another,"* he'd said when he handed me the box with a big red ribbon around it. He swore to my mother that it was an extra one he had, but I thought it looked brand new. I'd squealed and hugged him and he'd flushed bright red but looked very pleased.

I looked back at Jaxson until we had to round the corner and he waved each time. My steps felt heavier with every step away from him. I looked at Mum and tears were streaming down her face too. Afterward, I thought she must have known what we were going home to, but she didn't say anything on the flight.

We took a cab home and even then I still thought everything was okay. The house was dark when we pulled into the driveway and I looked at Mum. She patted my arm and the driver helped us get the luggage to the door. The note from my dad was on the table in the entry. It fluttered slightly when we came in the door, calling my attention to it. I picked it up and Mum snatched it from my hand. She read it then crumpled it into a ball with her fist and walked numbly to her bedroom, shutting the door behind her.

Something was wrong, but I wasn't sure what I could do about it. I knocked on my mother's door and cracked it open. Her room was dark and she was in bed.

"I'm exhausted, Mirabelle. Go to bed. We'll talk in the morning."

I nodded. "It was a fun trip, wasn't it?" I said softly.

I shut the door and dragged my suitcase to my room. All the excitement from the week faded into bleak loneliness.

―――

MUM DIDN'T COME out of her room until the next afternoon. I'd unpacked my suitcase by then and done laundry all day. I had to go back to school the next day and wanted to wear the new outfit I'd gotten in California.

"Mira?" she said, cracking my door open.

She looked like she hadn't slept at all. The rings around her eyes were dark and puffy.

"Are you okay?" I asked, stepping toward her. "What's wrong?"

"I've made a decision," she said. She smiled faintly and sat down on my bed.

"Okay." She was making me nervous, but I smiled back at her and waited for her to come out with it.

"I didn't tell you this because I wasn't sure how I felt about it, but Charles offered me a job with his company while we were there. I can start as soon as we get back there if I want. How would you feel about moving to California?" she said it calmly, as if her words wouldn't completely change my life.

My mouth hung open as I stared at her. I sat by her on the bed, taking her hand. "Are you serious? Yes! I love it there! When can we go?"

She swallowed hard and looked like she wanted to cry.

"Why aren't you happy about it?" I asked quietly. "What about Dad?"

"Your dad will stay here and sell the house. We'll let him worry about that. We only need our necessities—we can get new furniture out there. It was time for an update anyway," she said. "He'll meet us when he's quit his job and has everything squared away here."

"Okay."

I couldn't believe it. I looked around my room and besides my clothes and a few things I had collected with Jaxson, I didn't have an attachment to my furniture. It wouldn't take long to be ready, but I couldn't believe we were really going.

"What was the note about?" I asked. "You seemed really upset."

"I was upset Dad wasn't here when we got home, but he's going through a rough time. The move will be good for him. It'll be good for us." Her eyes were resolute as she nodded and smoothed her shirt. "Anne said Charles has already set up our flight. We'll go day after tomorrow."

"What? Day after tomorrow? Aren't there...things we have to take care of here first? Not just the house, but...our whole life!" I stood up and turned around in my room, panicked. "I don't have to take much, but seriously? Day after tomorrow?" I jumped up and down then went to pick up her hands and tried to get her to jump with me. "We're moving to California?"

She stood up and laughed with me. When we stopped, she hugged me and began to cry.

"It'll be good for us," she repeated over and over.

SO, just six months after Jaxson and Anne moved to California, there we were, following in their footsteps. I knew there was more to the story than what my mother would tell me. It was more than a job—I knew that. It was confirmed with the way Anne took Mum in her arms and held her as she wept.

"It'll be okay. We're here for you," Anne whispered to my mother.

Jaxson looked more serious than usual when he said, "I'm glad you're here, Bells."

"Do you know what's going on?" I whispered when I got the chance.

He shook his head. "I only overheard Mum saying she was angry with your dad."

I sighed, wishing someone would clue me in.

We stayed with Jaxson while we searched for a place. Three days into our search, we found a cottage five minutes from Jaxson's. It was tiny—but it was charming, and it had a view of the ocean that took my breath away. The best part about it was that we could move right in, and even though I loved staying with Jaxson, I hoped my dad would come sooner if we had our own place.

Our second week there, I started school. It was within walking distance and Jaxson met me out front, his grin split wide open.

"You ready?" he asked, falling into step with me. "You'll love it here. Everyone is so friendly."

I nodded. I wasn't ready; I was extremely nervous. I lay awake the night before, my stomach churning with nerves.

"I wish I had some classes with you," I told him. "Not the first time I've wished that though." I'd always hated being a year behind him, but I shrugged like it didn't matter and walked through the door he held for me.

"I have practice today," he reminded me. "If you want to stay, I can walk home with you; otherwise, call me later to tell me how it went." He saw a guy he knew and waved. He looked at me and shifted his bag into his other hand. "Smile. You look terrified." He put his finger on my neck and made me look down then tweaked my nose, laughing as he walked away.

I groaned. I fell for it every time.

I walked into class after class where everyone already knew each other. Too occupied to pay attention to the new girl, they didn't really notice me in the back until each teacher had me introduce myself. I got fleeting glances from a few people and a couple of girls introduced themselves, but by the end of the day, I wondered what Jaxson meant about everyone being so friendly.

I didn't see him all day and decided to wait for him after school. He was on the football field and stood out, even in his uniform. They seemed to be having a break because Jaxson and Derek were surrounded by cheerleaders. I pulled out my package of Reese's peanut butter cups and sat on the bleachers behind a group of kids, watching where I hoped he couldn't see me. He seemed to be in his element with all the pretty people hanging on his every word. Heather was in the group. She stepped closer to Jaxson and touched his arm, laughing at something he said. Over his shoulder, she looked up in the bleachers and saw me sitting there. Maybe it was for my benefit or maybe I was imagining things, but she leaned up on her tiptoes and whispered something in his ear then gave his hair a tug. He was completely oblivious to the fact that I was even there, and who could blame him? He had a beautiful girl who had claimed him before I even got here.

I stuffed the entire peanut butter cup into my mouth and savored the way the salty and the sweet filled my mouth. In that moment, it was the only thing that made me feel the tiniest bit better.

MY MOM WAS IN A FUNK. She said she loved her job and California; we even settled into our place quickly, excitedly furnishing it from the incredible flea markets and Goodwill stores we rummaged, but I heard her crying night after night when she thought I was sleeping.

It was even more evident something was wrong when my dad showed up a month later, suitcase in hand. Our house suddenly felt crowded. All this time I'd wished for him to hurry up and get here, and now that he was here, I was annoyed by everything he said.

"Why didn't you pick something a little bigger?" Dad asked. "It's like I turn around and you're on top of me. I'm already suffocatin' over the smog. Don't need you takin' my air in the house too. And it's always day after bloody day of sunshine," he went on. "None of these people have ever been through a hard winter, no wonder they're so bloody cheery."

This went on for a few weeks until my mother had enough. "You'll be glad to come home to it if you get yourself a job and get out a bit," she said, her face ruddy from anger.

My dad didn't like hearing that and let her know it. I left when he started yelling about looking for a bloody fuckin' job. I shut the door and then heard my mom say, "If you hate it so much here, you can always go back to Holmes Chapel...lord knows you can be the big fish in the pond there."

When I got up the next morning, he was gone. For good.

9

PRESENT

Diary, you have it made.
I want to live in your paper walls and never have to make
any decisions.
The End.
Mira

I WAKE up feeling like I have a hangover even though I'm stone-cold sober. Jaxson's words from the night before are at the forefront of my mind, no matter how much I try to push them aside. How could he say all of those things...now? The more I think about it, the angrier I become. All these years and he chooses now to realize he's in love with me after all? I don't think so.

Chad has been sulking since our night out and I know I need to deal with him, but I just haven't felt up to it yet. *Tomorrow*, I tell myself. Or maybe today if I hear from him.

I get ready for the day and walk into the living room where Dave is drinking coffee and reading the paper. We're still in the cottage, but we added a second story after my dad left. It's still cozy. I wondered if I would feel weird coming home with Dave living here now, but he's so quiet, it hasn't made much of a difference.

"There's more coffee in there if you need some," Dave says.

"Thanks." I pad slowly toward the kitchen and then he speaks up again. He points at a box.

"Almost forgot. That was sitting outside this morning when I went for my run," he says. "It has your name on it."

My heartbeat quickens. I know what it is from across the room. I just don't know what it's doing here. Our box. I left that buried when I moved across the continent. Jaxson and I talked a lot about it back then, sad that neither of us had a chance to bring it with us. He always said he'd go back and get it one day, but I assumed neither of us ever would.

I lift the lid and pick up the list. It looks the same. Hard to believe it could stay the same when everything about us is different now. There's an envelope in the box that I don't recognize. I open it and pull out the note first.

I DUG *this up a year ago. Can you believe I found it with no trouble?*

Give me another chance, Bells. I want your friendship back. I'd rather have it all, but I'll take anything I can get. The summer...can you give me that?

Or at least this trip?

CONFUSED, I pull out what's left in the envelope. It's a ticket to Paris, leaving in two days. I stare at it like it's going to tell me what to do.

"You okay?" Dave asks, setting his paper down and staring at me.

"He's lost his mind," I say, dropping the ticket into the box and putting the box under my arm. I look at Dave and he's looking at me like I'm the one losing it. I shake my head. "Thanks. Don't worry. I'm not going to fall for it again."

Dave's mouth parts and I realize he has no clue what I'm going on about.

"Never mind." I wave my hand in his direction.

His brows draw together. "Care to fill me in?"

"It just figures when I finally move on and get over him that he decides to go all in." I pace back and forth in front of the fireplace, my face heating with growing rage. "I mean... what is it—he meets my boyfriend and can't handle the fact that I'm finally going out with someone?"

"You, uh...you've gone out with more guys than Chad, right? Who are we talking about again?"

"He doesn't know that. At least I don't think he knows about Alex or Sam." I roll my eyes over the fact that I haven't gone out with more guys. I spent too many years agonizing over *him* to give anyone else a chance. "How dare he?" I yell.

Dave leans forward, elbows on his knees. "Right." He stands up and puts his hand on my shoulder. I pause my pacing and look at him. "Should I make a pot of tea?"

I give him a wobbly smile. His tea tastes like murky lukewarm water, but I'm touched that he's trying to help. My mum and I turn to tea for every occasion, good or bad, but especially when we need comfort.

"No, it's okay. Thanks for listening. I'm sorry for rambling nonsense. I'll just go put this upstairs." I hold up the box.

"Mirabelle?" he says. "I've never seen you so, um,

worked up. My guess is that anyone that makes you feel so *impassioned* must be someone you really care about. Might be worth hearing him out." He drops his hand and looks shy again.

"You're a good guy, Dave," I finally say. "Thanks. I'll think about what you said."

He nods and moves back to the chair and picks up the paper. "Ah, would you look at that. Dolphins have been spotted near our favorite beach all week."

My eyes fill with tears. I can't help but think of number seven on our list: **Go swimming with dolphins.** There is no escaping Jaxson Marshall.

WE NEED TO TALK.

I read the text and immediately type back: **Agreed. Starbucks in an hour?**

Chad is sitting near the front when I get there, scarfing down a muffin. "Hey," he says, and crumbs go flying.

I laugh and sit down by him.

"Sorry, I was saving some for you but couldn't wait." He holds up the last bite and I shake my head.

"I'm not hungry. I'm glad you texted," I say.

He sets down the empty wrapper and dusts off his mouth, avoiding eye contact with me. I've never been nervous with Chad, but he's acting so strange, my stomach turns over.

"What's up?" I ask.

"I'm just going to say it outright." His head drops down and when he looks back up at me, his eyes are full of guilt.

"I've met someone," he says.

"Oh!" I slump back in my seat. Not what I was expecting. "Okay..." I don't really know what to say, so I just sit there for a minute and wait for him to say something.

"I'm sorry. Things have been crazy this summer, but I didn't plan on this." He's so pitiful that I feel bad for not caring more.

"It's okay." I put my hand on his and he grasps it tight. "Really, Chad. I'm not mad."

He nods and looks down at the table. "I knew you wouldn't be."

And then I feel the guilt for not ending this relationship a while ago, when it was already dying.

"You've never been as into me as I wished you were," he adds. "I guess I thought in time." He shrugs. "I haven't had sex with anyone, I want you to know that...but I wanted to let you know before it got to that point."

What do I say to that? *You're right...and thank you?* I nod and smile awkwardly. "Be happy. Okay? And thanks for everything."

He nods back and stands up. "Well, I'm gonna head out. Take care, Mira."

WE NEED TO TALK. This time I text those words and then delete them...then re-type and hit send.

Seconds later, he responds. **Time and place. I'll be there.**

La Jolla Cove. Bring your suit.

I put my wet suit on and hop in the car, careful to not overthink what I've just set in motion. *It's already been set in motion*, I remind myself as I park. Jaxson is standing there already next to his surfboard, looking glorious in his wet suit.

"We've missed them every time for one reason or another," I say, not bothering with a hello or bringing up all the foul reasons we missed the dolphins before. "Today's the day to see the dolphins." I point out to the ocean and sure enough, in the distance, I see one jump in the water.

His eyes light up. "I haven't even looked out there yet. I was watching for you." His eyes roam over my body in the formfitting suit. "How about I just look at you looking at the dolphins?" He grins and I roll my eyes, moving past him.

When he doesn't immediately follow me, I turn around and he's transfixed by my lower half. My arse, what have you. We might be California people now, but *arse* will always stick.

I clear my throat and his eyes meet mine, no apology in sight, just brazen admiration. I stop and put my hands on my hips, glaring at him.

"There's no way the things on the list are going to get checked off. I don't know why you've got this idea that suddenly everything is just going to return to normal. I don't even know what that is anymore when it comes to me and you." I swallow hard and plow ahead. "Thank you for the ticket to Paris, but I won't be going with you. But this I can do...today. This will be the *only* thing we do and then we'll put the list to rest for good. Okay?"

His grin drops, and for a moment, I want to change my mind about everything.

"Dolphins it is," he says quietly.

We walk along the beach, the perfect light cast upon the water, and the sight of dolphins swimming closer than they've ever been. Something I've wished for my whole life is happening and I feel hollow inside. We lie on our boards and paddle out, going to the right side of where the dolphins are frolicking. When we are about a yard from them, we stop and Jaxson glances at me with excitement.

"Can you believe this?" he whispers.

I bite my lip as tears fill my eyes and grin, shaking my head. We float for a long time, watching as they swim and play. There are at least six and they're not paying any attention to us, lost in their own fun. Before long, they surround us and it is such a beautiful experience, my heart nearly explodes.

But then I sneeze...two times, three times...and the third time I sneeze so hard, I fall off my board. I bump into a dolphin and it turns and looks at me, making an aggressive sound that scares me.

It must scare Jaxson too because he grabs my hand and tries to help me on my board. The other dolphins get agitated at the one barking at Jaxson and me, and I hurriedly paddle through an opening.

"Hurry, let's get out of here," he yells when they swarm around us and look far more ominous than I ever thought dolphins were supposed to look. I get creeped out feeling the slippery skin of the dolphins against us, when before it seemed enchanting.

We paddle back as fast as we can. When it seems the dolphins are done with us and we're far enough past, I wait for a wave and surf the rest of the way in. Jaxson follows.

When we reach the sand, I turn and look at him.

"That was stressful," he says, still panting.

"Not exactly how I imagined," I add. "I didn't know dolphins could get that angry."

He starts laughing. "I thought that one was going to take your head off when you sneezed the third time."

I start laughing too. A part of me doesn't want to bring

this day to an end. It feels too much like another goodbye and I've already shared too many goodbyes with Jaxson.

He steps closer to me and moves a thick strand of wet hair off of my face. "No one I'd rather get eaten by dolphins with than you," he says.

I laugh and prop my board upright. Jaxson leans over and kisses my cheek while I stare straight ahead, still as a statue.

"I hope you'll reconsider Paris," he whispers.

10

PAST

2011

My British accent finally won me a friend! Maybe things will turn around, or maybe at the very least, I won't feel so out of place all the time. It's getting old, D.

IN THE MONTHS after my dad left, the divide between La Jolla and Holmes Chapel felt greater than ever before. Dad didn't call or write, and I didn't feel inclined to reach out to him either. For all I knew, he hadn't gone back home at all but was wandering around town and I might bump into him when I least expected at the grocery store or gas station. I constantly looked over my shoulder, hoping to see him. I imagined telling him off and begging him to come home. I'd show him pictures of my mum curled up in her bed, room dark and stifling. He hadn't been pleasant when he was around, but anything had to be better than this. In trying to keep my mother from crying nonstop, adjusting to being in a new country, and feeling behind in my school-work...I was exhausted.

Gemma left for school in New York, so Jaxson's house felt weird too, without Gemma's sarcastic comments flying all the time. It was too much change. Too many beginnings for everyone else felt like endings for me.

The silver lining was that I saw Jaxson most days and I also made a new friend. Tyra was in three of my classes and we had lunch together—I first met her at lunch when she was in front of me in line. She groaned when she saw the coconut cream pie they were serving.

"I am destined to be a plus-size model," she said. She swiped a few dreadlocks out of her eyes with her long, bright purple fingernail and turned to me. "Have you tried this pie yet? It's the best thing they serve. Trust me."

"I've been trying to avoid it," I admitted, reluctantly taking a piece. She looked pretty great to me. If she was plus-size, I was extra plus-plus. Most of the girls at my school were twigs. Still, I couldn't resist a good pie. "It's that scrummy, huh?"

"Scrummy? Is that what you said?" She looked at me over her shoulder.

"Uh...delicious?" I'd have to remember to strike *scrummy* from my American vocabulary.

"Scrummy. I like that." She smiled. "But it's even better than that," she moaned, dipping her finger into the creamy filling before moving forward. "I'm Tyra. I've seen you around. I'd kill for an accent like yours."

I flushed. "Thank you. Usually the noses are curling up before I have two words out...it's like I'm speaking another language."

She laughed. "The people at this school don't think anyone else exists out of these walls and maybe the beach down the street. My aunt and I moved here last year from Riverside. It's two hours away at most and when I tell someone where I moved from, they're like, 'Never heard of it.'" She shook her head. "Livin' in their own little world."

I didn't tell her I'd never heard of Riverside either—I didn't think that would win me any points—but I made a mental note to look it up later that night. Tyra motioned for me to follow her and sat down at the closest table. She chatted throughout lunch. It was nice to have someone to listen to. She asked questions here and there too, but she was so entertaining, I preferred listening to her talk.

When I took a bite of the pie, she stopped talking and stared at me. "Well?" She lifted an eyebrow.

I nodded. "Even better."

"Told you," she said.

THAT AFTERNOON TYRA and I walked out of class together. We'd discovered our lockers were across from each other after lunch, so we headed in that direction. When I got closer, I noticed Jaxson was leaning on my locker and started grinning.

"I'll expect you to fill me in on *that* the next time I see you," Tyra said, giving me her direct look that suggested no arguments. "Again...even better than scrummy. See ya later."

I waved and excitedly walked up to Jaxson. "Made a friend finally," I told him.

"You'd have lots of friends if you'd talk to everyone like you talk to me," he said.

"I like Derek," I said. "He's easy to talk to."

Sometimes Derek came over to say hi during the breaks at practice. It had shocked me the first time he did it, but I soon realized he needed a break from the girls going on over

Jaxson. He claimed they were *so annoying*. We were in agreement there.

Jaxson frowned, and I turned to my locker.

"Heather's your friend...and Elle, Danielle, Giselle... Raquel..." He rattled off a list of all the girls that hung on his every word.

I had my head in my locker and rolled my eyes. I wasn't going to spell it out for him, but I had a feeling they would act like I didn't exist if it weren't for him. Heather tried a little harder to be nice to me, but I suspected it was because she liked Jaxson the most. A couple of the girls were my age, but the rest of them were in classes with Jaxson or knew him from football. They were on the cheering squad and since Jaxson had been playing really well lately, their interest in him had escalated. They all had long, flat-ironed hair and size zero bodies. I felt like their eyes circled in on my lumps and frizzy hair every time I was around them.

"I'll find my own friends, thank you," I muttered.

"What?" he asked, tapping my shoulder.

I shook my head. "Nothing."

"Hey, after practice, a bunch of us are doing homework at my house. Stick around and walk with us."

I finished putting my books in my backpack and shut the locker door. Jaxson looked down at me, grinning expectantly. I leaned my head over on the lockers and groaned inwardly. As much as I didn't want to hang out with a bunch of his groupies, the thought of him hanging out with them *without* me was even worse.

"Fine," I agreed, sighing. "But I really have to get my homework done..."

"I'll even help you finish," he promised.

He put his arm around my shoulder and we walked

toward the field. I took my spot where I usually waited for him and pretended to read/not watch him practice.

Heather and the rhyming name girls practiced their routine and cheered extra hard every time Jaxson did anything. I wondered who would be the first to fight over him.

When practice finished up, I walked down the steps of the bleachers and sat on the row behind where the girls practiced. Belle looked back at me and elbowed Danielle. She whispered something and they turned and looked at me again, laughing.

My face grew hot and I moved closer to the edge of my seat, wishing I could disappear but not wanting to move while they were watching me. As soon as they looked away, I gathered my things and stood up to get out of there.

"Hey, don't let those girls get to you," Derek said. He bent down and picked up the book I'd dropped. "You're classier than th—"

Heather came up then and put her hand on Derek's arm. "Great job out there today," she cooed and I could see him physically melt, his shoulders going limp before he came to his senses again and straightened.

"Why, thank you," he said, grinning down at her.

He walked off with her still beaming up at him, and I thought I was forgotten until Heather turned around and waved at me over her shoulder.

"See ya, Mira." She lifted a brow and gave me a smug smile, almost as if challenging me, but the next second I thought I'd imagined it.

———

I WAS HOME when Jaxson called.

"Where are you?" he asked before I even said hello.

"I'm not feeling well," I told him. "Have fun, though."

"What's wrong?"

He sounded so concerned that I felt bad for lying to him.

"I'll be fine. I just need to lie down. No worries..." My voice trailed off.

"Okay, I'll call you later. Get better. I want to have everyone come over on Friday night and can't do it without you."

"Jaxson, I've gotta go. Sorry." I hung up on him and fell back on my bed, wishing for the days when it was just the two of us.

He didn't call that night and I was driven to school instead of walking the next morning, so I didn't see him until the afternoon. He looked relieved when he saw me.

"Sorry, it was too late to call when everyone left. You feeling better?"

I nodded.

"You look fine," he said. A guy bumped his arm and he nodded. "Hey, Max." He looked back at me and grinned. "So this party tomorrow night...everyone's coming. You can't miss it. My mom said everyone could stay until midnight." His eyes widened to match mine. "I know. I can't believe it either. She likes everyone coming to our house, she says...so she can keep tabs on me." He shrugged again and I noticed how American he seemed.

"You hardly sound British anymore," I told him.

His eyebrows lowered in the middle. "Impossible. I get made fun of every day for my accent."

"You do? I thought I was the only one." I laughed.

"We'll never get rid of it, okay? We're the only ones who sound proper around here," he teased.

I leaned my head on his shoulder and smiled. "I've missed you," I said.

"Missed you too," he said, not realizing I meant more than yesterday's homework session.

Heather walked by and stopped when she saw us. "Group hug," she said, putting her arms around us.

Jaxson smiled at her when we all let go. "C'mon, I've gotta get to practice," he said.

"I'm going to head home," I said quietly. "Too much homework."

A flicker of hurt crossed his eyes, but it quickly faded. "Promise you'll come tomorrow night."

"I'll try."

But the next night, when it was time for me to make a decision about going to Jaxson's, I thought of all those girls surrounding him, how out of place I would feel, my conflicting thoughts about Heather...and instead, I made a double batch of chocolate chip cookies and watched the *Twilight* movies until I fell asleep. I spent the first four hours checking my phone to see if Jaxson would call, but he never did.

11

PRESENT

DD, I think I have survived everything now. Get me on solid ground, STAT. There is a reason the good Lord gave us FEET. To walk and not fly.
If you help me live, I will (most likely) not attempt this lunacy again. (Hopefully.)
Yours,
Mira

I'VE PROBABLY LOOKED at the airline ticket a hundred times, each time hoping it will tell me what to do. The night before the flight, Dave knocks on my door.

"You packed yet?" he asks.

I frown at him and shake my head. "What made you think I was going?"

"Oh, I don't know. I guess it was the free ticket to *Paris*." He snorts and even though I'm exhausted and anxious I laugh with him. "What if you went and heard him out? Things can be clearer without all the excess noise around you…it doesn't mean you have to *be* with him. Hell, you can even ditch him once you land and just enjoy the city."

"I hadn't thought of that," I admit.

"I can take you to the airport in the morning," he says.

"You really think I should go?" I ask. I shift my feet to the floor, knocking a throw pillow off of my bed in the process.

"I think you might regret it if you don't," he says.

―――

I HARDLY SLEEP at all that night and don't pack a thing. I don't set the alarm and tell myself if I do fall asleep and wake up in time to get to the airport, that will be my answer.

So when the sun hits my eyes and I jump straight up, wide awake after, at most, two hours of sleep, I don't think, I just start throwing things into a suitcase. I hurriedly shower, brush my teeth, and put mascara on before walking out to see if Dave really meant what he said. He's waiting in the kitchen, a to-go coffee mug held out for me.

Mum is sitting there, dressed for work and beaming.

"Don't get any ideas," I tell her. "This means absolutely nothing."

She acts like she's locking her lips and not saying a word. I lean down and hug her and she whispers, "Have fun. Be safe. I don't need to become a granny just yet."

I groan.

―――

THE AIRPORT IS A NIGHTMARE. I get my bag checked with minimal trouble, but then it takes forever to get through security. As we divide into lines for the last round, I get cut off by a businessman who thinks he deserves to get through faster than the rest of us, namely me, as his bag gives my leg a painful swipe. By the time it's my turn to put all my things on the conveyor, I'm a pile of nerves. My shoelace breaks as I'm trying to get my shoes back on and I give up, leaving both shoes untied.

No sign of Jaxson, and to his credit, he hasn't hassled me since leaving the ticket a couple of days ago. Part of me wonders if he's changed his mind about asking me to go. Or maybe he's sending me alone! My God. I haven't even considered that possibility yet.

I hear the last call for my flight as I'm twelve gates away and start running. One of my shoes keeps sliding off of my heel, but it manages to stay on. When I reach the gate, the attendant is typing away at her computer, but no one else is around.

"Please tell me I'm not too late..." I lean onto the counter, huffing, and a drop of sweat glides down my forehead.

She looks up. "You're cutting it very close," she says.

I want to cry, but she takes my ticket and scans it through the machine.

"Enjoy Paris," she says, waving me through.

I TAKE a deep breath before walking into the plane, humiliated to be the last one. But there he is. Seated in the second row in first class, the relief in Jaxson's eyes is almost my undoing. I tuck that feeling away and give him a faint smile. He stands up and takes my carry-on from me, putting it overhead as I take the seat by the window.

When he sits next to me, he leans over and kisses my

cheek. "Thank you for coming," he says softly. He lifts a glass of champagne. "I got this for you, just in case."

"It's not even nine in the morning," I whisper. I look around like the police are going to jump out and catch me for taking an underage sip. Just a couple of months before I'm twenty-one...no big deal, right? I look around again. No one is watching so I gulp it down, enjoying the burn.

Jaxson's eyes widen, along with his smile. "There are no constraints on this trip...at least not where time is concerned."

I lean my head back against the seat and turn to face him. His face—his perfect, beautiful face—is so close my lips could almost brush against his. I swallow and he leans in closer, his nose touching mine.

"I want to say something and I want to be sure you hear me right from the very start." I lean back just enough to get my bearings but not by much. "This trip, while you really shouldn't have done it, well, I'm just going to say thank you. I *am* appreciative and once the shock goes away, I know I will be very excited that I'm actually going to *Paris*." When I say the words, my heart picks up a little more. "Paris!" I smile at him and his eyes crinkle at the corners with his happiness. "I want to be comfortable with you, Jaxson. That's all I'm after. It doesn't mean we're picking up where we left off or starting something new...it simply means I don't want to see you at a crowded party and wish I could run the other way."

The pain in his eyes makes me regret my words instantly, but I hold to them.

"I'm sorry if that's too harsh. It needs to be said. It's how I feel. I can't give you the summer, or even next week, but I will give you Paris." I lift a shoulder. "And you might not still want me around after saying what I've said, but we can put the animosity aside for the trip and enjoy the place we've always wanted to go."

"I don't have any animosity toward you," he says quietly. "I just want to prove to you that I've changed and that I'm clear on what I want."

"That may be true, but I've also changed, and now *I* want different things."

He pulls back, stung, and I don't jump in to make him feel better, as I would have in the past. I let my words sink in and feel a sense of closure that I've needed, just by updating him on my feelings. Or lack thereof.

Breakfast comes before the awkwardness is too consuming and we eat the cute airplane food that isn't half bad in first class. I comment on this just to make conversation, and the time passes quickly as we half watch a movie together on the TV screen in front of us.

Eventually, I lean my head back against the seat and close my eyes, the exhaustion of overthinking every little thing catching up with me. The next thing I know, I wake up to a loud noise and a jolt. The plane shudders and dives and the captain tells everyone to quickly get in their seats and fasten seat belts. Jaxson takes my hand in his and I realize that I'm shaking. Besides flying from London to California and back those times as a kid, I haven't flown and those flights weren't rough. This seems extreme. We lurch and my stomach dives into the floor while my food jumps up in my throat. People are crying out with each drastic drop, and the person in the row across from us searches frantically for a bag and gets it just in time, the sound of her throwing up making me feel sicker.

I look at Jaxson, wide-eyed, and he puts his arms around me, holding me close.

"It'll be okay," he says. But then we take another dive and several people scream.

"We are going to have to make an unscheduled landing, folks. Fasten your seat belts, and stay in your seat until we are on the ground. Everyone, please remain calm," the pilot adds.

"Where are we landing, did you hear?" I ask Jaxson, the panic making my voice shrill.

"He didn't say," Jaxson yells over the commotion.

When we drop this time, I grip Jaxson's hand as hard as I can. The plane shudders and dips and I feel sure we're going to crash in the middle of nowhere, but then a runway comes into view and we're heading for it. When we touch the ground, the passengers applaud and I turn my head in the crook of Jaxson's neck and breathe in the relief.

"We made it," he whispers, kissing my forehead.

I lean into him, my body soaking in every touch of his, despite my brain warning me to stay away. It's just the situation we're in. We nearly died, for goodness' sake.

The speaker system crackles and the pilot gets on, sounding somewhat calmer. "We've landed in Montreal and will get you to the gate as soon as we can to work out your next travel arrangements. Thank you for your patience."

"Montreal?" Jaxson says. He looks frustrated, but when he turns to me, his eyes soften. "Well, things have never gone as expected for us, have they. We'll get there…" His hand stays in mine and we both take a deep breath.

12

PRESENT

I don't think I have to tell you twice, Diary, but there's something to be said for good old-fashioned PAPER.
Always,
Mira

IT'S a shock when we step off the plane and into the airport. It's not just crowded...it's suffocating. The gates surrounding ours are all in the same state—swarms of people trying to get answers from the poor people at the counter. We step into the jumbled line.

"What's going on?" Jaxson asks the man in front of us.

"From what I can tell, the computer systems are down. Flights from all the airlines are canceling. I'm not sure if it's this god-awful weather we're having or something else, but it's not looking good for flights."

Jaxson groans. "I can't believe it." He puts his hand on my arm and leans in closer. "Let's see what they say though. Maybe it's not as bad as it looks."

Just then, there's an announcement saying our flight and the next are canceled. When we finally reach the counter, Jaxson turns to the gate agent, Earl, with his charming smile and the man's eyes stay fixed on his computer, his fingers tapping away.

Jaxson gives him our tickets and Earl's fingers fly over the keyboard even faster.

"Our computer systems are down," Earl says flatly.

"Why are you using your computer then?" Jaxson asks.

Earl glances up and gives a droll eyebrow lift with one brow, then resumes typing. "All flights to Paris are canceled for today and tomorrow. It's possible we could get you out the day after that, but it's unlikely. I'd suggest you get a hotel and check in with the airline tomorrow or the next day."

He looks past us like he's already dismissed us and Jaxson puts his hand on the counter, leaning in. "Does this mean the car rentals won't be available either, with this computer..." He waves his hand around, speechless.

"You'll have to ask that at one of the rental locations. Follow the signs." And with that, he is completely done with us.

"Unbelievable." Jaxson looks at me, eye twitching, and we start laughing. We shuffle through the agitated people in line and laugh harder. "Come on, let's go work on Plan B... and eat something."

"I could eat." I nod, taking his hand so we don't get separated.

We follow the signs to the rental places and it's nearly as crowded. We stand in line and by the time it's our turn, we're not laughing anymore.

"We'll take whatever you have available," he tells the girl behind the counter.

She grins while her lashes lower seductively and my eyes narrow at her, while also being impressed that she can do all of that at the same time.

"I'm available," she says with a laugh and then glances at me and quickly sobers. "Sadly, not much else is. But we do have a couple of cars in this range." She points at the laminated page of cars and we aren't choosy.

He fills out the paperwork and eventually we're pulling out of the airport parking lot.

"Tell me what you think of this," he says. "We spend a couple of days in Montreal, checking out the sights...if we can't get a flight to Paris day after tomorrow, we drive to New York." He shrugs. "Cross the Empire State Building off of our list." He glances at me, waiting to see my reaction.

I grin. "I like it. Solid Plan B."

He lets out a gust of air. "Whew. Okay."

He drives as if he knows exactly where he's going.

"Have you been here before?" I ask.

"No, never. I'm excited to see it with you," he says.

"When did you start saying all the right things again?"

"When I remembered to start saying what I really feel instead of what someone might want to hear..." He swallows and I watch the slide of his throat, mesmerized.

I look away, face heating, ashamed that he can so easily get me off-course. I'll have to watch that this week or it would be so convenient to slide into old habits.

About fifteen minutes later we pull up to a grand building.

A man in a distinguished uniform opens my door and I step out, feeling like I might burst out laughing again.

"Welcome to Hotel Le St-James," he says.

Jaxson hands the keys to the valet and we walk inside.

"Wow," Jaxson says under his breath. "This is a nice little layover."

It feels like we've stepped into another time. The ceilings are beautiful white domes, which balance out the dark wood elsewhere. The marble floors gleam with beautiful rugs toning down the acoustics. I admire the intricate furnishings and for a moment I don't even remember Paris. While Jaxson works on getting us a room, I wander around a little, venturing into an area that makes my mouth drop. Circular wooden bookshelves hold old and new books alike and I let my fingers run against the spines.

I feel Jaxson before I see him, the hair on the back of my neck rising in awareness when he steps close behind me. I feel his breath against my cheek as he leans in. I should step away, I really should.

"I won't be able to get you out of here, will I?" His voice sounds husky and my heartbeat picks up.

I look at him and it's a mistake. He's so close our noses brush against each other.

"I could eat," I whisper.

He laughs and the spell is broken. "Let's feed you then. Right after we check out our room...hey, about the room. I hope it's okay that I just got one."

"Of course. I already feel bad about you spending so much money."

We walk to the elevator and he grins, waiting for me—I will always be the kid who wants to push the elevator button. I smile back and jump when the elevator dings.

"Please don't think about the money, Bells," he says. "I've been saving for this trip since we made the list."

"*What?*" I stare at him.

He holds my gaze, his eyes bright. "You heard me."

"I didn't think you could still manage to surprise me, but..." I shake my head.

When he opens the door to our room, I realize how much trouble I'm in. The room is a dream. Inviting, romantic, with a plush bed and a fireplace. A trunk sits at the end of the bed and I sigh, my romantic sensibilities firing off in rapid speed. *One bed.*

"I can sleep on the floor, of course. This room just sounded the best."

I decide to worry about the bed situation when it's time to sleep, which fortunately, is not now.

"I'll just freshen up," I tell him.

I take my suitcase into the bathroom and stare at myself in the mirror, the panic forcing me to look away. *This is nothing,* I tell myself. *Just a few days with an old friend. Nothing is going to happen. It will give me closure. That's all.* "That's all," I tell my reflection fiercely, daring her to disagree.

When I've got my makeup just right and have washed and reapplied deodorant, I slip on my dress...one I haven't worn before. It's not overly dressy, but what I think of as a vacation dress. Black with a few tiny flowers, very short but not slutty...at least I hope that's the effect. I walk out and Jaxson's mouth drops.

"Your turn," I say nonchalantly. "I'm done in there."

I hear him curse under his breath as he takes his things into the bathroom. Before he shuts the door, he says, "You steal my breath, Mira." He pokes his head out the door. "You've always been the most beautiful girl I've ever seen."

My heart puddles somewhere between my ankles and the floor. I want to look away, but I can't. Finally, he pulls back and shuts the door. I hear him start the shower.

Shaken, I try to ignore my fluttering chest. I put on my

fabulous sandals that are just high enough that I won't wobble and sit on the chair near the fireplace. Staring at the bed, I think of his words and as much as I try to resist, my past insecurities bubble up to the surface. I lift my eyes to the ceiling and will myself to not cry. I can't mess up all the work I just put into my face.

He doesn't mean what he said. He's the best liar I know.

13

PAST

SEPT 2011

I'm going to die of sadness, D. I am one catastrophe short of death. I know you think I'm dramatic, but I mean it this time.
Truly,
Mira

A FAINT RAPPING on my door made me jump. I had my dress over my head and was frantically trying to pull it down over my lumpy stomach. It took me twenty minutes to get my new contacts in, so I was already late and crabby *before* trying to suck in enough to get this dress on.

"Mira? Can I come in?" my mother asked.

I tried to respond, but it came out muffled beneath the fabric.

She opened my bedroom door and I could barely see her through all the material still around my head, but she looked concerned.

"Oh dear, what happened? That fit when we bought it a few weeks ago."

I pulled and the awful sound of my dress ripping made us both gasp. My mum helped me get the dress off and when she found the tear, four of her fingers waved through the hole.

"I can't go to this party," I sobbed, plopping down on the bed.

"You can't miss your own party," my mother said. She set the dress down and put her hand on my shoulder, her gaze wandering down my body and narrowing in on the rolls. When she met my eyes again, she bit her lip and tried to put on an encouraging smile. "I'm sure there's something else you can wear. I know...why don't you look in my closet."

I groaned and cried harder. My mom dressed like an old lady, even my dad used to say so. She came back with a black dress slung over her arm. I recognized it instantly. She used to wear it on date nights with my dad, back before she went through her divorce weight loss. Nothing that a girl celebrating her thirteenth birthday should be caught dead in, but it was better than my new holey dress.

"This will be beautiful with your translucent skin," she said, handing me the dress.

"I'll look like a corpse. The sun hates me." I fell back on my bed and then curled up in a ball. "I told you I didn't want a party, Mum. I just want to hang out with Tyra and watch movies. Stay up late, make cookies..."

Her lips tightened with annoyance, but she sat down on the bed and took my hand.

"Has something happened between you and Jaxson, sweetheart?"

"No...we just don't..." My lip trembled and more tears

fell down my cheeks. "We're still friends. But it's different. *He's* different. He has so many new friends who are as beautiful and popular as he is and I'm still just me. And now to top it off, we're at different schools." I choked back a sob.

"Oh honey, popularity has never mattered to Jaxson. He's not about that." She sniffed and patted my shoulder. "And you'll be right there with him next year in high school…"

It took everything in me not to argue with her. These days Jaxson was riding high on all the attention he got. And now that they had endless money to spend, he had the best of *everything*. Sometimes I wondered if the boy who said he couldn't wait to explore life with me was gone forever.

"Come on, let's get your face washed and you'll feel better," Mum insisted.

I rolled my eyes until they hurt but let her pull me into the bathroom, where I tolerated her wiping a cold, wet washcloth across my face. It seemed to make her feel better. I still felt like dying inside, but she definitely perked up.

"We have fifteen of your friends coming in a half hour. I can do your makeup if you want."

"They're not my friends," I muttered, but she either ignored it or didn't hear me. "I can do my own makeup."

"Fine." Her shoulders sagged, but she let me move past her to my bedroom.

There wasn't much I could do to improve my puffy eyes, but I did my best. I thought about putting my glasses back on.

When Tyra got there ten minutes later, she screeched, "What happened to you?"

And instead of being mortified, I laughed. "That's what

I love about you," I told her. "You don't try to sugarcoat anything."

"I can help." She pulled out her cosmetic bag from her purse and held her bottom lip between her teeth while she fixed me up.

When I turned to look in the mirror, my mouth dropped. I looked like an eighties porn star. Or what I'd expect them to look like—I'd never really seen a porn star... that I knew of. My mom would die when she saw me in all this makeup. She'd only just started letting me wear it.

"I didn't know you had blue eye shadow," I said. "I've never seen you wear it."

"It's not good on me, but look how blue it makes your eyes look," she said. "We can really see them now that they're not hidden behind your glasses."

My lips were so glossed, every hair and dust mite in the hundred-mile radius would attach to my mouth like little magnet particles.

"Are you sure this is working?" I asked. I mean, she did always look so good. And it did make me look at least fifteen and a half.

"You look sensational. I just think you need a belt with that dress. It doesn't show your curves at all."

"I think maybe that's the idea..."

"All these girls are so skinny they don't have any boobs. Cinch that waist and your chest will be all any guy will notice."

I wasn't sure her theory was true, and I didn't really care about any guy but one...but there wasn't time to think about it. She threw a wide black belt at me as the doorbell rang.

"I'll answer the door. You wait here until everyone arrives and then make a grand entrance!" Her eyes were wide and she looked more excited than I'd seen her since *her* birthday. "You look beautiful," she said sweetly before she went out the door.

I wouldn't wait until everyone got there—that would be too much attention on me—but I looked out the window to draw out the solitude a little longer. A tree mostly blocked my window, but I could still see part of the driveway. A group of girls, Derek, and Jaxson were strolling toward the house, laughing, and taking their time. They all looked like they belonged here, with their smiles and tans and perfect clothes and bodies.

I swallowed hard and pulled away but then saw something that made my heart clatter inside my chest. Jaxson pulled Heather by the hand and then kept holding it...not friends swinging hand-holding, but the entwined fingerhold. Heather looked at Jaxson and smiled, hearts where her pupils had been.

I stepped away from the window like I'd been shot and sat down on the bed. And then I hopped back up. He'd been mine my whole life. I couldn't give up so easily, could I? I glanced in my mirror with uncertainty before I stopped living inside my head and went out to face the music.

———

THE ROOM WENT silent when I entered it. I smiled and then felt gloss on my teeth. I tried to turn and subtly swipe my teeth before turning to everyone again. Danielle and Giselle were closest to me and I heard them laugh.

"Oh my god, what is she wearing?" Giselle said.

I squared my shoulders and turned my back on them just as Tyra called me over. There were about ten people standing and sitting in various awkward arrangements, each looking as uncomfortable as I felt. Music played softly in the background and I was glad for that or the room would be silent. When the door opened and Jaxson came in with the others, I had to remember that if everything else went wrong with this birthday party, I'd make it right by fighting for him.

THE PARTY WAS TORTURE. My mom and Anne had a few games they wanted us to play, but none of the kids were interested in them. Tyra and I tried, but everyone else stood talking by the food or sitting against the wall. I had a hard time paying attention to anything but the couple huddled in the corner. Jaxson had come over to hug me and wish me a happy birthday, but then Heather had dragged him to the corner and they were in a deep discussion.

Anne saw me staring at them and gave me a sympathetic look, but our attention was diverted when the front door slammed. Jaxson followed Heather out the door, and I didn't think, I just moved quickly. They were already around the corner when I stepped outside, and I paused, not sure if she was crying or just whiny.

"It's our anniversary, I don't know why we have to be at this party," Heather said. "You don't even really hang out with her anymore."

I put my hand over my mouth and stayed still, wishing I'd stayed inside. *Anniversary?*

"Come back inside," Jaxson said. "I can't leave yet. I told you—my mom made me come. She said I'd be grounded for a month if I didn't get over here."

"Haven't you told your mom you don't want to be friends with Mira anymore? I thought you were going to."

"My mom wouldn't understand. She doesn't know how much Mira has changed."

Everything felt hot: my skin, my clothes, my shoes...the belt. I couldn't breathe.

"She's so serious now, always lurking in the corner, watching me, following me...trying to be part of the crowd when she doesn't fit in. I think she's insecure about her weight, but I wish she'd do something about it if that's how she feels."

My fist squeezed tighter against my mouth, and I tried to stop it but a sob broke out.

"What was that?" I heard him ask and I turned and ran before he could see me.

I shut the door quietly and was going to run up the stairs, but Derek blocked me. "Mira, what's wrong?" He put his hands on my arms then led me into the office when he saw that I was crying.

"I don't fit in here. I never will," I told him.

He put his arms around me and let me cry. I appreciated that he didn't try to tell me otherwise.

―――

JAXSON AND HEATHER came back in around the time I was opening presents. When I got to his present, he came and stood next to me, smiling sweetly. Such a hypocrite. I stared through him until he became fidgety.

"Aren't you going to open it?" he asked when I just held the box in my hands.

Instead of answering, I finally ripped the package open. Inside the box was a huge leather-bound book with my name engraved on the bottom right corner. It was beautiful. I looked at it for so long, my mom bumped my arm.

"You still journal, hopefully?" He looked at his mum to make sure he had it right—that it was, in fact, a journal.

"That's gorgeous, isn't it, honey? Jaxson, that is so thoughtful. Tell him thank you, Mira," my mum said.

I found Anne and held up the book. "Thank you, Anne. This is really thoughtful."

Anne tilted her head and smiled. "Jaxson picked it out, but you're welcome."

I looked at Jaxson then and leaned in so only he could hear. "You have everyone fooled but me. I wish you'd told me yourself that we aren't friends anymore. It would've saved you all the time and money you put into this gift. Oh, wait...you have more than enough money to waste now."

His mouth dropped and he grabbed my arm. "Bells, what's going on? What do you mean? You're my *best* friend," he whispered urgently.

I yanked my arm away. "You're a liar, and I never, ever want to see you again. Ever!"

I backed away from him and then while everyone stared at us in confusion, I ran to my bedroom and locked the door.

I didn't speak to Jaxson again until I was forced to the following year.

14

PRESENT

*He sings and I am putty in his hands, Diary.
I don't dare tell him that, but I just thought you should know.*

"IS SOMETHING WRONG?"

We're at the hotel restaurant, which is one of the prettiest places I've ever seen. The bite of food I try is out of this world, but I'm moving it around on my plate, swirling it when Jaxson speaks. I look up at him and set my fork down.

"I'm fine," I answer quietly.

"Something changed while I was in the shower. You've been looking at me like...you hate me again."

"Who says I ever stopped?" I ask, picking up my fork and continuing to make pictures on my plate with the pretty food.

"Bells," he whispers, his voice plaintive and sad.

I would feel bad for him if not for the fact that he's the one who created this divide.

"I don't know how to get past everything, Jaxson. I really don't. I thought I could, but then...I remember."

"You said you'd give me Paris." He tries to smile, but instead, he looks in pain. "I know we're on Plan B here, but can we please put everything in the past for this week?"

"You say that—put everything in the past—but you don't mean it because the very list itself is the past. Our friendship is the past and you want to pull it out when it's convenient and skim over the parts where you screwed up. That's not really putting things in the past at all."

He's staring at me with a piece of steak hanging on his fork, eyes unblinking. "I like when you get indignant," he says finally. "It suits you. Eyes all fiery and whatnot."

I take a sip of my wine—the legal drinking age in Montreal is eighteen, how convenient is that—and then decide, what the heck, I'll guzzle the whole glass. Jaxson pours another glass and I take a few bites of food before having the second glass.

"You're right, you know. Guilty." He makes a goofy face but quickly sobers. "I guess I keep hoping there is a new us. One that remembers what is beautiful about us but also makes new and better memories." He leans in. "When I think back on us, I only feel the love. And I'm afraid when you look back on everything, all you feel is the sadness." He looks so devastated that my eyes fill and I have to look away. "I really would like a chance to change that."

"Let's just try to get through this week," I tell him.

"Like you're being tortured," he mutters.

"No..." I jump in. "More like I don't want to figure out who we will be after this week. I just want to be right here, right now."

"I can do that," he says.

He clinks his glass to mine and we manage to enjoy the rest of our dinner.

———

"*I DIDN'T KNOW what I had until she was gone,*" he sings in my ear as we stumble down the hall. "*Her eyes haunt me from sunset until dawn...If I could tell her one thing, it would be this...I came alive with her kiss.*"

We stop at the door and fumble for the lock, him still singing the sad song.

"What song is that? It's too sad." I shake my head, fumbling with my shoes as I step inside.

"It's your song," he says. "Our song. One of the many songs I've written about you...with a consistent theme of you being gone. We need new ones where you stay..."

Once my shoes are off, I fall back on the bed, my head spinning. "So I'm your muse?"

"Do you even need to ask?" He laughs, falling on the bed beside me.

"Apparently so. What are your plans with your music? That night I heard you...you sounded even better than I remembered, and I always thought you were bloody fantastic." I turn my head to face him.

He grins. "Thanks, Bells. I didn't think you...liked it. I'm glad you did. I've been working on the music a lot. At school, I really thought maybe I would pursue a music career full-time, but while I still love it so much, I'm just not sure that's who I really am. I love doing other things too, you know? For now, I've decided to keep working at Charles' company. It's fulfilling, I'm good at it, and I like making money." He laughs. "And I'm still playing music around town, so that outlet is there. I don't really want to go on tour for months at a time. We've had several opportunities to do that, and I've told the guys if they want to pursue that, they should, but my life is here. I feel like for the first time I'm finally becoming more grounded. A life on the road doesn't sound so appealing. Especially when I have a heart to win over." He yawns and closes his eyes when he says that and I feel like I've just been jump-started.

"You're not staying because of me, are you?"

"Everything is because of you, Bells. Don't you know that by now?"

His face relaxes and I realize he's fallen asleep that quickly...clothes on, outside the covers and all. I get up and put my pajamas on. I had too much to drink, so I take a few Advil and get under the covers as best I can.

When I wake up the next morning, his still fully-clothed body is wrapped around mine. We're spooning like we were born to do it, and it feels so good, so comforting, that I close my eyes and fall back into a deep sleep. I sleep better than I have in years.

―――

WE'RE shy with each other when we wake up. He smiles sweetly at me when I turn to see if he's awake and I wonder how long he's been watching me. I jump up and get my shower and when I come out, he's getting off of the phone.

"It's not looking like an option to get out of here any time today or even tomorrow," he says. "They're calling it the biggest airline crisis in history. Can you believe that?" He pulls his clothes out of the suitcase. "I'm sorry, Mira. Not how I pictured our Paris trip of a lifetime."

"No more apologizing. There's no way we could have known this would happen."

"Well, how about we explore around here today and then get back to our list tomorrow...drive to New York sometime tomorrow?"

"Or the day after tomorrow even..."

His smile brightens. "Plan C, I like it.

"HOW LONG SINCE you've been on a bike?" he asks, as we step outside.

"Holmes Chapel."

"Jeez," he teases. "Nearly as long for me. Why did we stop riding?"

"You were too busy surfing." *With Heather*, I nearly add but stop myself.

"Surfing is overrated. Kidding," he quickly amends.

He grabs my arm and we veer to the right, where we try to figure out the rental station. Once we have our bikes, I look over at him and see him as a kid in Holmes Chapel, where we spent nearly every day on a bike. I must look wistful because when he catches me staring, he flushes slightly.

"Ready?" he asks.

I nod, emotion stuck in my throat.

We start out slowly and while we're in traffic, I'm a nervous wreck, but once we're on a quieter path, it gets easier. The breeze through my hair and fresh air on my face are intoxicating. I can't believe I ever stopped doing this.

We make it to the canal and the way the sun hits the water is perfection. We stop here and there to catch our breath and take it all in but don't really talk much. It's a comfortable silence between us, but that shy feeling is still there. We ride for a while and on our last stop, my stomach growls so loud, a nearby squirrel stops running and stares at me.

Jaxson's laugh bounces off the river, making my stomach twist further. I've always loved the way his eyes and nose both crinkle up when he laughs. He motions toward one of the street food places behind us.

"I think it's time," he says.

I roll my eyes but laugh along with him.

We get burgers and share an order of poutine so we can say we've tried it. While we're eating, a little curly-haired boy catches our attention and we watch him trying to walk with his mom close behind, hands out at all times to soften the blow when he falls, which is often.

"Do you still want kids?" Jaxson asks, taking a big bite of his burger.

"I either want none or several," I tell him. "After Tyra..." I take a bite of food to stall all the feelings that stir up when I think of her.

He reaches over and squeezes my arm, letting it linger there on my skin.

"First you and then her...you both made being an only child a lot easier. But once you were gone...that changed everything. Maybe it would be different if I were really a present mother, you know? Someone who likes to hang out with her kid and is really there for them. Maybe it wouldn't matter then if I had more kids to keep that first one company. But how does a person know ahead of time if they'll be that way?"

"You will. I know you will. You don't do anything halfway. You go all in, no matter what you're doing."

"Maybe. I mean, hopefully." I shrug. "What about you? Kids?"

"Definitely. Someone once told me two's good, but

three's..." His eyebrow quirks up and he waits for me to remember.

"Better," I finish and feel flushed with the sudden heat. "You better hope you can find a woman who will put up with three little Jaxsons running around then."

He doesn't say anything, just smiles that same satisfied smile he's smiled all day.

"So Dave seems really great," he says finally.

"He's the best thing to happen to my mum and me," I agree. "He loves her and doesn't act bothered by me being part of the picture. And he gives good advice...in fact, he's the one who nudged me to take this trip with you."

"Dave is the best thing to happen to me," he says, laughing. "I'll have to find a way to properly thank him when we get back."

"You just don't quit, do you?"

"Nope," he says. "As Nana would say, I've lost the plot over you."

"Aw, I'd love to see her. The last time I saw her was..." I pause because the last time I saw his grandmother was one of my least favorite memories.

"Yeah, that Christmas," he says, and I know by his expression that he remembers just how awful that night was.

15

PAST

CHRISTMAS 2013

Oh D, there are times I just can't keep up.
It's a good thing I have you. I don't want to be a snitch.
What to do?
This is yet another time when it would be really nice if you could talk.
~M

"I REFUSE TO GO, Mum! You cannot make me!" I yelled across the house and slammed the door to my bedroom.

She stomped up the stairs and came in without knocking. I hated when she did that.

"For the last time, you don't have a choice. They are like family to us. You've known Jaxson your whole life! I can't help it if you aren't speaking to him right now. Maybe it's time to get over yourself and give the poor guy a break. He's nearly beaten that door down trying to figure out how to win back your friendship."

"Because his mother made him!" I yelled. "At school,

we steer clear of each other. The only time we've spoken in a year is when you made me go to his stupid birthday party last year. If that's what you call beating my door down, yeah, he's really going full-throttle."

I didn't tell her he had thrown rocks at my window throughout that first year we weren't speaking, seeing if I'd come down and talk. His mom had probably made him do that too. Before, anytime he really wanted to see me, he climbed up to my window. He was relieved to be done with me—I knew it in my heart of hearts.

"I shouldn't be put through the torture of being around him any longer," I said quietly. "Please don't make me go."

"I don't make you go over there regularly, but it's Christmas...*please*, Mirabelle. Gemma will be there. Things are good with her, aren't they? I remember you talking with her at the party last year."

"Yeah, Gemma is on my side," I told her.

When Gemma saw me standing in the corner at Jaxson's birthday party last year and asked why I was there and not in the thick of things, she'd assessed the situation without me having to say a word. She'd stood by me the rest of the night, making wisecracks about all the girls tripping over themselves to get attention from Jaxson.

"He's an idiot if he doesn't see what he has with you," she'd said.

By that time, I'd built a shell around my heart so thick that I almost didn't feel what she said, but somewhere down deep, what she said penetrated. Yes, he *was* an idiot of the supreme kind.

"Why is there a *side*? I wish you'd just tell me what happened," Mum snapped. "It's been two years. Get over it already!"

My eyes filled with tears. "Why can't you just have my back?"

She put her arms around me and hugged me close. "I do. I have your back, I promise. I just wish, for both your sakes, you could work things out. You've been miserable without one another. Anne says he's not the same without you."

"The two of you are seeing what you want to see, and I'm sorry, but it's not happening—you're not going to get your little fairy tale with us. He's moved on and so have I; we're different people now."

"If you'd moved on, it wouldn't bother you so much to see him." She took my face in her hands and studied me. "Sweetheart, for this one day, don't you think you could set things aside and simply wish him well for the upcoming year?"

When she put it like that, it did sound appealing. More than wishing him well, I wanted to stop thinking about him, period. In a dream world, I wouldn't be in turmoil over Jaxson Marshall for another second, but I didn't know how to stop. I'd loved him much longer than I'd hated him.

I put my hand on my mother's and held it tighter against my face for a moment longer. "Okay, I'll go. It'll be good to see Gemma. But can I bring Tyra?"

She crinkled her nose. "Not tonight, okay? Let's just have it be us tonight."

I didn't like it, but I agreed. I needed someone besides Jaxson's sister, just in case she hated me by now. Derek and Jaxson were together so much that after everything changed with Jaxson, it meant I didn't really see Derek anymore either. He smiled when he saw me in the hall, but as far as having an ally at the party, I didn't think I could turn to him. My mother would forget me once she got to Jaxson's house.

She and Anne were still like kids when they got together, giggling over nothing and in their own little bubble. I didn't begrudge my mum's time with her best friend—being a single parent was hard and I didn't want or need all of her attention on me, so most of the time I was glad of Anne's distraction.

Once Mum left my room, I FaceTimed Tyra. She answered and was on her treadmill, sweating like she'd been at it a while.

"Guess where I'm going tonight?" I pulled a long face and whispered the next bit into the phone. "Mum is making me go to Jaxson's."

She rolled her eyes and toweled off her forehead. "Well, go in there looking good and like you *know* you look good. You're so much better than all of them, Mira. Never, ever forget that."

"I wish I had your self-confidence. Someday I'll catch up with you."

She laughed. "My confidence is off the *chain*. I *dare* you to catch up."

"I love you," I said, still laughing. "I'm gonna go obey you now and look as hot as possible."

"That's my girl. Love you. Merry Christmas!"

"Merry Christmas." We'd celebrated the day before, but I still wished she could be with me tonight.

We hung up and I smiled while I walked to my closet. Tyra had a way of making everything better, always. She didn't care what anyone else thought and lived life exactly the way she wanted. It was impossible to wallow for very long around her.

I picked out some of the outfits she'd given me. Since working out every day and joining track, her clothes swam on her, so I had a new wardrobe with far better choices than my mum's closet. I settled on jeans and a nice shirt. It probably wouldn't be as dressy as everyone else, but I squared my shoulders and tried to channel some of Tyra's sass.

Thanks to YouTube tutorials, I could safely say I'd mastered makeup and hair. I still wasn't up to California standards—I couldn't seem to give up the junk food and the last thing I wanted to do was physical activity, but give me a curling iron or a new makeup palette and I could put the most perfect waves in anyone's hair, mine included. And I could make my face look flawless. After that makeup debacle two years ago with Tyra's heavy hand, I decided to teach myself how to do it.

Act like you know you look good, I reminded myself on my way out the door.

"You look lovely, Mira," my mum said as we walked to the Marshalls' house.

"Thanks, Mum. You do too."

The party was underway already when we got there, the beach behind Jaxson's house full of kids playing volleyball and standing by the fire pit. I got mad all over again that Mum hadn't let me bring Tyra since all of these other people were here. It wasn't just our families like she'd made it sound like it would be. I went inside to get a drink before going out there and watched through the window. Jaxson's long arms shot up and he got the volleyball over the net, the other team missing the shot. He looked happy. I wondered what it would be like to be on the inside of his life again.

I stood there longer than I should've, the only non-adult in the house, but something kept me rooted to that spot. From this height, I had a better vantage point. I didn't see Heather right away. Normally, she was within a few feet of Jaxson at all times, but she wasn't in the game and she wasn't on the sidelines. I kept looking for her but didn't spot her anywhere.

"We're ready for dessert. Come on out, Mira," Anne said, waving for me to follow her.

"I need to use the restroom and then I'll be right out," I promised.

"Excellent. I want Jaxson to know you're here." She smiled and gathered things to carry outside.

Jaxson's nana followed Anne and winked at me on the way out. "You need to weasel your way in between Jaxson and all these dimwits," she said under her breath. "You have more depth to you than most of these girls have in their big toe!"

I laughed. "Thanks, Nana. I don't know—guys seem to like the dimwits."

She cackled and went out the door.

Someone was in the downstairs bathroom, so I went to the second floor and heard someone in there. I waited for a few moments and then went completely still. Oh god. Heat flooded to my face and I looked around, wondering if anyone else was hearing this. Someone was having sex in the bathroom! There was no mistaking that—I'd managed to catch the peak moment, so to speak. A hissed, "Shhh!" and a muffled groan followed. I rolled my eyes. *Too late.* When it got completely quiet and I heard the sound of a toilet flushing and the sink turning off and on, I realized I was going to get caught if I didn't move quickly. I was backing away just as the door opened.

Derek walked out first and quickly stopped, staring wide-eyed as he saw me standing there. He turned to prevent the girl from coming out, but it was too late. Heather walked out and there was no hiding for any of us.

16

PAST

2013

That saying about hindsight...it's haunting me now.
I am terrified of loving another person ever again.

HEATHER'S HORROR smoothed over as she took a breath and worked on conjuring up a smile. She stepped toward me, and my eyes narrowed. When I put my hand on my hip, she stopped walking, and I could clearly see the fear in her eyes.

"This isn't what it looks like," she whispered. "I don't know what you're thinking you heard or saw, but you know nothing. I love Jax and nothing you tell him will change the way he feels about me."

Derek looked equal parts hurt and ashamed.

"Something tells me that if you can have sex in Jaxson's bathroom during a *Christmas* party, you're being all kinds of careless. I doubt I'll have to say a word." I shrugged. "I also doubt I'm the only one who'll find out. You're both idiots and Jaxson is smart—it might take a while, but he'll figure out that the two of you are lying snakes." I pointed at Heather. "Can't say I'm surprised about you…"

The vein on Heather's forehead popped out as she grew redder. She didn't enjoy being called out, but I didn't really care.

"You though…I really thought you were better than this," I said to Derek.

When I looked at Derek, he swallowed hard and put his fist over his mouth. "Mira, please…" he said.

I turned and went down the steps, with them on my heels.

"Jaxson!" I called out, as I rounded the corner and came face to face with him.

He looked startled and I knew it wasn't just from not expecting to see someone coming straight for him, but because I hadn't spoken to him in so long.

"Hi, Mira," he said softly. "I'm glad…" He looked at Heather and Derek and seemed puzzled to see us together. "Thanks for coming," he told me.

"Can we talk for a moment?" I didn't know where I was going with this, but it was out of my mouth before I could stop it. Heather gripped my arm and squeezed. Hard.

I glared at her and she dropped her hand, smiling. I rubbed where her hand had been and looked at Jaxson.

"What's going on?" he asked, looking back and forth between all of us.

"Alone?" I said.

"Jax, Derek and I have been working on your surprise and it's ready n—"

"Surprise," I scoffed, and they all looked at me. I shook my head and laughed. "Yeah, it's a surprise all right."

Jaxson frowned and I felt sorry for him. He didn't

deserve this. No matter how hurt I'd felt by him, he didn't deserve *this*.

"Heather and D—" I started, but Heather cut me off.

"Really, Jax, come on. We've been working so hard on it. Jeez, Mira, I know you've got a crush on Derek, but *not now*," Heather said, tossing her hair and smiling at Jaxson like *can you believe this girl?*

"What?" I sputtered.

"Heather," Derek snapped. "Shut up."

Heather smirked and Jaxson looked so confused. He shook his head.

"What's going on?" he asked.

"God, you're all so serious. I was just joking. Now, can we go get your present already?" Heather put her arm around his waist and he moved along with her, giving me an apologetic look over his shoulder.

"I'll talk to you later, Mira? Okay?"

"Merry Christmas, Jaxson. That's really all I wanted to say tonight. And I wish the best for you this year." There, I'd said it. And it felt good, liberating. The rest would work itself out. I didn't need to be the bearer of bad news—especially not today. He'd resent me for it forever.

He moved Heather's hand, which was still gripping his arm tightly, and moved back toward me. "Thank you, Bells. That means a lot."

I think he meant it. I didn't stop to question if he did or not. I nodded, found my mother to tell her I was leaving, and walked home.

I WOKE up to noise outside and got up, heart pounding. It had been so long since Jaxson had reached out to me. I missed it...I missed *him*. Desperately. I could only admit that to myself in the dark.

Instead, when I looked out the window, it wasn't Jaxson at all. It was someone slim—it looked like a girl with a hoodie on, holding a can of spray paint in each hand. I grabbed my robe and threw it on, running down the stairs as fast as I could. I flung the door open and ran out. By the time I got outside, she was gone. It was no use anyway: I was too late.

The word *pathetic* was written over and over on our house in red spray paint. Even our car had *pathetic* covering it in huge block letters. I sobbed as I tried to scrub it off of the car and house, frantically running back and forth. It didn't make a difference; in fact, with every smear I made, it only made it more chilling. I felt the word in my bones. I agreed with the word...I'd thought it about myself before, so this only solidified it. *I am pathetic* rang out in my mind like a noon church bell.

I lost track of time out there, and when I came in, the sun was rising. Exhausted, I barely heard my mum before I bumped into her. Coffee sloshed from her mug and she set it down, taking me by the shoulders.

"Mira? What's going on? Are you bleeding?" Her voice rose with concern and she sat me down on a barstool while she looked me over.

I couldn't catch my breath to tell her, as the tears kept coming down. Just then the phone rang, and she was about to ignore it but saw who it was and held up her phone.

"It's Charles. I'm sorry I should take this. It might be about our meeting this morning..."

I didn't say anything, and when she heard what he had to say, she looked more distressed. She glanced at me and rushed outside.

"Oh my god," I heard her say over and over.

Someone else—Charles, I could tell as I walked to the door—was out there too.

"I didn't know if you'd seen it yet," he said. "I was on my way to the gym and couldn't believe...who the hell would do this?"

They both stared at me when I walked out.

"Do you have any idea who did this?" Charles asked me.

I shook my head. Of course I did, but there was no way to prove it. This was a warning. What would Heather do if I said it was her and no one believed me?

Mum started crying and took my hand.

"I'll send someone over to take care of this right away," Charles said. "Don't worry about a thing, okay? You know our crew at the rental properties will be happy to do this for you. I'd like to install cameras too...make sure this doesn't happen again."

"I can't let you do all that," Mum said. "It's too much..."

"Consider it part of your raise," he said. "You closed on that massive property for me just this week—this will be an addition to your compensation. How's that?"

She nodded and smiled, wiping her eyes. "Thank you, Charles."

"We take care of our family." He looked at me again. "We haven't seen as much of you as we'd like lately, Mira, but you know Anne and I are always here for you, right?"

I nodded. "I do know that. Thank you."

I didn't want to embarrass myself by sobbing in front of him any longer, so I went inside and got in the shower. It was a weekend. Most of the kids from school would be sleeping late from holiday break, especially after Jaxson's party. I didn't know how long it would take for it to be painted over, but maybe no one I knew would see it.

If I'd known how small the whole thing was in comparison to what else would happen that weekend, I wouldn't have shed a single tear over Heather. I would've rushed to Tyra's house and made sure we didn't leave the comfort of her family room for the rest of the weekend. We would've painted nails and watched movies all day long.

But, too caught up in my own drama, I didn't talk to Tyra all day. A crew of painters came, and between feeding them and doing what I could to be helpful outside, I didn't talk to her the next day either. Sunday night, around six p.m., after the house was finished and the car had been towed away for a new paint job, Charles and Anne came to the door. I thought their faces were somber because of everything that had happened, but the way Anne wept when she hugged me, I knew something else was wrong.

"Mira, I'm so sorry," she cried, "there's been a car accident. Tyra and her parents..."

I felt myself falling back and Charles held me up. I heard the words *they didn't make it* from somewhere far away, but I couldn't hold onto what that could possibly mean. Tyra had more life in her than anyone I'd ever known. There was no way she could be gone.

17

PRESENT
SUMMER 2019

Traveling is not for the faint of heart. Maybe if you're not accident prone, this doesn't apply, but D, this trip, the cosmos have aligned against me and are saying, "TAG! YOU'RE IT!" before raining down fiery missiles.
But other than that, it's really fun.
Always,
Mira

WE'RE on our way to New York. We spent another day in Montreal and loved the city, but the list is on Jaxson's mind, and if we can't get to Paris, he wants to make sure we at least get to New York. We've only been driving a few hours, but we're both anxious to get there. Jaxson won't settle on a song and keeps switching it just as I get into it.

"What's up? You're so anxious," I say, reaching out and stopping him from changing the song *again*.

"I haven't known whether to bring it up..." He glances at me and grips the steering wheel harder. "I started to say it the other night when you mentioned her, but...I lost my nerve."

"What? Just say it."

"I feel awful for not being there for you more after Tyra. And that craziness with your house being painted all happening around the same time...I didn't know what to do or say. We'd barely talked for two years, but I remember you sort of reaching out to me that one Christmas. I didn't want to make things worse. Even later, when we—" he clears his throat and chews the inside of his mouth nervously, "—you know..." The pregnant pause is excruciating. I know exactly what he's not saying, but I'm not going to make it easy for him. "I, uh...well, I wish I'd said it then and I didn't. I was so stupid and I'm sorry. I'm *really* sorry."

I swallow hard and look out the window. The view whips past me and I wonder if my eyes are doing that creepy fast movement I've seen in movies.

"Honestly, the year after Tyra died was a fog," I finally say. "Most of it still is." I don't go into the parts I do remember. Some things are better left in the past where they belong. "It was a miracle I got through my sophomore year. I kept my head down—I didn't want any trouble. I remember you trying to talk to me a few times, but I stuck to being alone. It was easier that way."

"I was dying for you to let me in," he says quietly.

I sigh and shake my head. "In your memory, maybe that's how you remember it, but no. You were preoccupied with one thing, and one thing only...well, two things that went hand in hand for you. Sex. And Heather."

He groans and I turn up the radio, so done with this conversation.

―――

IT'S early evening when we arrive in New York and I've barely said two words to Jaxson since our conversation. I look at all the buildings and lights around me, and it doesn't feel real that we're really here. We check into a nice hotel, freshen up, and go to a restaurant that the concierge recommends.

"What can I do to lighten things up here?" Jaxson says after trying to start a conversation numerous times.

"I don't know what to tell you," I reply. "I've never been good at being fake."

"I'm not asking you to fake anything," he says, eyes snapping. "Talk to me, let me have it. Yell at me. I can take it. I deserve it."

I take the last bite of my burger and stuff two fries in my mouth. When I'm finished chewing, I swig my Coke until my eyes burn. Then I stand up and walk out of the restaurant. I hear him calling my name, but I walk faster.

We're in a busy part of the city and the sidewalks are crowded. It's easy to lose myself in all the people. I walk and walk, looking in the windows, sometimes admiring the pretty displays, and other times seeing scenes of the past flashing before me. When those pictures get too vivid, I walk faster.

It's two in the morning before I find my way back to the hotel. My feet hurt and even my little purse holding my phone and lipstick feels heavy across my shoulder, but I'm so exhausted that I'm hopeful sleep will come.

Jaxson is in the hotel lobby, elbows on his knees, eyes rimmed red, and hair going every which way. He jumps up when he sees me and hugs me to his chest.

"Thank God," he says. "I was worried sick." He doesn't sound mad, but worse—desolate. It makes my heart hurt. "I'm so glad you came back," he whispers.

When I lift my head, his face is close and his lips softly brush against mine. It surprises me, but I'm too exhausted to acknowledge it. He puts his arm around me and leads me to the elevator. When we get to the room, he pulls the comforter back and I crawl into bed. I'm filthy, but I'm too tired to do anything else. He crawls in on the other side and pulls my back to his chest, holding me tight the rest of the night.

THE NEXT MORNING I feel bad about how I've acted and decide I'll make an effort to try harder to keep the peace. Just a few more days...

"So coffee, then the Empire State Building?" I ask when he comes out of the bathroom, showered and looking far better than he should. It would really help if he were ugly.

His eyes assess me too and I can tell he likes what he sees. He lingers on my bare legs and the dip of cleavage—my sundress was strategic: I'm not trying to win Jaxson's heart; I'm trying to make him suffer for all the times he's broken mine. If I can look damn good every time he sees me from now until eternity, I've done my job. Not that there aren't a million girls prettier than me...I know this. But any time he has a tinge of regret or looks at me with longing, it feels like justice.

"Can I just say, you look especially gorgeous today. You do every day, but this is...next level. That color on you. Your mouth. That hair. Your legs. And..." He motions toward my chest and flushes. "Speechless."

I laugh. "You seem to be doing just fine. Thanks. You ready to go?"

He nods, swallowing again and looking a bit shy. "Should we talk about last night?" he asks.

"Nope." I put the key in my purse and we walk to the elevator.

We tell the cabdriver the name of a coffee shop near the Empire State Building and he drops us off. I feel much better once I've got caffeine running through my veins. We walk a block and the crowd of people is insane. Streets are blocked off and everything is at a standstill.

"What's going on?" Jaxson asks someone.

"They're making a movie over there." The guy points behind him. "They've shut down the Empire State Building and the area surrounding..."

Jaxson curses under his breath. "You've gotta be kidding me." We look at each other sadly and then he straightens his shoulders. "Plan D?"

"Plan D." I laugh.

When we walk away from the crowd, he mentions a few things we could do and I agree to Central Park, maybe even the museum if we have time. I don't know how it happens—I think it's a combination of a skateboarder running into me and my foot hitting a pothole—but I go flying. The next thing I know, my face is planted on the sidewalk and my ankle hurts. A lot.

I turn so I'm on my back and look at Jaxson, whose eyes are huge.

"Oh, your face is bleeding," he says in alarm. "It doesn't look deep, just skinned," he quickly assures me. "What else hurts?" His eyebrows crease together and he helps me sit up.

"I think I've broken my ankle." We look down and my foot is turned in a really weird direction.

"Oh shit," he says.

FIVE HOURS LATER, I have a cast on my foot and we're getting back to the hotel.

"Room service and more meds?" he asks, as he helps me hobble onto the elevator.

"Room service and more meds." I grin. "I love these meds. They are the best thing to ever happen to me. I'm hardly even thinking about Tyra anymore." The smile falls from my face and my eyes fill with tears. "That's not true. Not a day goes by that she's not right here." I put my hand on my head and shake it. "I miss her so much," I say, leaning onto his shoulder and sobbing.

He guides me into the room and I cry until I can't breathe. He reaches behind him, still holding onto me so I don't lose my balance, and grabs a tissue.

"You're not so bad, Jaxson," I tell him, blowing my nose.

He chuckles. "Now I *know* the meds are talking. First the tears and then buttering me up?" He moves a strand of hair behind my ear and smiles so sweetly my eyes fill again.

"Olive you, Jaxson," I tell him.

His eyes widen and he puts his hands on my cheeks. "What did you say?" he asks.

"I said, '*Olive you.*'" I try to enunciate better, but I might be slurring. I can't tell.

He laughs. "How about I run a bath for you? You can wrap your cast in this plastic bag and prop your foot up on the edge of the tub." He holds up a bag from the ice bucket. "I'd be happy to be of assistance, should you need help washing your back...or whatever." He lifts an eyebrow and smiles his deadly smile.

"That sounds bloody fantastic," I say.

He laughs again.

"You're so cute when you're happy," I tell him. "And when you're sad. It's not right."

"This is the best night I've had since that Christmas, you know the one..." His eyes twinkle. "Stay right here while I get your bath ready." He helps me move to a chair and when I sit down, he pauses, looking down at me.

"Olive you too, Bells," he says.

18

PAST

2014

*One step in front of the other, one day at a time.
That's been my new motto and the only way I can survive.
Life without her is void of color, of spark, of substance.
I miss her like I miss breathing. She is a part of me that will
never be whole again.*

"I JUST WANTED you to know I'm here, if at any time during the day the load gets too heavy to bear," the school counselor said.

"Thank you. I don't want to talk about it." That had been my line for the past month.

To my teachers, to the kids at school who meant well. To my mum. To Jaxson.

He'd come over the night of the funeral and sat with me outside. I hadn't cried since the morning after she died; crying all night, I'd felt like I would never be able to stop, but once I did, I was all dried up.

He brought his guitar over and sang to me, and I curled

up in the grass and fell asleep. When I woke up, I was in my bed with the blankets up to my chin. I never thanked him for that, but I was grateful nonetheless.

It was a drunk driver who took her from me. A man, who when they arrested him, was still saying he wasn't drunk. That's what the news reported and what I'd heard around school. No one tried to talk to me about it anymore though. I didn't know how I got through the day because I blinked and I was home again, crawling into bed, barely sleeping at night, and getting up the next day to do it all over again.

That I passed sophomore year was thanks to the teachers who'd loved Tyra. They looked out for me, and until my head cleared enough to function more easily, they let things slide. Months later, when the circles under my eyes weren't quite as dark and I was more present in class, I was able to catch up at my own pace.

Heather sniffed around some to see if I was ready to fight back and expose her secret, but when she saw how I could barely get through the day, she left me alone. I didn't thank her for that either, but I was grateful. Nothing mattered anymore.

OVER THE SUMMER, when I started to feel more like myself, the pain of losing Tyra really hit. When my mum left for work and returned and I still hadn't gotten out of bed, she came in and pulled the covers off of me.

"Get up. I need my daughter back," she said. "Tomorrow I expect you to start looking for a job. If you don't get one in the next week, I'll make you come work at the real estate office with me, and you know how boring that will be."

I rolled my eyes and stood up, stretching, and my mum gasped.

"Since when are you so much taller than me?" She pulled me over by her and we looked in the mirror. I was a good four inches taller than her. "You must have grown half a foot since summer started." She pinched my side and I yelped. "What the bloody hell?" she hollered. "There's nothing to ya. You're skin and bones. Are you not eating?"

I plopped down on the bed and fell back. "I could never be skin and bones," I told her. "I'm eating. Just haven't been as hungry."

"What did you eat today?" she asked, her eyes narrowing in on me, as she cinched my shirt together.

"Toast and fruit for breakfast, chicken salad on a croissant for lunch, and I was waiting to see if you'd make dinner," I said.

"Hmm. Well, I know I've seen you mostly horizontal for months, so this skinny, stretched out business has me gobsmacked." She glared at me again. "You promise you're telling the truth about eating?"

"Yes," I groaned. "Fix me dinner and I'll show you," I said and she smiled.

"It's good to see my girl," she said. "Tonight, we're measuring you against the doorframe. I can't believe it. I know I've always said you were just a late bloomer like me and your gran, but I *was* beginning to wonder if you were gonna be a shorty like your Grammy Hart." She laughed and went to the door. "How about we go out for dinner and get you some new clothes?"

"I don't know..." I frowned. I didn't want to leave my room.

She held up her finger. "No arguing...you'll need clothes for this new job you'll be getting."

"Right," I dragged out.

I HADN'T REALLY BELIEVED my mother, but when I got in a dressing room and all my normal sizes were too short and super baggy, I realized she was right. I asked her to get a size smaller and it was still too big. Four sizes smaller and I stared with shock in the mirror.

I could hear Tyra's voice in my head. *"Damn,* girl, you're looking *good!"*

And for the first time since she'd died, I giggled. I shimmied into a pair of jeans I wouldn't have been caught dead in before and stared at myself.

"Weird," I whispered.

I was still curvy, but for someone who'd always had extra rolls and dimples and had been termed *pudgy* since I'd moved to California, there was now definition.

I WENT HOME with a new wardrobe, and the next day, I got up and looked online for jobs. I didn't see any that looked exciting, but I filled out applications anyway. That evening, when Mum came home from work, I told her about the places I'd tried.

"None of them look interesting though," I said.

"Well, keep looking. I want you to find something that's at least somewhat fun."

A few days later, she sent me to the grocery store while she ran into another store nearby, and on the window of a salon I'd never been in but had always wanted to try, there was a sign about a job.

I walked inside and admired the place. It was bustling, but cheerful and clean. The receptionist asked if I had an appointment.

"I wondered if I could fill out an application."

"Lord, yes. We are in dire need. I'm Liesl, the owner, and I'd rather be cutting hair, but I'm answering phones and trying my best to keep the place clean." She was petite and spoke almost faster than I could keep up with, but I knew right away that I liked her. Her hair was blond with pink streaks and her makeup was divine. "Fill this out, make sure to let me know your availability, and I'll look it over as soon as you're done."

Once I'd given the form to her, we had the interview right then and there, and I went home with the job. I started the next morning and quickly fell in love with the job, the regulars, and my co-workers. I worked hard that summer and the best part of being around Liesl was that she carried on where Tyra had left off in one regard—she helped me find my confidence.

LIESL CAME FLYING in the door one morning. "I have a wedding this weekend and Sajel has pneumonia. Are you free? I know you're ready. I'd much rather have you do makeup than take someone from Sajel's team that I don't know."

"Are you sure I'm ready?" I asked, my heart pumping with excitement. "School starts the week after next, so I am *free.*"

"Hells yeah, you're ready," she said, grinning. "This is

going to be way more fun. I've been dying for you to come do this with me. I'll show you pictures of what the bride is thinking when we have a lull later."

I went home and opened up the pictures, practicing on myself until I thought I had it right.

The day of the wedding, Liesl came to pick me up at seven in the morning, but I'd already been up for hours. Since I was too excited to sleep much, my hair was in perfect shiny waves, pulled back on top so it wouldn't get in my way. My makeup was on point. I wore a top that made my blue eyes bluer and dress pants that fit perfectly.

It had been nine months since Tyra had been gone, but I felt like she'd put in a word for me up above—good things were happening. I still missed her every minute of every day, couldn't talk about her yet—who knew how I'd feel once school started—but she was with me. She'd be proud of me for getting back up.

"Whoa," I said, as we pulled into the circular drive of a house even bigger than Jaxson's. We'd done a practice run at the shop with the bride the day before and she'd been so down-to-earth. "*This* is where Jenna lives?"

"I think it might be." Liesl laughed. "Damn, I should've charged her a lot more."

We were still laughing when we got to the door and it opened before we could knock.

"I'm Sandy, Jenna's mother. Come on back." She led us through the jaw-dropping house and knocked on a bedroom door.

Liesl and I got to work setting up our stations. I did Sandy's makeup while Liesl curled Jenna's hair and then we swapped. They sipped champagne and got happier the more time passed. When I finished Jenna's makeup and turned her toward the mirror, she lit up when she saw herself, fanning herself to stop the tears. I decided then that I wanted to spend my life trying to make people happy like this.

Bridesmaids trickled in and I continued working, feeling energized by the hour. I loved pulling out each person's best features and making them feel good about themselves.

After their pictures, we freshened up hair and makeup and packed up our things as the wedding was about to start. Since the wedding was to be in the back garden, we were leaving as guests were arriving.

I took a load out to the car and came back in to help Liesl, turning to go down the hall and colliding with someone.

"Watch it!" she said. Then she stared me up and down, having to look *up* at me now instead of down—*so* weird—and her nose curled up in distaste. "What are you doing here?" she finally asked.

"Heather," I responded.

"Well," she said, waving her hand for me to come out with it.

"None of your business," I said quietly.

She looked me up and down again, her expression darkening.

"You have something to say or can you just bugger off already?" I said, trying to move past her.

"You've lost like a hundred pounds, good for you," she said.

I could tell when she got her bearings back because she grinned then, like a tiger about to go in for the kill.

"For a while I wondered if Jax was saving himself for, I don't know...a childhood friend...it's crazy, but I did wonder. It was ridiculous though, because this summer..." She shook her head and bit her lip, her teeth slashing white daggers against her dark red lips. "Well, let's just say, we've had quite the summer. He had a *lot* of time to make up for."

Liesl walked out then, saving me from making a fool of myself. She took one look at my face and grabbed my arm.

"There you are," she said and hustled us out of there.

"See you at school." I heard Heather call out before I shut the door behind me.

I didn't know which hurt worse: that he hadn't been having sex with Heather as long as I'd assumed and now he was, or if I'd gotten my act together sooner in the summer, maybe I could've done something to prevent it.

19

PRESENT

DD, Apparently pain meds and I should never dare meet. This tongue of mine gets me in trouble...I can tell by the twinkle in his eyes and the relaxed shoulder that he was not carrying around before I partook.
Save me,
Mira

WHEN I WAKE up the next morning, Jaxson is sitting next to me in bed, hair still wet from his shower, and *reading*.

"I've never seen you read a book. You finally learned to read?" I tease, wincing when I move.

"Very funny. Are you in a lot of pain?" he asks, adjusting the pillow under my foot.

"It hurts like a mother," I groan. "Where are my happy pills?"

He laughs. "You were happy all right. And so entertaining," he adds, tapping my nose. "And sweet."

I glare at him and decide to try to make the trek to the bathroom. "Did I do anything to embarrass myself? I don't really remember anything except for a supreme state of well-being."

His grin grows and it makes me nervous.

"What? What did I say?" A vague memory of us chatting while I was in the tub comes back. "Did you see me *naked*?" I yell.

He stands up and hurries to the other side of the bed and helps me hobble to the bathroom. "No, I did not see you naked. You had bubbles, and I kept my eyes averted the whole...most of the time. I *might* have seen the tiniest edge of your, uh, your areola, but I very quickly looked away."

I shake my head and scoff. "You're such a perv."

"What can I say? You're beautiful. It was excruciating to look away—everything inside me wanted to stare—but I did not take advantage, I promise. Are you okay?"

"Yeah, but now I'm terrified to take the pills. You look far too smug for my liking."

"You didn't say anything embarrassing. You were refreshingly honest," he says.

"Refreshingly honest," I humph.

I shut the door on him and scowl at myself in the mirror. I wonder what I said but decide I can't worry about it; my ankle hurts too much to go without the meds today. I clean up and Jaxson taps on the door.

"Do you need me to help you get dressed?" he asks.

"You've lost your mind!" I call back.

He laughs. "And she's back," he says.

"I don't even want to know what that means, do I?"

"Nope," he says, stepping away from the door.

It takes forever, shuffling around to get into clean shorts and a tank top, but I manage to do it without his help. I put on a little mascara and lip gloss but still look out of it. When I hobble out, his eyes zero in on my chest. I look down and my nipples are standing at attention.

"Get your eyes back in your head. I can't bra today. Sorry. Besides, it's not like you haven't seen them before."

"And I've dreamed of them every day since," he says, rubbing his lips together. "It's like a gift from the nipple gods. Thank you."

He turns around and I think he's adjusting himself.

I roll my eyes. "Boys are such dolts."

"I'm a dolt for you, that's for certain."

I have to suck in my cheeks to keep from laughing at that. I climb onto the bed and he brings the room service menu to me.

"How about we order one of everything? I'm starving," he says. "And the doc said today and probably tomorrow, we should try to beat the pain with the meds, so let's get you fed and medicated."

"Mm-hmm, you just want to have an arsenal to make fun of me with…"

He makes a face of mock horror. "Never."

———

LATER, after we're flipping through the channels after pigging out, I look at him. "I'm sorry for ruining our day in New York."

"Are you kidding? I'm having the best time. I don't care what we do, Bells. I mean…it's kind of weird that every time we try to follow the list, it backfires, but…I like what we've done with it. Don't you? Except for the part where you broke your ankle because that really blows…" He shakes his head and looks up at the ceiling. "I'm an idiot. It all blows, doesn't it? We're supposed to be in Paris and we're stuck here in this hotel room."

"We've definitely made the best of the situation." I look at him and he puts his hand on mine, slowly tickling my fingers. We both watch his hand as it traces little swirls across my skin and I shiver.

"Hey, I've been wanting to ask...well, not really, but I have to know anyway. What's going on with you and Chad?"

"We broke up," I say and he threads his fingers through mine. I give him an incredulous look and pull my hand away. "Which changes nothing."

"No, it doesn't change much," he agrees, "but it's a step in the right direction."

"Not for you," I say cheekily. "I do miss sex though. How long has it been for you?" I turn to face him and spit out a string of curses for the stinking albatross that is my ankle.

He puts his hand on my arm and his expression is pained. "What can I do?"

"Nothing. It's not so bad if I don't make sudden movements." I get comfortable in the new position and motion my hand for him to talk.

"I don't want to talk about this with you."

"We can't talk about sex? Why not? You want to be friends, right? Isn't this what friends do—talk about everything?"

"No, I don't want to be—I mean, I do, I *do* want us to be friends, but I want so much more than that. I'm afraid anything I say about this will just make you hate me more—"

"Because you're a manwhore?"

He rubs his hand across his face and laughs, but it

sounds bleak. "I'm not. Not anymore. Never, really...not in comparison with most of my friends, anyway."

"I'm kidding. I can't talk really. I've given it up for more people than I expected to by now."

He groans and pounds the back of his head against the headboard. "I really, *really* don't want to talk about this with you."

"Either we're going to be friends after this trip or we're going our separate ways once and for all, don't you think? Why not say everything?"

"I refuse to let us go our separate ways," he says. "And you might not remember everything we say anyway, while you're in this state—maybe that's a good thing," he adds. "I have so many regrets, and it makes me sick when I think about all the roadblocks I put between us. I acted like a raging hormone and lost sight of everything for a while. But when I woke up..." He looks at me and his eyes are so sad, I reach out and touch his cheek.

His bottom lip is so full and begging to be touched. I stare at how perfect his mouth is and then up to his eyes, which hypnotize me. *Come closer*, they whisper. I'm powerless when he looks at me like this. Our lips barely touch, but one of us shocks the other, a tiny electric spark that jolts us. We pull back, his thumb sweeping across my lips, and he groans before pulling my mouth to his. He keeps one hand on my face and the other drags through my hair, gripping me tighter. The kiss deepens and there is no awkwardness trying to recall how we best work together. Our memory serves us well. It's still magic. And something more, something explosive that time apart has only magnified.

We explore each other like our taste fulfills every craving, and it's how I feel—I never want it to end. He's everything I want, everything I need. When he pulls back, I whimper and he kisses along my jaw and up to my ear, teasing me. His fingers slide back and forth under the strap of my tank top, and then his mouth moves down my neck and lower, but not past the material. His nose dips into the valley between my breasts and his tongue traces a trail from there and up, up to my neck so painfully slow, until he reaches my lips again. I can't take it anymore, and I pull his face to mine and kiss him until we're breathless.

I yank his shirt off and he stares at me then, chest heaving, pupils dilated. My nipples hurt, straining against my shirt and he flicks his thumb across one, making my back arch.

"God, Mira. I want you so much," he whispers, his mouth crashing against mine.

His hands grip my waist and one hand slides under my shirt, cupping my breast. I lean into it, willing him to do whatever he wants with me. Instead, something changes in that moment, it's almost as if a big bucket of ice water pours over us. He suddenly goes still and leans his forehead against mine, shaking it slightly.

"I'm not gonna mess this up with you again, Bells. I'm sorry—I lost my head there," he says shakily.

I pull away and stand up. It takes me a moment to get my balance, and I can't believe I can't stalk away when I need to. He gets up and puts his hand on my arm.

"Don't." I hold my hand out, and his hand falls. I can't look at him.

"I just...did I botch it up by kissing you or by stopping?" he asks. "Because there is nothing I want more—"

"I think it'd be best if we went home."

20

PRESENT

Have I mentioned you-know-who is a DAMN good kisser? Heavens to Purgatory and Beyond, he can kiss the booty off of Kim Kardashian and that is no small task. It's a shame I keep shutting him down, because those lips are all I can think about...
SOS,
M

CHARLES IS able to arrange flights back for us that night. We land at San Diego International Airport at ten p.m. and there's a car waiting to drive us home. The plane ride and the fifteen-minute car ride are painfully long. I haven't taken any pain medication since this morning and my ankle is making me aware of it. But the silence between Jaxson and me is much more excruciating.

He's tried to talk several times and I've been polite but shut him down every time. All I know is I can't be around him right now. I can't be in love with Jaxson Marshall anymore. It didn't work in the past, and it won't work this time. I'm embarrassed I let things go as far as they did. I think he believes our lusty moments were because of the meds where I'm concerned, but as soon as his lips touched mine, I was fully aware of what I was doing. I'm just glad one of us had the wherewithal to stop when things got out of hand.

We pull in front of my house and I turn to him. "Thank you for everything, Jaxson. This trip was what I needed in so many ways. You helped me see that I can talk about Tyra and not fall apart...it actually helps to talk about her. You were a gracious host and took great care of me when I fell. I appreciate that. And I needed this closure."

His brows crinkle together in the middle and he opens his mouth.

"Thank you." I turn to open the door and he puts his hand on my back to stop me.

"What do you mean by closure?" he asks.

"Do I need to spell it out?" I ask, looking over my shoulder. "I think we both needed to see that our past is just that, the past. Everything we've tried has backfired, even when I was willing to have sex with you this morning."

"So I did wreck everything when I stopped. Stopping was the last thing I wanted to do! I was trying to do the right thing..." he rushes to say.

The driver turns the lights off and it's the first time I think about him hearing this whole conversation.

"You did do the right thing," I assure Jaxson. I kiss my fingers and put them on his cheek. "I'm so glad you did." He starts to respond and I shake my head. "Let's just leave it at that, okay? Good night, Jaxson. Goodbye. I wish you well."

I step out of the car and he gets out to help me to the door, muttering, "I hate it when you say that. *You wish me well*," he sputters. "Don't talk to me like we're strangers,

Mira. We're not. I know you love me. You're just afraid. You told me you loved me last night. Did you know that?"

I look at him in horror. He sets the suitcase down at the door and nods.

"It's true. You did. And I told you I loved you back. It was the best night I've ever had. And we can have a lifetime like that, if you'll just let us."

I laugh. "We're kids, Jaxson. I'm not even twenty-one yet. You're twenty-two and aren't even a hundred percent sure of what you want to do with your life. I'm not knocking it—it's normal. We have time to know those things. This —*we*—are not normal."

"I don't need to be older to know how I feel. And I'd rather not be normal with you than to be normal with anyone else!" he yells. "You're breaking my heart, Bells. How can you keep shutting your heart to me? And what can I do to crack it open again?" He puts his head in his hands and rubs his eyes. When he looks at me again in the glow of the porchlight, he looks raw and empty. "Please don't make me live another day without you. Please," he says softly. He steps closer and puts his hands on my face. He looks from one eye to another as if willing me to hear him, but I take one of his hands from my cheek, kiss his palm, and walk inside, shutting the door softly behind me.

———

WHEN MY DAD LEFT, my mom cried every day for a year. I vowed then that no one would ever break me that way. It didn't work. I've been broken more than once, but I keep thinking eventually I'll learn.

Jaxson is my weakness. He asked how to crack my heart open and he doesn't realize that he does every single time we're together. I'm not immune to him, and I'm afraid if I let him in one more time and he breaks me again, I'll never get over it.

DAVE AND MUM hover over me for the next few days, concerned over my injury, concerned over my state of mind.

"I'll take off work today, sweetie...keep you company," Mum says each morning when she wakes me up before she leaves for work.

I roll over and put my pillow over my head. "Absolutely not," I insist. "Let me sleep, Mum. Go to work."

Dave checks on me when he gets home from work. "Can I get you anything? Need help getting down the stairs? I can set you up down there...it'll give you a change of scenery," he says, trying to get me out of my bedroom.

"I'm good here. I need the space. It's okay," I tell him.

I try to withdraw into myself, the place I go when I feel too precarious. But no one will give me peace.

Jaxson texts and calls regularly, checking to see how I'm feeling, and if my ankle is improving as it should. And whatever is on his mind at the time. I want him to leave me alone, but he's like a persistent fly swarming around in my head. Sometimes I reply, sometimes I don't.

I THINK **that cast makes your leg look extra hot. And my god, imagine when the cast comes off. Your ankle will be abnormally small compared to the other one. I can't wait for that.**

Me: I'm so over this %*@(&@# cast. And you have the wrong number. Perv.

Are you working this Saturday?

Me: Not this week but next. Why?

The guys and I got a last minute gig at Brigley's Saturday night. You should come. Speaking of work. I didn't even ask how your job is going.

Me: I still love making people beautiful on the most important day of their life. We stay busy and make way better money than we used to. The occasional D-List celebrity wedding can be surprisingly good money. I can afford to keep Sundays free for homework!

It's incredibly sexy that you're pursuing what you love. Also, that was the most appropriate use of an exclamation—great placement, and not three thousand of them.

See, not the wrong number at all.

Me: Weddings will be tricky with this cast. It can be done, but I'll have to get a stool or something. !!!!!

You sassy bugger!

Liesl will bedazzle the stool if you're not careful.

Areola.

Me: What?

Just seeing if you're still here.

Me: Nope.

Can I come over?

Me: No.

. . .

BETWEEN HIS RIDICULOUS TEXTS, I reorganize my bookshelves and closet while catching up on Netflix shows. Maddie comes over and we eat ice cream while watching more Netflix. After days of not accomplishing much, I don't even feel guilty about how bedraggled I look. My hair is a dirty, tangled mess, I'm wearing a pair of old glasses that are crooked, and I haven't worn makeup since I got back from New York. This is a record for me.

WHAT ARE YOU DOING NOW?

I IGNORE him and keep watching *Doctor Zhivago*. A box of tissues is clutched to my chest and I swipe my eyes every few minutes. The starkness of the desolate winter and the tragic love between Yuri and Lara are more than I can take. I sob into the tissues but can't look away. The movie is almost over when the doorbell rings. I ignore it and it keeps ringing and ringing.

Finally, ticked, I pause the movie and stand up, moving as cautiously and quietly as I can with this dumb cast toward the window to see if I can tell who it is.

The ringing stops and then I hear, "I'm coming up."

"What? What are you doing here?" I twist around in a panic and wince as my ankle doesn't move along with me as fast as I'd like. I catch a glimpse of myself in the dresser mirror and want to die. "Do not come in," I tell him.

Just as he's saying, "I'm coming in. If you don't want me to see anything, cover up."

When he opens my door, I give him the death stare. "I

said 'do not come in' and I meant it. How did you even get in?"

He grins. "The key is still where you guys have always hidden it. Listen, you've been avoiding me long enough. I've tried various approaches with you and letting you stew has not worked well for me in the past. So I'm here." He shrugs. He takes a closer look at me. "Have you been crying? Bells, what am I gonna do with you?"

"I was watching a sad movie...nothing to do with you, so you can move along."

"I'll watch it with you. What are we watching?" He gets on my bed and pats the covers next to him.

"Why are you so annoying?"

"I like to think I'm older and wiser this time around," he says quietly. "And I've always had an annoying streak, right?" He laughs and then frowns when I don't join him. "We don't have to talk today if you don't want to, but I need to be near you." He pats the covers again and unpauses the movie. "Ooo, did you know that the author who wrote this based Lara on his real-life mistress, Olga?"

"Shhh."

"Sassy bugger," he whispers and turns back to the movie, a satisfied smile on his face.

21

PAST

2014

You know what, D? There is a God in heaven and her name is Tyra.
XO,
Mira

AT SCHOOL, I'd always done whatever I could to hide, with exception to my hair and makeup—I never went without those two things in top form once I learned how to do them properly—but the rest of me was usually in baggy, nondescript clothes and I stayed under every radar. I didn't answer questions unless called on. I didn't try out for anything, didn't do any extra clubs. I decided to change that when I went back junior year. I wanted to make sure Tyra was not forgotten.

On the first day, I dressed to kill. Nothing over the top, but more deliberate than I'd ever been. I wore a pair of kickass boots. My jeans were ripped in all the right places and fit like a second skin. My shirt was snug and accentuated my newly discovered waist, which also drew attention to my chest. I had dusted a fine shimmery powder on my skin that gave it a radiant glow, I tried out one of the makeup palettes I'd used on a bride the weekend before and nailed it, and my hair, which I'd always thought was my *only* redeeming feature, was in top form.

"Go in there looking good and like you *know* you look good," I said Tyra's words to myself in the mirror and walked out the door.

I didn't have my license yet, so I lost some of my rock-star vibes when my mum dropped me off in front of the school since I'd taken too long getting ready. It felt like every eye turned on me when I started walking to the door. I turned around to see if anyone was behind me when I saw a few gaping mouths and elbows knocking other elbows to see if the person next to them was looking, but it was just me. Tyra would've *loved* this moment.

Better yet, when I walked through the door, Jaxson, Derek, and another guy I didn't know were standing there. A guy almost as cute as Jaxson. When Jaxson saw me, his eyes widened and he did a double take, standing up straighter.

"Bells? Holy—what did...you look fantastic," he stuttered. He looked at the guys who were also gawking at me.

"You look fucking hot," Derek said.

Jaxson hit him in the chest. I rolled my eyes at Derek but bit back a grin at Jaxson.

"That's no way to talk to Bells," he said.

Derek laughed. "But it's true. You look great, Mira," he added.

"Thanks."

The guy next to Derek held out his hand for me to shake. "I'm Miles," he said. "Just moved here, junior..." He motioned to Jaxson. "My stepdad works with his stepdad, so we met in the summer."

"Oh, my mum must know him too then. She's one of the agents. Nice to meet you," I said, smiling. He was really cute. "I'm a junior too."

His grin widened and my heart skipped a little faster.

Jaxson stepped forward and took my elbow. "Got a minute?" We stepped away from Derek and Miles. "I came over a few times this summer but never got a chance to see you. You doing okay? You look so...*different*. I can't believe it."

"Not as fat, you mean," I said.

"No! You were never...that's not what I meant. You're like, tall now too. You've always been beautiful, Mira. And you look...well, I know it's been really hard since Tyra. I just wanted to make sure you're really okay. You're healthy? And you're, uh...you're eating, right? I've never...seen you this skinny." He cringed with those last words and ran his fingers through his hair.

I looked at him, incredulous. "Of course I'm eating. I'm trying for healthier choices more often, and yeah, I finally grew taller. Mum always said I'd be a late bloomer. She was, Gran was. As for how I am? I've lost my best friend. Twice. I'm doing about as well as can be expected."

I walked away, his stunned expression lingering in my mind. He had the nerve to think I'd confide in him after all this time? Unbelievable. And what was the deal with him and my mum thinking I'd starved myself? I wasn't *that* skinny.

My inner rant threatened to ramble all day, but midway through the morning, I reminded myself of what I'd set out to accomplish this year. I went to the office when I had a few extra minutes and asked to speak to someone about an idea I had. Within minutes, I was speaking to Leigh, the counselor who'd tried to talk to me several times after everything happened with Tyra.

"I'm so glad you reached out to me," she said. "I've thought about you over the summer. How has it been?"

"It's been hard, but I'm not really here to talk about that," I told her. "I've been thinking there must be ways we can keep Tyra's memory alive. I can't talk about her yet. I don't want to," I reiterate, just in case she thinks this is a counseling session. "But I need everyone not to forget her. She loved clothes and—" The lump in my throat grew too big to ignore, but I swallowed it down and tried to change the course of the conversation to be about the end result I wanted. It was still so hard. "Everyone should feel their best, whether it's prom night or at school every day. I'd like to organize clothing donations. We could call it Tyra's Closet. No one has to spend any money and it'd be a tax write-off. It can be as simple as people around here cleaning out their closets, but I'd also like to visit businesses and clothing stores who might want to donate new items. We can do three big pushes so there are gowns to choose from for Homecoming, Winter Formal, and Prom...but I'd also like to provide things like flannel shirts and nice sweaters..."

I took a breath then and began to worry when Leigh didn't say anything right away.

"If I need to simplify it, I can, but this—"

"I love the idea," she jumped in. "Love it. You've obviously put a great deal of thought into it, and Tyra's Closet—that's perfect!" She clapped her hands together and I laughed. "I know just who to talk to about this. I'm positive she'll love it as much as I do and will help us get the ball rolling. Can we talk again tomorrow around this time?"

I nodded, a relieved smile stretching across my face. "Yes. Thank you so much."

My last class of the day was physics and when I walked in, I bumped into Miles.

"Finally! I've been hoping to have a class with you all day," he said.

"Oh!" I rubbed my lips together nervously and then smiled. "Hi." I groaned inside at how lame I was. "How has your day been?"

We sat next to each other in the back.

"It's been long. You're the nicest person I've met so far," he said. "Jax is pretty nice too. You guys go way back, he said?"

"We do, yes."

"Cool." He flipped open his notebook and then faced me, elbows on his knees. "Hey, would you want to go get some gelato after this? Compare notes on our classes? I'm addicted to that place on Girard."

"Um, sure," I said. "I won't have my license for another couple of weeks, so I just walk," I added.

He grinned. "You can ride with me."

The bell rang and I pulled out my notebook, the thrill of being asked out on my first date—if you could count going for gelato to discuss school a date—doing a crazy dance in my chest.

―――

WHEN CLASS WAS OVER, Miles waited for me to gather all my things and then walked to my locker with me. His locker was across from mine and when we saw that, we smiled shyly at one another. When we had everything, we walked outside. It was one of those perfect days of sunshine with a faint breeze; the fragrance of flowers, salt water, and car fumes wafting in the air.

"I'm this way," he said.

We walked a few feet and I stopped when I saw Jaxson and Heather walking toward us. Heather had become a pro at schooling her expressions when Jaxson was around. The most I'd heard her say anything negative around him had been at his party so long ago; typically, the times I'd been around them she'd done a good job of acting. When she saw Miles, she smiled so big.

"Hey, Miles. How was your first day?" she asked.

I did an inner eye roll. Figured they were already friends by now.

"Great. I met Mira. Survived lunch..." He laughed.

Jaxson looked between Miles and me, his expression cloudy. I couldn't tell if he was mad or constipated. Maybe hangry.

"We're going to Bobboi...no practice today for once," Miles said.

"You play football?" I asked.

"Oh, we were thinking of doing that too," Jaxson said at the same time.

"We were?" Heather asked.

"We should join you." Jaxson nodded.

Miles looked at me, lifting his eyebrows in question.

"Come on, it'll be fun." Jaxson was almost perky now.

What are you doing? I lasered in on him and he just grinned.

I didn't say anything. This wouldn't count as my first date after all.

———

WE ONLY HAD a few minutes to talk on the ride, but Miles was easy to talk to.

"I've never lived near the beach," he said. "Do you surf? I've always wanted to try."

"It's been a while, but yes, I do. You'll catch on fast and love it, I'm sure. Where did you move from?"

"Maybe you could teach me," he said, glancing at me quickly then back at the road.

I smiled. "Maybe."

"We've moved around a lot. My mom and I. But the last place was Indianapolis, Indiana. She met my stepdad at a wedding a year ago—he had just moved here—and they got married at the beginning of the summer."

"A whirlwind relationship. Do you get along well with him?"

He shrugged. "It's been an adjustment, but yeah, he's pretty nice."

We parked and I reached for the door handle, but my door was opened first.

"There you are," Jaxson said, holding out his hand to help me out.

"Why are you being so weird?" I said under my breath.

He looked hurt. "I've missed you, Bells."

I shook my head and stepped past him, moving in step with Miles.

"What do you usually get here?" Miles asked.

"I love the pistachio," I answered.

"Hmm. I'll have to try that one today."

Jaxson sighed heavily on the other side of me and I looked at him. "What?" He looked at me like I should be able to read his mind, but I wasn't in tune with his thoughts anymore.

Heather scooted between us, and we ordered our gelato

then took it out to the deck where we could see the beach nearby.

"I love it here," Miles said, scooting his chair closer to mine. "Mira, did—"

"Miles, did you have fun at that party the other night?" Heather interrupted. "You and Danielle were cracking me up."

Miles looked like he was trying to remember what she was talking about and then laughed. "Oh yeah, I had to loan her my sweatshirt. She got pizza everywhere! That reminds me—she never gave that sweatshirt back."

I knew what Heather was doing, but the guys seemed oblivious.

"She thinks you're hot. Might not ever get that sweatshirt back," she said, licking her spoon in a way that usually got the guys around her to do whatever she wanted.

Why did it always work? I shoved my spoon in my mouth and realized Miles had turned to look at me instead of her. He put his hand over his eyes and discreetly made a face in my direction, which made me giggle. Maybe it didn't work on everyone.

"What's so funny?" she asked.

"Nothing," I said, smiling at Miles.

Jaxson leaned his elbows on the table, studying both of us. He hadn't taken a single bite of his gelato from what I could tell. "My mum said you got a job, Mira. Where is it?"

I pointed at the cute salon next door to us. "Right there. And then I do makeup for weddings on the side with the owner. I really love it."

"That's so great. I'm happy to hear it," he said, and he looked genuinely pleased.

Jaxson and Miles both tried a few times to draw me into conversation, but it would remind Heather of something they'd done during the summer, her and Jaxson, or the three of them. I was exhausted by the time I got home.

"I enjoyed this," Miles said, when he pulled in front of my house. "Can we do it again? Maybe just the two of us next time, so I can get to know you better?"

I smiled. "Sure. I'd like that."

Hmm. I looked up at the sky while I walked inside. Things like this didn't just happen to me. Tyra was definitely working her magic up there.

22

PRESENT

FINALLY! I have finally met the love of my life! And he's mine, all mine. Well, Jaxson says I have to share him, but... he's MINE.

MY LAZING around does not fly on Saturday morning, with both Dave and Mum in the house. They insist that we go out for breakfast, so I begrudgingly fix my hair and put makeup on. I do feel better after leaving my room and getting out of my pajamas—more like myself, more energetic even.

When we get back home, I show my mum the donations I've accumulated for Tyra's Closet, a program that's still going strong at the school, and we work on her closet for a while.

My ankle hasn't hurt as much, and when I sit down to take a break, I'm happy with all we've gotten done. I grab a pen and check off several things on my mum's to-do list.

My phone buzzes on the table.

BE READY IN TWENTY MINUTES.

Me: I'm in for the night. It's been a busy day.

I'll be by to pick you up then.

Me: Why does it feel like you're not hearing me?

Because I don't like the answer you're giving me.

Me: You have the wrong number.

Eighteen minutes now.

I LAUGH EVEN though he's being completely rotten. Dave comes through and sees me smiling.

"What's up?" he asks.

"Jaxson is insane. He says he's coming by in less than twenty minutes to pick me up. He's playing over at Brigley's tonight."

"Oh, that's a great venue. Doesn't sound insane to me." He grins.

"You're all in this conspiracy together," I moan. "I can't get ready fast enough. It takes me twenty minutes just to get in and out of clothes and back down the stairs."

"You better hurry then."

I shake my head. "Whose side are you on?"

"Yours, always yours," he says.

JAXSON WHISTLES when I open the door, looking me over. His eyes land on the cast and he shakes his head. "Damn, that cast is really working for you."

I shuffle out and he takes my hand and puts his other arm around my waist.

"You don't look like a granny at all," he says.

"I can't keep up with you right now," I say.

He slows. "We don't have to go so fast."

"I meant your brain. You've lost your mind." I laugh.

"Oh, well, yeah. Desperate times call for desperate minds, or something like that. Haven't you heard?" He opens the door for me and leans against it once I'm in, smiling down at me. In the sunlight, his eyes are a collision of green and blue and a touch of grey. "I have a surprise for you first."

"Yay," I say weakly.

My defenses are wearing down fast. I might have to call for backup.

———

THE LAST PLACE I expect him to pull up to is an old yellow building. He helps me out of the car and I question him all the way inside, but he doesn't answer.

When the door opens, the sound of dogs barking echoes around the high cement walls. Jaxson gives his name to the lady petting a dog at the front desk, and she smiles.

"Oh hello, I'm Emmy, the one you've been speaking to. Follow me," she says. "Grinch has been waiting."

"Grinch?" Jaxson and I say at the same time. We walk through a gate and then there are dogs everywhere. Different sized dogs are sectioned in separate areas, with various people either looking at them or holding them. Some stand pitifully, waiting to be noticed.

"Oh, we name them once we rescue them. If this works out, you can name him yourself. Wait right here."

I look at Jaxson and he looks as if he's going to bust, he's smiling so big.

"What did you do?" I ask.

He makes a giddy face, and Emmy walks out holding a pitiful white fluff ball of a dog wearing the cone of shame. He has the saddest eyes and the top of his head is stained yellow, but he's cute in spite of it all. Around his feet and belly, his hair is choppy.

"He was rescued from an Amish puppy mill a week ago, neutered yesterday, so you'll need to give him the rest of his medication. Don't bathe him for another two weeks, just to make sure he's all healed up from surgery. He hasn't been off of a wire-bottomed cage, so his paws are a bit deformed. His nails had never been cut until this week, so he's walking funny," she scoffs. "You just can't believe the things we see."

She hands Grinch to me and I melt. He nestles into me and doesn't budge. My eyes fill with tears. "He's so sweet," I whisper. With one touch, it's like I can feel all of his sadness seeping into me and I want to protect him from every bad thing that could ever happen to him, ever.

"It might take some time for him to get used to everything. Like I was saying in our interview," she motions to Jaxson, "rescue dogs are skittish. He's around eight months though...not as old as a lot of our puppy mill rescues, so hopefully, he'll come around quicker. Give him time. Keep a leash on him whenever you're outside. If it goes well and you decide to keep him after this fostering process, come back in two weeks and we'll make it official."

"Thank you," he says. "Did you say an *Amish* puppy mill?"

She nods grimly.

"What the hell?" He looks at the dog and shakes his head. "We'll take good care of him. His name won't be Grinch though."

"Suit yourself," she says. "Bye, Grinch-for-now. You're a good boy."

She walks back to the front desk and I look at Jaxson. "You just got a dog? Just like that?"

"*We* just got a dog," he says. "Technically, he's our foster dog, but...he's not coming back here. Do you need me to carry him while we walk out?"

I shake my head. "No, I'll go slowly."

Jaxson snaps pictures of me with the puppy in the building and then when we step outside, he takes selfies of the three of us together. I move gingerly, wishing for the millionth time that I could get out of this cast already. When we get in the car, the puppy settles into my lap, angling his head to try to get comfortable with the cone. I take it off and he looks up at me gratefully.

"There you go, buddy."

"It's been a long time coming, but we can finally get started on number nine," Jaxson says.

"Number nine?"

He gives me a look. "Number nine: Always have a dog," he says, reaching over to pet him. "What are we gonna name him? How about Paul...Frank?"

I look at him like he's crazy but end up laughing.

"I know-I know. *Larry*," he says.

"You're terrible at this," I tell him.

"Larry," he calls, and the dog looks up at him. "See? He likes it."

"How about Edwin or Bennett?" I suggest.

"Ah. Something a little more refined...I can go there. Eugene?"

I crinkle my nose.

"Clarence?"

I shake my head.

"Right. That sounds too Amish. We can't feed into his memories. Oh...I've got it...Winston," he says.

"Aw, that reminds me of—"

"I know, me too..." he finishes.

Mr. Winston was one of our teachers in Holmes Chapel and we loved him. He had hair coming out of his ears and was hard of hearing, so he talked really loud, but he made fourth grade English come to life.

"Winston. I love that. It's perfect. And I love you," I tell the puppy. He sniffs my nose and lays his head back on my lap. I look at Jaxson with stars in my eyes and he puts his hand on my cheek.

"I should've started with number nine," he says, his eyes crinkling up with his smile.

I love it when he looks this happy. It's been so long I almost forgot.

"Who needs stinkin' Paris and New York?" I say, my heart thumping fast.

———

THE GIG IS on the patio and Jaxson had already made sure it was okay to have the dog out there while he plays, so he gets me settled and then goes to set up with the rest of the band. I sit as far from the speakers as I can get, just in case it scares Winston, but he's content to sleep on my lap all night. I think he's extra sleepy from the traumatic day before, so he doesn't really budge. It's like having a toasty live teddy bear curled up on my lap all night.

Jaxson and the band blow me away. He has something really special, and together, he and the band are incredible.

On the way to my house, I tell him so. "Have you really thought this through enough about the music career thing? Because I think you absolutely have what it takes."

He reaches over and runs his hand over my arm. "You really think so? Thank you, Bells."

"It's hard to imagine you having all that talent and *not* doing it full-time…it's kind of a crime. Everyone deserves the honor of hearing you sing your songs. Your whole stage presence…it just…well, I'm gushing, but it's just true," I trail off, embarrassed by how much I'm going on.

"I don't know what to say. That means everything to me," he says quietly. "I guess I just think California, and the whole rest of the world for that matter, is full of talented people trying to make it. There are other things I can do well, that feel a lot safer."

"Just throwing it out there. If it's something you want deep down inside…run after it."

"The only thing I feel *that* strongly about is you," he says.

"I walked right into that one, didn't I," I mutter.

He laughs. "You did." When we're almost to my house, he says, "So I talked to your mum and Dave about the puppy and they're good with it. Great, actually. But if you're not ready for a dog yet, or even if you'd rather me have him until your ankle is better…I'll take him home with me. I know I sprung this on you. Ideally, soon we'll be living together and can both take care of him, but baby steps!"

"You're not taking him from me and we are not cohabitating. Slow down there, Romeo."

He parks in front of my house and holds his palms up like he's giving in.

"But thank you for Winston. He's a dream. And proof that our list isn't jinxed."

23

PAST

2014

Dear Diary, I have so much to say, but all I'll say is: there is a first time for everything and that was quite the first. You can read between the lines—you always do.
All my love,
Mira

BY THE TIME I was getting ready for bed, I'd decided as weird as it was, my first date still hadn't been all that bad. Miles was sweet and cute. He wanted to go out with me again, so that was a good sign.

I pulled my nightie over my head and thought I heard something at my window. I smoothed my hair down and heard it again. Moving toward the window, I stopped to look out before lifting it up.

"Can I come up?" Jaxson stood under the tree, smiling.

"Uh, sure?" I hurriedly looked around for my robe to cover up more before remembering it was in the bathroom, and it was too late anyway—he was already at the window crawling in.

Something about the way he looked at me made me shiver and I rubbed my arms. He zeroed in on the middle of my tiny racerback nightie to the word *bombshell* that sparkled across my chest. I felt like I should pull it up because it was so low, but it was already so short that he'd see the scrap of lace to my thong if I pulled it up even an inch. I should've thrown on a shirt. A coat. Anything. He grinned like he could hear my racing thoughts and moved closer, rubbing my arms with me.

"You cold?" he asked.

I shook my head and he stopped rubbing my arms but kept his hands there, looking down at me.

"Today, when you said you'd lost two best friends—that hit me so hard. I know things have changed between us, which I hate...I hate the way things are between us, Bells. It might sound crazy to you since we haven't talked in so long, but...I still think of you as my best friend. You're the closest friend I've ever had and it might not seem that way since I have all these other friends too...and a girlfriend. I still wish you'd tell me if there's more to why you've been mad at me, but—I've just thought we'd get back there eventually. Because it's you and me, you know? You're still the one I want to tell everything to, the one who knows me best of all."

He paused, maybe waiting for me to say something, but I didn't know what to say.

"We have the list we've committed to," he added, smiling.

I rolled my eyes, laughing, while inside I wanted to cry. "The list is a moot point now, don't you think?"

"Absolutely not!"

I thought he was joking, but when I looked at him again, his face was red and his eyes were intense. I'd hurt his feelings.

"I think you don't know what you want," I finally said. "You're confused because I'm like, new and improved, I got attention today from a hot guy...and all of a sudden, you remember your good ol' bestie."

His jaw clenched. "I came to your window twenty-five times this summer. Yeah, I counted. Twenty-five. And the year before that, probably a hundred. I haven't seen you making any effort to talk to me...in years. Well, except at that Christmas party you came to, which made me hopeful, but then this year, you were a no-show." He lowered his head. "I knew you were grieving, so I didn't hold it against you, but Mira, I've tried. I don't know what else to do here."

"I heard you talking to Heather about me at my birthday party a long time ago," I said. "That Anne made you come, that you didn't want to be my friend anymore, about my weight...all of it."

The color left his face and he took a step back. "I didn't say that."

"You did. I heard it. You said it."

"I'd told Heather you were acting so different here, different than you were at home, and she might've thought I didn't want to be your friend, but that's not how I ever felt."

"Well, that's how you let her think you were feeling, which is just as bad. You think I want to be some hanger-on that your mum forces you to be around? No, thank you."

He put his hands on my cheeks and stepped closer. "I'm so sorry. Please, forgive me. I promise you I have never felt forced to be around you. I love you. You're my family."

Tears welled in my eyes. I knew he meant what he was saying, or at least thought he did, but hearing that I was his family felt about the way it had when I'd heard Heather say I was like his sister. A tear dripped on his hand and he wiped it away.

"Bells," he leaned closer, "please tell me you're hearing me."

I nodded and his forehead softly bumped mine. We stayed suspended in that moment, staring at each other, not saying a word. But then the air shifted. His hand moved to my hair and he tugged on it, making the tiny hairs on the back of my neck stand on end. My heart thumped so loud I knew he could probably hear it.

I licked my lips, suddenly dry, and his eyes followed every move. He looked hungry and my eyes widened when he came closer, closing the gap between us. His lips were soft and full and better than I'd ever imagined, and I'd imagined them plenty. I wrapped my arms around his neck when he deepened the kiss and his hand gripped my waist, bringing me even closer. When my hands found his curls, I thought I'd truly gone to heaven. I couldn't get close enough, even on my tiptoes. We kissed like we were starving.

He stopped long enough to grab my legs and wrap them around his waist, his hands landing on my bare backside. When his hands squeezed, we both moaned and the sound embarrassed me but made him kiss me harder. Somewhere in the back of my mind, a thought niggled and I pushed it away until finally, I had to catch a breath and that was when it all rushed back.

"Heather," I whispered. "What about Heather?"

He was already moving forward to kiss me again but stopped when the question hit him. His eyes widened in alarm and he rubbed his lips together, setting me down carefully.

"I'm sorry. I didn't mean to...do that—I mean, I wanted to...I really, really wanted to," he stuttered. "Mira, that was —" he started.

"You should go," I interrupted whatever he was about to say and moved away from him, walking to the window.

"The best kiss," he finished.

I flushed and couldn't look at him as he walked to the window.

"I can't believe I kissed you," he said. "I've always wondered what it would be like to really kiss you, and *damn*...that..."

He couldn't seem to stop talking and I just wanted him to leave. He was going to leave anyway and everything would be different again.

"I shouldn't have kissed you when I have a girlfriend," he said. "Mira, look at me." He lifted my chin and I finally looked at him. "Did I just wreck everything even more?"

So many things crossed my mind to say. *Your girlfriend has cheated on you with your best friend before, so maybe this is not so bad—oh, and she's also a bitch. And yeah, you probably have wrecked everything because how am I going to be around you and not want to kiss you like that every time?*

But instead, I squared my shoulders. "No, you didn't. I'm fine."

"Will we be fine?" he asked.

"Sure." I nodded. "We're Jaxson and Bells...we'll be fine."

That was the answer he wanted to hear. He beamed, pleased and happy and hopeful. He climbed out of the window and down the tree, waving when he reached the bottom.

I went to bed, a mass of confusion. My first date and my first kiss all on the same day and with two different people...

JAXSON AND I KISSED!

That was the theme of every thought I had overnight and while I got ready for school the next morning. I replayed the kiss and his reaction afterward. Maybe it was such a good kiss, he'd break up with Heather and want to be with me.

I made kissy lips in the mirror and then grimaced. I'd turned into an annoying girl overnight. One night of (phenomenal) kissing and I thought I was the shit. I grinned, remembering Jaxson saying it was the best kiss. I sighed and then saw the time and flew out the door.

I was jittery when I walked into school, and I wiped my sweaty palms on my bag. I saw Heather first, and she was holding Jaxson's hand. My stomach fell, but I swallowed back the pain. It had been so stupid of me to think I could change anything between them. They were walking to their lockers and stopped to say hello to Miles on the way. I held back, trying to wait until they walked away before going to my locker.

I leaned against the wall and scrolled through Instagram. *I have five minutes until the bell rings*, I told myself. *Deep breaths.*

"Bells," Jaxson called. "Hey, come here."

I looked up and the three of them were looking at me expectantly. Another deep breath later, I walked to Miles' locker.

"Why does he call you Bells?" Miles asked.

"Her name is Mirabelle," Jaxson answered.

"But no one but my mum or his ever calls me that," I said quickly.

"*Mirabelle.*" Heather laughed.

"I like it," Miles said. "Bells is nice too." He grinned.

Jaxson's face darkened and he stared at me like he wanted me to correct Miles. I walked to my locker and looked back at Miles shyly. "Thanks."

"There's a party at my house this weekend," Jaxson said. "I was just inviting Miles. You should come too."

I was already shaking my head. "You know I'm not a party girl, Jaxson." I looked pointedly at Heather then and said, "Your Christmas parties are about all I can take."

She shuffled on her feet and I wondered if I saw a glimmer of fear in there. That would be a first.

"I know, but this weekend will be fun. We're going to surf and then have a bonfire. Simple," Jaxson added. "Come on."

Miles walked over to me. "And I'll be there this time—it'll be fun," he said.

I smiled at him. He really was so easy to look at.

"Come on, Jax, we need to get to class," Heather said.

"One sec, I'll meet you there," Jaxson said.

"See you last period?" Miles asked over his shoulder.

"See you there," I said.

Heather had walked a few feet away but stood waiting for Jaxson, watching as he moved closer to me.

"I'm going to make things right with you, Bells. Be the friend I should've been all along," he said.

"You don't owe me anything. Really. We cleared the air last night. Let's leave it at that. We're good."

He glanced at my lips for a long moment and he flushed. He cleared his throat. "Right. Okay, I know. I don't feel I owe you anything. I just want to be with you."

I thought of all the times I'd wanted him to say those words, but even now, as he was saying them, it wasn't how I wanted to hear them. But I'd try. I'd try not to think of him that way, once and for all. We were friends. Our lips were transcendental together, but that was beside the point. *Friends.*

"Fine, I'll come to the party. Maybe Miles will bring me. I need to teach him how to surf."

His mouth opened like he wanted to say something, but his jaw flexed and he nodded. "I'll see you there."

24

PAST

*Scum accumulates in the most unexpected places.
I am finding that out the hard way.
I am more fortunate than I realized and for that, I say thanks
to the heavens tonight.
Mira*

"MUM!" I yelled. "I need a wet suit! It's an emergency!"

I ran down the stairs and she was in the kitchen making dinner.

"Why an emergency?"

I leaned over and tried to catch my breath before spilling it all out in a rush. "Miles is taking me to Jaxson's tomorrow night. I'm gonna teach him how to surf. My wet suit sags everywhere and my swimsuit is just...not attractive. I think it's been three years since I wore one."

"You're going to Jaxson's?" she said, setting her wine glass down. Her excitement was immediate. "I'll take you right now."

"Shouldn't we eat first?"

"We might have to look at more than one place. Things are good with you and Jaxson again? When did this come about?"

"*Miles*," I enunciated dramatically, "is the new guy that I went out with a few days ago. He's so cute and nice, and he's taking me to Jaxson's."

She tried to hide it with a smile. "But things *are* good with Jaxson?"

"We talked and things are better," I said. "And we kissed, but it was nothing. He has a girlfriend!" I added hysterically and then slapped a hand over my mouth.

She gasped and then looked elated. "Well, not if he's kissing you, he doesn't...right? He ended things with her?"

I raised my head to the ceiling and groaned. "Nope."

I really missed having someone to talk to...kissing Jaxson was something Tyra and I could've dissected for hours; I didn't want to dissect it with my mother. I was just glad the bum groping didn't slip out because I'd replayed that moment at least a thousand times in slow motion and my thoughts just seemed to be flying out of my mouth.

"He will. Don't worry. He should have done things in the right order, but...I knew this would happen," she whispered excitedly.

"No, no, it's not like that. We're not pursuing anything, so get it right out of your head. I shouldn't have said it out loud."

"Oh, honey. This was your first kiss, wasn't it? How was it? Was it everything you dreamed it would be?"

I sighed, annoyed with myself for opening my mouth. But I couldn't help but smile.

"It was...perfect," I said. I looked down at the floor while my face burned with embarrassment.

She squealed. "I knew the two of you would eventually get there..." She clapped her hands and grabbed my arm. "Come on, we'll eat quickly and go get you a suit that will have him eating out of the palm of your hand."

"Ew, Mum. Gross." I stopped her. "Listen to me. I'm not dating Jaxson, and we won't be kissing again. It was a one-off. Okay? But I do need a suit for tomorrow."

She smirked and twisted her lips to the side. "Whatever you say. We'll see."

I shoveled food in my mouth and between bites told Mum about how great Tyra's Closet was going. We'd made an announcement and put up flyers. I'd made a Facebook event for it and it was getting a good response. Students were going to start bringing in clothes the next week.

"I mentioned it to the ladies at work too, and they all agreed to contribute."

"Thanks, Mum. I'm excited about it. Hopefully it will make a difference for someone."

THERE WAS a surf shop near work that I'd never been inside. It was sad to wake up to how much I'd missed out on. I'd given up things I loved because of how I looked and how out of place I felt, but I couldn't do it anymore. Every time my stomach jolted with nerves about going to Jaxson's house, I tried to turn my focus on surfing. And Miles. It felt good to have a new friend, and as crazy as things were with Jaxson, it felt good to have him back in my life too.

My eyes were immediately drawn to a short pink floral wet suit.

"Oh, that's the cutest thing I've ever seen," I said,

rushing to it. And then I saw the price tag. "Ugh. Not that cute."

"Well, wait a minute, let me see," Mum said. "How long has it been since we've bought you a wet suit? You should get the one you want." She held up a black and white polka dot ruffled bikini and waved it. "And this."

I shook my head. "I can wait on a swimsuit. Even if I did get one, I can't do a bikini."

"Just try it," she said.

THE NEXT NIGHT, with my wet suit zipped up to just the right place to be enticing but not *too* enticing, and cut off shorts, I grabbed my bag and opened the door. I was all set to run out, but Miles was there at the door, hand up to knock.

"*Wow*," he mouthed when he saw me.

My mother rushed forward. "Oh hello. I'm Vanessa, Mira's mum. So lovely to meet you."

Miles shook her hand and smiled his perfect smile and I think my mum swooned right then and there. She looked at me and grinned, eyes twinkling.

"Aren't you sweet?" she said to Miles. "Have fun, you two."

"Should I have Mira home at a certain time?" he asked.

"Oh, I like you," she said. "You're going to my best friend's house, so I know where to come looking if she's not home by midnight. In fact, I'll probably be over there myself tonight..." She held up her hands. "Don't worry, I'll stay out of sight."

I giggled. "Love you, Mum. See you later."

She winked and we left.

"She's cool," Miles said.

"She has her moments."

"I love her accent," he said. "Makes sense now why you still sound different..."

"Different, yeah." I cringed.

"No, I love it. You sound exotic," he said, grinning big.

My face heated and I hurriedly looked away. "You know, we could actually walk if you want. It's really close." I picked up the surfboard leaning against my garage.

"Sure, I'm good with walking. I can carry that for you." He pointed at my surfboard.

"I'm good. Gives me something to hide behind," I said under my breath.

"You look...incredible," he said.

"Thank you," I whispered. We shared a sweet smile, and I was relieved he was with me.

Jaxson's house was a palatial spread ahead of us. There were torches lit along the path that led to the beach behind the house.

"I still can't get over how huge this place is," Miles said. "And he doesn't act like some of the other people around here—like he's better than everyone." He looked at me. "You're not like that either."

"Well, you saw where I live. My house is a bite-sized snack next to this twelve-course meal. Not nearly so grand. But Jaxson and I—we come from the same place, the same beginning..."

"I don't think you have an arrogant bone in your body," Miles said.

I smirked. "Maybe I haven't shown you the real me yet."

"Guess we'll just have to keep hanging out so you will."

I smiled and nearly bumped into Jaxson, whose eyes were about to pop out of his head.

"What's wrong?" I asked.

He took another look at me, lingering on my mouth, down the length of me and slowly back up again. My skin broke out into goose bumps. He dragged his hands through his hair and ran a hand across his face.

"Killing me," I thought I heard him say. When his hand came off of his eyes, he let out a shaky breath. "Miles! Hey," he said weakly. "Party's this way. Glad you guys could make it."

"I'll just go set down Mira's board." Miles took it from me and pointed to the other boards. "I'll be right back." He walked down the path, and Jaxson and I watched him go.

"You like him?" he asked.

"Yeah, he's great," I said.

"Did you tell him we kissed?"

I looked at him sharply and then around us to see if anyone else had heard. "No! Why would I do that?"

He scowled, moving forward until his feet bumped into mine. "Are you trying to pretend it didn't happen?"

I put my hands on my hips and wished I had grown six *more* inches so I could be nose to nose with him. "Are you saying you told Heather?"

"Told Heather what?"

Jaxson and I backed away from each other, both breathing hard. Heather stood there, panting and red-faced, like she'd been running.

"That Jaxson and I are friends again, and his mum isn't even making him this time!" I said, grinning at Heather.

"Oh. Well...cool. Sort of seemed obvious though," she said, looping her arm in Jaxson's. "Are you ready to get in the water?"

Jaxson looked at me. "You ready to surf, Bells?"

"Sure. You still have all those extra boards? Miles needs one."

"Right this way."

SURFING CAME BACK to me like slipping on an old glove. I'd been worried I'd lost it, but by the second time out, I had my footing back. Miles was a natural. Between Jaxson, Derek, Heather, and me, he had advice coming at him from every side. After we'd paddled out and surfed in at least a dozen times, Miles looked like he'd been surfing forever. He was still doing the smaller waves, but a few more times out on the water and he'd be legit.

When the sun began to fade, we headed back to the shore and went our separate ways. Jaxson went to see everyone hanging out near the bonfire. Miles went into the poolhouse to change and since it was pretty full, I went up to the house. I ran up the steps and when I reached the top, I rounded the corner too quickly and ran into someone. He put his hands on my arms and held me in place.

"Who do we have here?" a man slurred. "I don't recognize you."

I didn't recognize him either, and the way he was leering at me made my skin crawl. He was tall and muscular and old enough to be my dad. I pushed his hand off one arm and when he still held the other firmly in his grasp, I got scared.

"Let go," I said.

He laughed and let go. "Relax. I don't bite. Not here anyway." He laughed and the smell of whiskey permeated the air. "What's your name?" He licked his lips and put his mouth up to my ear. "Where are all your little friends?"

I backed away from him, but he moved along with me.

"You're beautiful. I would remember if I'd met you before," he said.

"Mr. Latham! What's going on?"

I hadn't seen Jaxson coming and when he put his arm around my waist, my shoulders relaxed.

"Ah, Jaxson, it feels like you're everywhere I turn," Mr. Latham said. "Where's my stepdaughter?" He motioned to me. "Heather better keep an eye on this one." His eyes got stuck on my cleavage and Jaxson moved next to him and put his arm around his shoulder, forcing him to walk away.

That was Heather's stepdad? I shuddered. God, what was he like at home?

"Why don't I get you some coffee? Did Mrs. Latham come too?" Jaxson asked, leading Mr. Latham to the house.

Jaxson looked at me over his shoulder, concern and fury on his face.

Thank you, I mouthed to him.

He nodded and I went in behind them. Mum was the first one I saw. She and Anne were with another woman—I could tell right away that it was Heather's mother. She looked like an older sister instead of her mother. She was a stick, tinier even than Heather, and she looked utterly miserable.

I got out of my wet clothes and Jaxson was still in the kitchen when I went back in there.

"You doing okay?" he asked.

"I'm glad you came along when you did," I said.

"Stay a—" he started.

Miles, Heather, and Derek came into the house then, interrupting whatever it was that Jaxson was trying to tell me.

"There you are," Miles said. "Are you ready for

s'mores?" He held out his hand, and I paused a second before taking it. When I did, he threaded our fingers together and my face grew hot.

All of the sound sucked out of the room, and when I looked up, everyone was staring at us. My mum looked amused, and I couldn't tell what Jaxson was thinking. He looked like he wanted to hit something, but it was probably still about the whole Mr. Latham thing. I swallowed and turned to Miles.

"Lead the way," I said, and he smiled his perfect, sweet smile.

25

PRESENT

DD, I don't need anyone ever again because my dog completes me. He loves me unconditionally, enthusiastically, and with such consuming passion, it's hard to imagine anyone loving me any more than that. When I enter the room, it's as if his world is complete—what could be better than that?

I FALL in love with Winston. It's hard not to when he so quickly attaches to me. The day after I get him, he's still out of it, but by the third day, he's off of the meds and has more energy. He sits on my feet when I brush my teeth. He doesn't let me leave his sight, and when I put his food out, he won't eat unless I sit next to him. It takes him a while to work up his nerve to eat. He's jumpy around everyone. On day four, he growls when Mum or Dave come to my door.

"Oh dear, maybe the name Grinch was more fitting after all," Mum says.

I make a face and try to lull Winston out from under the bed, but he won't come. When she's gone, he runs straight to me and falls on his back, rolling around on the floor, nuzzling my hands.

"Gah, you have issues, don't you." I laugh. "Don't we all."

Liesl lets me bring him to work. He sits on my lap or in a little bed under the reception desk while I answer phones, and I guess he's nervous enough with all of the extra people in the room that he doesn't make a peep. When I get up to clean, he rushes out of his bed to follow me. Between my cast and him being underfoot, I nearly trip over him all day long.

Jaxson comes to see him every day and that afternoon when I get home from work, he's there in a suit, talking to Dave outside. When Winston sees him, he growls.

"What's this?" he asks. "Did he just *growl* at me?"

"He's growling at everyone but Mira," Dave says, laughing. "He's claimed her."

I pick the puppy up so Jaxson can pet him, and Winston's body stiffens and he buries his head in my armpit. Jaxson looks hurt.

"He'll come around. Right?" I ask.

He smiles but still looks sad. "It *is* adorable the way he loves you. But I have a bone to pick with those Amish for wrecking him." He brightens up a little. "He just needs to get used to me. I need to be around you more, that's all." He lifts a brow. "How about we take him to Fiesta Island Dog Park? Take dinner with us. If he doesn't like the water, he can still run around for a while...maybe see if he likes other dogs."

I hesitate a few moments. I don't know what I'm doing

with Jaxson. My head tells me to run, but my heart begs me to fall headlong into him.

"I just need to go change," he adds.

"Shame," I say under my breath. He looks damn good in a suit.

His eyes light up. "Second thought, I'll leave the suit on the rest of the night," he says.

I laugh. "Let's both get changed and I'll get Winston's things together. I can be ready soon."

"I'll be back in thirty," he says. "Good to see you, Dave." He gives Winston's head another pat and leaves.

Dave smirks at me. "That boy has it bad for you, Mirabelle. Like, he'll-move-heaven-and-earth-for-you bad. Like, your-wish-is-his-command bad. Like, he-worships-the-ground-you-walk-on bad..."

"Enough!" I laugh, letting Winston down to do his business. "I still don't know why he's pursuing me so hard now. And I don't know what to do about it."

"My guess is he knows what he's been missing and doesn't want to live without you any longer. But if you don't feel the same, you should tell him so. Better to devastate him now than later."

I cringe, the weight of his words heavy on my chest as I walk to the door, Winston on my heels. "That's the kind of stuff he's spewing...doesn't want to live without me any longer, blah-blah." I sigh. "You really think he's sure of his feelings? I feel certain that he wants my friendship in his life and maybe always will. Time will tell. But our feelings have never aligned at the same time for very long when it comes to romance...especially where he's concerned."

"Sometimes it takes longer for guys to get their act together. I wasn't pulling out all the stops for a girl at Jaxson's age, that's for sure."

"You sure are rooting for him." I roll my eyes, but I smile at him.

He barks out a laugh.

"And I'm glad you got your act together just in time for my mum. You give me hope that I can have a good guy like you someday."

He flushes and ducks his head. "You girls are worth it," he says. We smile at each other for another moment and he motions for me to go. "Your guy will be here before you're ready if you don't get after it."

"Not my guy," I mutter.

I go inside and try to hustle. I don't know what to wear; it's been unusually hot all week. Running out of time, I put on my newest bikini—the green reminding me of Jaxson's eyes, even as I try NOT to think of them—under a short, cream crochet cover-up and a sandal on my good foot. I gather Winston's food, treats, and a leash and am walking down the stairs when Jaxson walks inside. I miss the suit, but he still looks too good for comfort.

"Dave told me to co—" He stops in mid-sentence, eyes bugging out of his head when he sees me.

Winston growls, but neither of us pays any attention to him.

"What?" I ask.

"That is a great—" he points to my dress, words not coming right away, then finally, "I can see right through it."

"It's a cover-up." I make a face and laugh at him. "You act like you've never seen a bikini before. People wear far less than this at the beach."

"It's like a holey peek of the bikini, like if I stuck my eyes up to one of the holes, inside would be a kaleidoscope of bikini, which is *fascinating*," he says. "I do want to get a better look at that amazing suit and find out what all those straps *do*, but this way makes me feel like I'm seeing something I'm not supposed to."

"You're ridiculous."

He walks around me. "The back is just as impressive," he says.

"Knock it off." I laugh and hand him my things so I can pick up Winston. "You ready?"

"More ready than you can imagine."

I look at him and he waits, smirking, to see what my comeback will be.

"You're in a good mood," is all I say.

"I'm with you. Nothing could be better." He grins as Winston hops in his car. "And our dog...who doesn't like me...now *that* could be better."

"Should we stop for food?" I ask when we're almost to Fiesta Island.

He points to the big canvas bag in the back seat. "I hope it's okay—I stopped at The Taco Stand already."

"Are you kidding? I haven't had it in so long. Always okay." I looked at the bag again. "That's an awfully big bag. What else are you hiding in there?"

"Surprises for Winston. Towels." He shrugs.

My eyes narrow on him. "I can't figure out why you're going to all this trouble. What do you want?"

"I want you," he says simply.

My face warms. "And if you had me, what would that look like? We've never had a normal dating relationship, not really...I think if we got together, you'd be over it as fast as it began."

He's quiet, but I can tell what I've said bothers him. We drive around the island and when he finds a place to park, he turns off the car and faces me.

"My feelings for you did not begin overnight and they won't die overnight. I'm in love with you, Mira. I don't know how much clearer I can make it. If you don't want to be with me, I will be devastated, but I hope to at least have my friend back."

I close my gaping mouth and blink slowly, trying to process what he's saying.

"I will always regret hurting you," he whispers, reaching over to move a strand of hair out of my eyes. "Do you see yourself ever being able to forgive me?"

"I can forgive you and still doubt that you really want the things you're saying," I say, eyes filling. "You've said things that I believed before."

"Are you willing to let me prove it to you?" he asks.

His eyes bore into me and I nearly let myself sink into them, to sink into him. Something holds me back. I take a deep breath and look down at my clasped hands.

"I think I need us to just be friends," I tell him.

He leans his head onto the steering wheel. The heat in the car is stifling, while we sit there in suspended silence.

When he lifts his head, his face is red and he doesn't look at me right away.

"Okay," he says quietly. He taps the steering wheel again and nods, his shoulders lifting with a deep breath. "Okay," he says again, more resolute this time.

TWO WEEKS LATER, I take Winston to get a haircut and he looks like a brand new dog. I call Jaxson and let him know. We've hung out regularly since that day at the dog park. It's been awkward at times, but we're getting better. I really think I did the right thing. Now that the topic of being more is off the table, we can concentrate on our friendship again. There are times it's still hard. My heart still pounds when I see him. I still want to kiss him and get distracted when he comes over from work in his suit. He still stares at my lips a lot and his eyes get hazy at times, making me wonder what he's thinking. But I did the right thing. I did. It will get easier.

"You should come see him. After work, wanna stop by?"

"Sure. Should I bring tacos?"

"Um, yes!"

Jaxson freaks when he sees Winston. "He's actually the cutest dog *ever*," he says, staring at me. "Who knew he'd be freaking adorable under all that straggly, stained hair?"

"He was adorable then too," I say, kissing Winston's cheeks until his eyes flutter closed.

"We should go make the adoption official. If we don't do it soon, they'll start hounding us about bringing him to adoption functions."

I squeeze Winston tighter. "I can't give him up." I already feel like I've had him forever. He doesn't leave my side. Even when I'm showering, he's lying in the corner on a little rug. It might be an unhealthy attachment for both of us, but not one I'm going to trade in. "Over my dead body."

"Easy there, you sure your major isn't drama?"

"Very funny." I make a face at him.

THE FOLLOWING SATURDAY, Jaxson picks Winston and me up and we make the adoption official. I try to pay, but he won't let me.

"I'll let you pay for things after we're married," he says, winking.

"Jaxson," I groan. Every now and then he'll make jokes like this and it makes it awkward again.

He kisses my cheek and helps me hobble to the car, and for a moment I let it feel like we're a family.

26

PAST

2014

I hate boys. That is all.
Hate. Hate. Hate.
And especially Jaxson.
I hate him. I hate him. I hate him.
Like, hate *him,* hate him*. I hate Jaxson Marshall.*

ABOUT A WEEK after surfing at Jaxson's, I finally took my driving test and passed it. I'd flunked it a few times and then lost my nerve to take it again right away, so I was elated when I waved the slip in my hand. Mum was as excited as I was, if not more. She'd been teasing me that I'd be seventeen before I got it, at this rate. I'd been worried she was right.

"Let's celebrate," she said.

There was a line going out the door at The Taco Stand.

"Do you still want this?" she asked.

"Of course." I could eat there every day and not get sick of it.

As we got out of the car, I heard something and looked over at the same moment Jaxson lifted Heather up, hands on her backside, her legs around his waist, kissing her the exact way he'd kissed me.

I put my hand to my mouth and Mum turned to see what I was looking at and gasped. They were oblivious, groping each other as if no one else existed. When he opened the door of his car and bent down, leaning over her across the back seat, Mum grabbed my arm and we practically ran back to our car.

My eyes blurred with tears and I shook all over.

"I'm so sorry, honey," Mum said again and again. "So sorry."

Finally, I dried my face. "I told you he has a girlfriend."

"Yes, you did, and the fact that he kissed you while having a girlfriend is reprehensible."

She hadn't minded so much before, knowing he'd kissed me. I hadn't minded enough either. But for Mum, the fact that he'd kissed me and hadn't changed his status with Heather was another story.

"I can't believe he didn't break up with her after realizing his feelings for you! Boys that age are all about sex, Mirabelle. It's good you're not with him right now when he can't think with anything but his willy."

"I'm not going to be with him ever!" I gasped. "He was going to have sex with her in the parking lot!"

"No, surely he wasn't!"

I glared at her. "You saw them. They were about to have sex. You just got done saying boys are all about sex."

"Well, I'd hope he'd have more sense than that. I don't doubt that they *are* having sex, just not...oh, Anne is going to die of mortification."

"You can't tell her," I yelled. "And if you say sex one more time, *I'm* going to die of mortification."

"I have to tell her. I'd want to know if she saw you doing something like that."

"Please, Mum. You can't. Jaxson will be so mad."

She patted my hand. "No, he won't, and if he is, he's not the person we thought he was, is he?"

———

I WENT to school on pins and needles and didn't see Jaxson right away. When I did, he waved and said hello… acted normal. I felt like hitting him, but I managed to wave back.

It was the next day that things turned on me. I got to school and Jaxson was waiting for me at my locker.

"You and your mum saw me with Heather?" he asked.

I couldn't tell if he was more angry or embarrassed. Feeling feverish, I actually didn't know which emotion I felt the most either. Definitely both.

"I tried to tell her not to say anything," I told him. "I'm sorry."

He dragged his hands through his hair and looked worried. "You met Heather's stepdad. This is not good," he said.

My brows creased together. "Why? What will he do?"

Just then, Heather came down the hall with a splotchy face. I had the thought that it wasn't fair that she could still look so beautiful even after obviously crying for a long time. When she saw Jaxson talking to me, she looked livid.

"Hey," Jaxson said, putting his arm around her.

She flung it off and got in my face. "You want to ruin my life?"

I immediately shook my head while she was still talking.

"Well, that's what you've done." She looked up at Jaxson and tears ran down her face. "My mom and Chase said I can't go to Homecoming with you now. It's three weeks away! I can't go anywhere with you. We have to break up."

"What?" Jaxson asked. He tugged her to the side and she leaned into him, crying harder.

Miles walked over while I got my books out of my locker. "What's going on with them?" he asked.

"Long story. My mum and I kind of saw something and she told Jaxson's mum about it." I shook my head. "I feel bad."

He looked confused, but I didn't bother to enlighten him. The bell rang and Jaxson looked at me over Heather's head.

"I'm sorry," I said quietly.

He nodded at me and rubbed Heather's back. It felt wrong, seeing his hands on someone else. My brain flipped back to him leaning over Heather in the car and I felt the familiar anger surge up again.

―――

BY THE END of the week, it was all over the school that Jaxson and Heather had broken up. Various rumors about her being pregnant and losing the baby, he'd been cheating, she had feelings for someone else...and then occasionally, I'd hear someone get it close to right. She was homebound for the month, grounded, and she couldn't see Jaxson again because they'd been caught having sex in public...at school. So not perfectly right, but even I didn't know all the details at this point. Jaxson had stayed away from me, and

Heather shot daggers through me anytime we were near each other.

I felt bad. I didn't like Heather, and I really didn't like them together, but after meeting her mother and stepdad, I'd softened toward her somewhat.

Friday afternoon, during our last period, Miles leaned over and handed me a note, his expression hopeful.

Will you go out with me tonight? Just you and me, a legit date…

I paused—I didn't know why. I bit my bottom lip and glanced up quickly to see if he was looking. He was. UGH. His hopeful expression was long gone.

"It's okay," he whispered.

"No, I…it's just…I don't know," I finished lamely.

"We can talk after class," he whispered.

I nodded and then all during class I tried to think of what I'd say to him. *What is wrong with me?* I argued with myself until the bell rang, not having any idea what I'd missed in class.

We walked to our lockers, neither of us saying anything.

"I'm an idiot," I said finally. "You are so cute and so sweet…I have so much fun with you."

"And I'm *so* not who you're interested in," he finished.

I looked at him, alarmed. He put his hands in his pockets and smiled, but it didn't reach his eyes.

"I'm not saying I could never," I told him. "I'm just not there right now."

"Understood." He cleared his throat. "Can I ask you something?"

"Sure."

"Is something going on between you and Jax?"

I swallowed and shut my locker door, facing him fully. I took long enough to answer that he nodded.

"Enough said," he said.

"No, it's not like that—nothing's going on with him, not really."

"But you want there to be," he said.

I looked at him and my eyes welled up.

His face softened and he looked like he felt sorry for me.

"Well, if you change your mind about me, I'll be right here," he said.

He walked across the hall to his locker and turned around one more time.

"Thanks, Miles," I said. "You're as near perfect as anyone I've met. You deserve the very best."

He gave me a close-lipped smile, and I walked away.

―――――

I WENT HOME and Mum came in from work not long afterward.

"We're going to the Marshalls' for dinner," she said.

"What? No, I think I'll just stay home and do homework," I told her.

"I already told Anne you'd come and you will," she said. "No arguments tonight about it," she said. "Wear something pretty."

I sulked the entire time I dressed, wanting to look a mess to spite her but too vain to go through with it. I came out with my hair and makeup spot on, an extremely short skirt, and on anyone else, a top with a modest neckline, but on my body type, it showed a good amount of cleavage. A jean jacket tempered the whole look. Liesl was with me when I tried on this outfit and she'd screamed that I looked like a movie star. Of course, I had to buy it.

I carried my boots and sat on the couch to put them on.

Mum winced when she saw me. "At least put some tights on."

"The boots cover a lot of my leg." I stood up and she eyed the boots that came well over my knees.

"I can't tell if you look like a slag or quite stylish," she said, brows furrowed.

"Let's go with quite stylish."

WE WERE ABOUT to sit down at the dining table when Jaxson came in, apologizing to his mother for being late. He halted when he saw me, grinning as he looked me over.

"*Hello*, Bells," he said, moving to sit next to me. "Every time I see you, you're knocking me arse over tit."

I giggled. When we were kids, we'd laugh hysterically any time we heard anyone else say that.

"Jaxson!" Anne admonished him.

"Like the two of you haven't said it plenty—am I right, Bells?" he said, pointing to our mums.

Their shoulders started shaking and Anne tsked a bit more, but all was forgiven.

Conversation was light the rest of the meal. We mostly laughed at our mums—they were endless entertainment when they got together.

"Are you still liking your job, Mira?" Charles asked.

"I love it," I said, smiling at him.

"You hoping to own your own salon one day?"

"That's a possibility. I'll probably focus more on being a freelance makeup artist." I looked down, shy now that all the attention was on me. "It'd be fun to work on films, or I might just stick with weddings. They pay well. And I could be a lot busier than I am with that."

"Just make sure you go to college—a business degree will help you, no matter what you decide," he said.

Jaxson rolled his eyes. "Here we go," he whispered. Then louder, "Want to go to my room, hang out for a while? Or we could go out by the pool..."

"Sure."

We took our dishes to the kitchen and went to his room.

"It's been a long time since I've been in here. Looks a lot different," I said.

"We redid it two years ago," he said, picking up his laptop. "We could watch a movie..."

"Okay." I didn't know where to sit exactly, and it was weird being alone with him...I hadn't been alone with him since we'd kissed.

"I don't really have chairs, sorry." He sat on his bed and leaned against the headboard. "Is this okay?"

I nodded and sat beside him. I didn't want to put my boots on his bed, so I unzipped them and pulled them off.

"Those boots are the sexiest things I've ever seen," he said.

I flushed. "Badass," I corrected.

"That too," he agreed.

He turned on a show and we looked at the screen. I couldn't focus on anything but how close Jaxson and I were sitting, the air popping with awareness between the two of us.

"Are you and Heather really broken up or are you just acting like it to make her parents happy?" I asked, my skin getting hotter with every word.

"We're broken up," he said. "It's...complicated. She has a hard time at home. We've always looked out for each other."

I wondered if she ever still "looked out" for Derek in the

same way. It took everything in me not to tell him she wasn't as innocent as he thought she was, but I actually felt bad for her at times too. Maybe I had made her out to be worse than she really was.

"Who knew you'd turn out to be such a slut?" I said.

His mouth fell open and he busted out laughing. "I haven't...not that many people...only two."

"Two! What the hell! Who else?"

"There was a stretch when Heather and I weren't... doing anything...and I slept with Danielle."

"I am so disgusted with you right now."

"I know," he groaned. "It's not like I'm proud of it," he added. He was quiet for a moment. "Bells?"

"Yeah?" I turned to look at him and our faces were close to each other.

"I'm really glad you're here," he whispered.

"Me too," I whispered back. "But you stay on your side of the bed, you filthy manwhore."

"Yeah." He laughed, his hand drawing a line down the barely there space between us. "Whatever you say, Bells."

27

PRESENT

AUGUST 2019

*Biceps are the one redeeming quality of the male sex.
I mean, there are other things, like excellent kisses...but those
get you in trouble. For the most part, biceps are pretty
awesome and far less trouble than kisses.
Peace out,
Mira*

"IT'S about time I see you. Where have you been all summer? I hardly saw you," Maddie whines, wrapping her arms around me.

"I stayed pretty busy. But I did miss you," I tell her.

She pets Winston and he doesn't growl. *Yet.* Hopefully he won't when she catches him off guard later, but chances of that are slim. He's still a jumpy guy. We're moving into an apartment right by school that allows small animals. Winston barely passed the mark, being twenty pounds. Our lease is through the school year and we're on the first floor;

it's not the cutest space I've ever seen by any means, but it's a thousand times better than the dorms.

She kisses me on the cheek and goes back to unpacking. "I forgive you. Once I realized how much Jaxson is in the picture, I couldn't be too mad at you. That boy is too hot to pass over."

I laugh and move a box to the counter to start unpacking it. "Jaxson is a friend," I tell her. "Nothing more."

"Pssh. *Right.* He wants to be your *everything*," she sings. "You forget, I heard "Blue-Eyed Shadow" or "Black-Haired Beauty"...whatever that song was called. He wants you *bad.*"

I roll my eyes but don't encourage her further. The less she thinks about Jaxson and me as a couple, the easier it will be. Once she gets her mind on something, it's hard to veer it elsewhere.

"Is anything happening with his music? His band was incredible. I've thought about him a lot and know they have what it takes to go big."

"He's working with his stepdad right now. I know he likes the work, but I think deep down, he'd rather be doing music. He fought to go to Berklee—I can't figure out why he argued with his stepdad so much over going there if he was just going to do music on the side..."

It's something I've brought up more than once, and while I love Jaxson's strong work ethic, I want him to be sure he's doing what he wants to do.

"That is weird. Well, let me know when they're playing next. We can go hear them," she says, wiggling her eyebrows.

I groan. "If you keep making that face every time we talk about him, we will NOT be going to hear him play...ever."

She scrunches her face up. "You're no fun."

She dumps the utensils into the drawer and then tries to organize them. I don't bother to tell her there could've been a simpler way; she does things her own way.

"If we're not lusting after Jaxson, that means everyone else is a potential subject," she says. "I should see if Alex has any friends!"

"No. Back off. I'm good," I tell her. "I just want to focus on school."

"*No FUN,*" she reiterates.

WHEN CLASSES START and I find myself missing Jaxson far more than I'm comfortable with, I rethink my stance with Maddie. Maybe meeting someone new is exactly what I need to get my heart and libido back on track.

That's never made much of a difference before, my heart argues with me.

But he's back in your life, and that's all you've really wanted, my brain shuts down my heart.

And he doesn't make it easier, sending me flowers the first week of school, and filling my nights with sweet text messages.

I drove to Fiesta Island today, missing you and Winston. I can't let Winston forget me—he was just starting to warm up to me. When can I come see you? I mean...him. :)

Me: Soon!

And on another night...

I read a book—can you believe it? It was called "How to Win the Heart of your Best

Friend"…or maybe it was "I'm Hopelessly in Love with Her and Other Truths"…something like that. Great read. Hopeful. Bittersweet. Infuriating. And very, very hot. You should check it out.

Me: eye roll emoji

And another…

I sold a hugely lucrative property today. Success! It feels dim without you here to celebrate it with me. You're not that far away. Please have dinner with me. I'm beginning to think you're avoiding me.

Me: When did you become so annoying?

Is it working?

Me: Let me get used to this new schedule and we'll put something on the calendar.

UGH. It's not working as quickly as I'd hoped. Pencil me in soon, please.

PART of me is relieved to have the smallest bit of distance between us. It had been too easy to blur the lines when we saw each other regularly. I immerse myself into my classes and Winston and wedding jobs on the weekends.

During the third week of classes, I walk out of my marketing class and run into the guy in front of me. My papers go flying and I look up, already apologizing.

"Miles?" I say, grinning.

"I can't believe it," he says. He bends down and helps me pick up the papers, handing them to me as we both stand back up. "Mira Hart, how are you?"

"I'm great. How are you? I had no idea you were here!"

"I transferred closer to home. My mom is going through a divorce," he adds, eyes clouding over.

"Oh no. I'm sorry to hear that."

"Thanks." He gives me an appreciative look. "You're even more beautiful than I remember. Damn," he adds, grinning wide.

"You're pretty spectacular too," I flirt back. "I don't remember these arms in high school." I eye his muscular arms and then get embarrassed at the way I'm ogling him. He was cute before, but now he is *hot*.

"We should get together, catch up," he says. "Are you doing anything Friday night?"

"I have an early morning Saturday, but I could go out for a bit," I tell him.

We exchange numbers and I walk away smiling. I've always had a special place in my heart for Miles. He looked out for me when I needed him most. It's so good to see him again.

WHEN FRIDAY ROLLS AROUND, I try to get out of the apartment without Maddie knowing I'm going out. I change into clothes that are cute but not *too* cute, and when she asks me to go with her and another friend to the restaurant a block over, I tell her I'm going to hit the library.

"I miss my Mira," she sulks.

"We can do something fun on Sunday," I tell her. "I have to work tomorrow, but Sunday is yours."

"Deal," she says.

I meet Miles at a restaurant he wanted to try and we hug shyly when we see each other.

"Is there a reason you insisted on meeting here instead of me picking you up?" he asks.

"I have a very nosy roommate," I answer. He laughs and leaves it alone.

We cover the small talk of what we've been up to since senior year and then he hits me with the question I know he's been dying to ask.

"So, are you still hung up on Jax Marshall?"

I choke out a laugh and take a sip of my Coke. "Jaxson and I have recently been in each other's lives again," I answer. "We're friends. He thinks he wants to be more. I don't. Seems like maybe we'll always be complicated, but bottom line, we are friends." I tap out the last three words with my hands on the table.

He leans in, his eyes twinkling in the low lights. "Hmm. Complicated." His lips move to one side as he studies me. "Would you say that there's any hope for me yet?"

"I'd certainly put you at the top of the list for options," I tell him, smiling. "If I was looking, I mean..."

"Oh, right...when will you be looking?"

My heart ping-pongs along with our banter. "I always had a bit of a crush on you, in spite of being hopeless about Jaxson in high school."

"Had I known that, I would've tried a lot harder." His eyes fall to my mouth then and I flush, wondering if he's remembering.

He seems to know exactly when to move the conversation to lighter, safer territory, and the rest of the night, we both talk freely about anything and everything. I'm shocked when I look at my watch and see that it's eleven o'clock. I look around and see that the restaurant is closing and we're the last of the remaining customers.

"I think they've been shooing everyone out of here but

us. They must have known we needed the time," he says, grinning.

He walks me to my car and there's the first twinge of awkwardness as we look at one another.

"It's really good to see you again, Mira," he says.

"It's great to—" I start and am cut off with his kiss. I'm so surprised, I don't kiss him back at first, but then I snap out of my daze and kiss him back. I hold onto his firm biceps and swoon into his mouth. When we finally pull away from each other, I feel weak.

"You're not going to run this time, are you?" he asks, wiping his thumb over my bottom lip.

Still breathing hard, I shake my head. *I hope not*, I think. "No," I say.

He kisses me again, smiling this time when our lips first meet. "Good," he says when we part. "I could get used to this mouth," he says, leaning in for one more kiss. "You better go before I kiss you all night."

I drive home smiling and tapping my steering wheel, giddy over a great night and a great kiss. *I've hardly thought about Jaxson at all.* Things are looking up.

I'm walking into the apartment when I turn the sound back on my phone and a slew of messages go off. At least five from Jaxson and twelve from Maddie. I race into the apartment and Jaxson is sitting on the couch with Winston by his side. He smiles up at me and then takes another look at my face, my lips, and what I imagine is a red chin from the razor stubble that I was basking in all the way home, and his face falls.

28

PRESENT

HEY, D,

When you see that I'm on a downward spiral, could you at least have the decency to give me a heads-up? We've been friends a long time and I could use your help.
∼M

I FEEL Maddie's eyes on me during the brutal silence, but I stay focused on Jaxson. Winston rushes to me and dances around my feet, doing the spastic dance he reserves for me when I come into a room. Normally, it makes me laugh my head off, but tonight, I pet him quietly while still watching Jaxson.

"I shouldn't have just shown up here," he says finally. "I apologize. Winston does let me pet him a lot more when you're not around, so that was...cool." He leans his head back and looks at the ceiling. "I'm afraid I'm going to keep saying stupid things, so I'll just get out of here." He stands up and grabs his keys.

"Jaxson, wait. I'll...walk you out."

Winston trots happily beside us and stops every few seconds to sniff a leaf or the grass. I guide where I want him to go with the leash.

"You'll never guess who's back in California," I say, clearing my throat. *Why am I so nervous?* I square my shoulders.

"Who?" he asks politely.

"Miles. He's going to UCSD..."

He stops walking and turns to look at me. "Is that who you were with tonight?"

I nod. "We went to dinner."

He starts walking again and nods...a lot of nodding. We reach his car and after he unlocks it, he turns to look at me. He holds his hand out for Winston's leash and attaches it to his mirror, almost like he's stalling.

"Are you trying to hurt me?" he asks.

"What? Why would you say that?" I step closer and put my hand on his arm.

"I was a real asshole in high school. I'd understand if you wanted a little payback if you've ever felt about me the way I feel about you...what goes around, comes around and all..."

My hand drops and I take a step back. "You think I'm trying to pay you back? I would never intentionally do that to you or Miles. And I would hope you weren't trying to get back at me for something all that time in high school!" When he steps toward me, I hold my hands up and they land on his chest.

"You're killing me, Mira. I thought you needed time. That I needed to build your trust...that I could show you how much I care about you and...eventually, you'd be with me. You're not going to be, are you?"

"I told you I thought we should be friends," I say, my voice cracking.

He puts his hands on my cheeks and stares into me, his eyes stormy. And then he closes the distance and kisses me. A tear falls down my face and he wipes it away with his fingertips, his tongue tracing my mouth before diving inside. I get lost in it, my heart thudding as he turns and presses me against the car. I groan as he grinds into me, kissing me like we will never get another chance. I pull on his waves, driving my tongue deeper into his mouth, while my body melts, like liquid seeping into the pavement.

When he drags his lips from mine, he kisses my forehead, and panting, says, "Look at me and tell me that's all we are…friends. Tell me, and I'll let it be."

My stomach and hands and knees feel like they are shaking from the inside out. I move past him and lean over, putting my hands on my knees. When I'm steadier, I unwind Winston's leash and don't look at Jaxson as I take off running.

THE NEXT MORNING I drag myself to the wedding venue and meet Liesl out front.

"Geez, rough night?" she asks.

"Don't ask," I say, taking the coffee she holds out for me and lifting it in thanks.

"I just hope you have a steady hand," she says with wide eyes.

"No alcohol contributed to this foulness," I assure her.

We lug our things inside and fortunately I am too busy to dwell on the night before. Random screenshots still float across my mind, and I dismiss them repeatedly. As in, so many times that by the time we're done for the day, I'm exhausted from trying not to think about it.

"Okay, what gives?" Liesl asks when we have everything packed up.

I lean against her car and sigh. "I kissed two guys last night."

"Hussy!" She laughs and when I don't, she rubs my arm. "Oh, honey, I'm teasing. What happened? You look miserable."

"Jaxson and Miles."

She looks confused. "But...didn't you...? Weren't they...?" she trails off.

"Yeah, high school."

She'd heard bits and pieces about them back then.

"Well, do you want to be with one of them? Or do you not know, is that the problem?"

"I want to be friends with Jaxson and see where things go with Miles."

"That sounds straightforward enough. So what's the problem?"

"I'm afraid I'm never going to get over Jaxson."

I put my face in my hands and weep.

"Well, there's your answer—why aren't you with him?" she asks, her hand on my back.

"I don't trust that he'll stay," I whisper. "And if things don't work out with him, I will lose him for good."

―――

AS IT TURNS OUT, things fall into place sooner than I expected. I see Miles in class on Monday. We go out on Tuesday and Friday, stealing kisses in the car and at the park. Another week goes by, and it's fun with Miles...

exciting even. I like him so much. He makes me happy without making me feel like I'm losing my mind. I feel confident and in control, which is liberating.

And I hear nothing from Jaxson.

Another few days go by and I come to the realization that I have probably lost him for good either way. It hurts... terribly...but I distract myself with a jillion other things so I don't have to think about it so much.

And then...

I've been waiting for your answer and then realized that WAS your answer...when you left me standing there. Duh. Why haven't you told me before how slow I am?

I see the dots showing he's typing and wait.

Anyway. I am gearing up for another round of pursuing and/or only friendship and thought I better let you know I'm still here. Whatever we are, whenever, however, wherever, and all the other evers...that's me...right there...evering.

There's a brief pause and then ding.

It sounded better in my head than typed here, but hopefully, you get the point.

P.S. Can I see Winston soon? I know you have full custody, but I'd really like at least every other weekend...in some capacity.

I'm a mess, laughing and then crying...and laughing again.

Dave calls while I'm reading over the texts again and I answer right away. He never calls.

"Is everything okay?" I don't even say hello.

"Yes!" he says. "Everything is fine. I wondered if you

could come home this weekend. I need to talk to you about something."

"Oh. Sure! I've been meaning to get home before now anyway. And I don't have a wedding this weekend. I can come Friday night and spend the weekend. Does that work?"

"That will be great."

"You're not gonna give me any hints?"

"Nope," he says.

"You're being very strange, but I'll see you Friday, I guess."

I don't give it too much thought and type before I can change my mind.

Me: I'll be home this weekend. Hang out on Saturday?

I will live for Saturday.

Me: Such a flair for the dramatic.

Only where you're concerned.

I call Miles and he picks up on the first ring.

"Hello!" He sounds so happy, I smile.

"Hi! Weird, we've never talked on the phone."

"I know. It's nice, though. You've got a sexy voice."

"Ha. Yeah." I laugh. "I wanted to let you know I need to change our plans for this weekend."

"Oh, okay. Sure." He sounds bummed. "That's fine."

"Dave asked me to come home to talk about something and then Saturday I'll be seeing Jaxson. I need to see my mum too," I add.

"Right. Okay." He doesn't sound quite as lighthearted anymore, and I hate that I've put that worry in his voice.

"I'll see you tomorrow...and a rain check on our date," I say.

WHEN I SEE Miles on campus the next day, he's subdued. Finally, I just confront it head-on.

"What's up?" I ask.

His jaw clenches and he turns to me, a confused look on his face.

"I can't help but wonder if I'm crazy to fall for you," he says.

"You're falling for me?" I ask, smiling.

"Can you not tell? I know we're taking things slow here, but...yeah...I've always been crazy about you. I just...I want to say..." He takes my hand and runs his thumb along the top of it. "I've always regretted not fighting harder for you in high school. And when I hear you're going to hang out with Jax, I can't help but feel I'm right back there all over again." He tugs me to him and smooths one of my curls back. "This time around is much, much better, now that I can do this anytime I want." He kisses my face and I laugh. He puts his arms around my waist and I look up at him, getting nervous by his expression. "When I asked you about him before, you said he wants more and that it's complicated. Does he know you've been hanging out with me?"

"Yes."

"Okay...when you say you're friends...are you friends with benefits?" he asks.

"We're not having sex, if that's what you're asking..."

"Are you kissing friends?"

My face heats up and I remember the kiss. It makes my stomach turn over just thinking about it. "We've kissed, but it's not a regular thing."

"When was the last time?"

I pull away from him and stare at him, the blood

pumping in my throat. "He was at my apartment when I got back from my first date with you. I didn't know he was coming...he just showed up."

"And you just happened to kiss him that same night that you kissed me..." He balls up his fists and turns his back to me. "God, Mira. I thought this was a dumb little tirade I was going on...but turns out it's not. Were you ever going to tell me?"

"You and I weren't exclusive and I think Jaxson knew he and I weren't going to continue in that direction, so no, probably not. Should I have? I'm sorry."

He turns around and looks so hurt. I feel like a horrible person. "Yeah, you should've. No—I don't know. I think I've gotta take a step back. I like you so much. But I think you're going to break my heart all over again."

I hold my hand out to him and he takes it.

"I know I just said I should've fought harder, but...I don't think I'm cut out to fight. I want someone to only want me."

"It's what you deserve," I tell him. "You're the perfect guy in every way."

"I'm just not Jax."

He walks off and I don't try to stop him. At this point, I don't need to be with anyone. I can't keep hurting people.

29

PAST

2014

It'll take a few days to write about this night. I'll be back later...

AFTER THAT NIGHT at Jaxson's, things were good between the two of us. He'd occasionally chat with me at my locker before school started and we went surfing a few times. Miles was still being nice and even went surfing with us once, but he didn't ask me out again.

As far as I was concerned, I was ecstatic with the way things were. I had my friend back and I hadn't lost my new friend either. Heather looked like she wanted to kill me whenever we crossed paths, but I made sure to stay out of her way as much as I could.

I was doing homework one night and got up to stretch for a few minutes when I heard rocks at my window. I walked over and lifted the window.

"Come on up—what are you waiting for?" I called down.

"Permission," Jaxson said, grinning. He bounded up the tree and crawled inside, dusting off a few stray leaves. "I can't stay long. Charles is hounding me about my college choice and I have to go back and fight it out with him..." He waved off my concern. "It'll be fine. I'm okay working for him the rest of my life—I actually love it there—as long as I can go study music too."

I made a face. "Okay, hold your ground." We bumped fists.

"So, I have a question and you can totally say no, but I hope you'll say yes." His shyness was so out of character, I got nervous.

I tilted my head. "Okay?"

"Will you go to Homecoming with me?" He shifted from one foot to the other, antsy.

"Oh! I was not expecting that," I said.

"Are you going with someone else?"

"Uh, no."

He lifted his brows waiting for an answer.

"Yes! I'd love to go with you."

"Yeah?" He walked over to me and took my hand, then wrapped his other arm around me, hugging me tight. "Thanks, Bells. It'll be great."

I closed my eyes and completely floated into dreamland with his hug. He chuckled quietly into my hair and turned us around so that I was facing where he'd been before...the mirror. I cringed. He'd seen me bask in his hug.

I pulled away from him, my face on fire.

"Hey, come back here," he said. "That was feeling really nice to me too." He put his hands on my shoulders and leaned down, kissing the tip of my nose. Then he kissed my left cheek, and my right...and paused over my lips.

"Did you know, in a way, I've always idolized you,

Bells? Put you on a pedestal. You are..." He licked his lips and I could see his pulse in his neck. "My ideal. My dream girl. Someone I could never be good enough for, but when you look at me the way you do, I want to try to be. One day I hope to be someone worthy of you...if you'll even have me by then." He nuzzled his nose into my neck and I melted into him.

Is this really happening? But when I really thought about what he was saying, I pulled back, my hands resting on his chest. "You're worthy of whoever you want, Jaxson. I'm the same person I always was, even if circumstances have changed along the way, and so are you. You don't have to do anything to be good enough for me. You already are. Just as you are," I added, giggling.

"So very Darcy of you," he said, laughing.

We'd had to put up with our mums watching *Bridget Jones's Diary* at least five times one summer and that was just the first movie. For years, I could recite nearly every line. I hadn't hated it as much as I'd pretended to with Jaxson. Or at all really, but I'd take that to my grave.

He tugged me to him for another hug and sighed. "I just don't ever want to wreck this again with you."

"Then don't," I told him.

I TOLD my mum about Homecoming, and she was beside herself, but other than that, I didn't say a word. I didn't want people talking about it...I didn't want Heather to feel like we were rubbing it into her face when she couldn't even go. And maybe a small part of me was still pinching myself that it was even happening.

I found my dress with Liesl. It was the perfect mixture

of demure and sexy, with blue lacy appliques over a simple, nude A-line dress. My waist looked tiny in it—I kept turning sideways, in shock still that I even had a waist—and my boobs didn't look like I could topple over at any second. It was as if I'd finally grown into my body; everything had stretched out and found its rightful place.

"Teenage metabolism," my mum must have said with envy a hundred times over the past few months.

When the night finally came, Liesl did my hair in a low updo with loose braids tucked into artful swirls, and I had fun with my favorite Charlotte Tilbury eyeshadow palette and red lipstick. Mum flitted in and out, bringing hot tea and cookies and salad. I was too excited to eat, which was a first.

When we were done, I turned to face Mum and she gasped.

"I've never seen your eyes look so blue," Liesl said in awe. "You have to recreate this—you have found your look."

"It's a little much for school, don't you think?" I laughed.

"Never!"

Mum was still staring at me when the doorbell rang and she jumped out of her skin. She clutched her heart, laughing, and ran down to let Jaxson in.

It was like a dream when I walked down the stairs and Jaxson stared up at me, looking crushingly handsome in his suit. His waves were tamed and his eyes glistened like the water we used to snorkel in...he was devastating.

"I'm speechless," he said, his voice gravelly.

"You look...so handsome," I said quietly.

"You...take my breath away," he said. He chuckled somewhat awkwardly and then held up a pretty box. "I couldn't get the typical thing for you. Because you're not... typical. I hope you like it. It reminded me of you."

I opened the box, my fingers shaky, and inside was an antiqued champagne flower bracelet with a brooch in the middle, held together with two strands of pearls.

I looked at him, wide-eyed. "Jaxson!"

Pleased, he stepped forward and helped me put it on. "You like it?"

"I love it." I held out my arm, admiring the way it looked against my skin and my dress.

Anne had asked if we could take pictures at the beach behind their house, so we drove over there, Mum included, and as soon as we stepped out of the car, they had a picture fest. It was a bit uncomfortable just *how* excited they were. I didn't want them to scare Jaxson off; I still wasn't sure this was even a date. For all I knew, we were two friends going to a dance. But he put up with every picture—his arm around my waist, smiling down at me, standing with my back to his chest and both arms around me...we covered them all.

On the way to the school, we kept glancing at each other and smiling. One time he stared a little too long and shook his head, rubbing his hand over his face.

"It's hard to concentrate on driving or anything else when you look like that," he said. "Eyes on the road..."

I laughed, feeling a rush of butterflies take flight in my chest.

We'd spent so much time taking pictures that the dance was well underway when we got there. When we walked in, it felt like every eye in the room turned and stared at us. He laced his fingers through mine and we walked straight to the dance floor. It was a fast song, but he pulled my waist flushed to his, arms wrapping around me, and his forehead leaned on mine.

"I don't want this night to end," he said. "This is every dream I've ever had, right here, with you."

My heart galloped away from me and I drank him in, soaking up every word. "This is all I've ever wanted," I whispered. "You and me..."

His lips lowered to mine and it was the sweetest, softest, breath of a kiss. We swayed in time with the music and I pulled him in closer, kissing him harder. His breath caught in my mouth and I loved knowing I affected him that way.

And then I was yanked out of his arms and pushed back, forcing me to bump into the other couples dancing. Heather stood in front of Jaxson, shaking and enraged. I watched in slow motion as she slapped him and then ran out of the auditorium. Jaxson looked at me, stunned. When it switched to apologetic in the next second, it was like mud dousing all the butterflies. I staggered backward and he ran after Heather.

I felt a hand on my elbow and turned. Derek led me off of the dance floor and to the punch bowl. He handed me a glass and I took it from him, numb.

"She won't let go of him so easily," he said. A pained laugh burst out of him and he rubbed his mouth as if to shut it back inside. "Believe me, I've tried everything."

"You love her?" I asked.

He nodded. "Since third grade. But I'm not the one she wants."

"I'm sorry," I said softly.

I didn't like that he'd gone behind his best friend's back, but I understood him more than I had before. A little too well.

"You're a smart girl...beautiful...I'd be rooting for you to be with Jax so I could have a clear path to Heather, but I don't wish this feeling on anyone," he said. "You should run while you've got a chance." He ducked his head and walked away.

I looked around and didn't see any sign of Jaxson. I walked to the nearest table and sat down and then couldn't be still, so I stood up and fidgeted. The tones from all the dresses swished together like a watercolor. I don't know how long I stood there waiting for him to come back, but eventually, the floor cleared and people began to leave.

"Are you okay?"

I felt a hand on my shoulder and turned. Miles stood there, concerned.

"Do you have a date tonight?" I asked.

"N-no..." he said.

"Do you think you could take me home?"

We were quiet all the way home, and when we pulled up to my house, Miles stopped the car and turned to face me.

"I'm just going to say this. You look like an angel tonight." He put his hand on my cheek and moved closer. "I'm sorry you're sad," he said softly.

He looked so sincere and I was so grateful; when he closed the distance between us and kissed me, I didn't stop him.

30

PRESENT

When the bottom drops out, that's when the good fills in the spaces, sinking into every crevice until you can't remember there was ever a hole.
The good came just in time, Diary.
I need to remember that it always will...sometimes in its own time, but it will.

BEFORE I STEP inside the house, I chant out loud, "Be positive. Be positive. Be positive."

"Who are you tryin' to convince—me or you?" Dave asks, stepping around the corner of the house with the garbage cans rolling behind him.

I laugh, embarrassed. "Caught me."

"What's up?"

"Ah...it's been a long week," I tell him. "I don't want to talk about that, though! I want to hear what was so important that you called me on the *phone...*"

"I know—that ancient device that no one actually ever

talks on anymore." He parks the garbage cans and motions to the door. "Come on, let's go in. It's good to see you."

"You too."

Dave washes his hands and I sit at the kitchen table, waiting for him. Once he dries his hands, he holds up a finger and leaves the room. Really curious now, I nearly follow him out, but he's back before I stand up...holding a little black velvet box.

He sets it on the table and my eyes go wide.

"Is that what I think it is?" I ask.

He motions for me to take a look. I carefully open the box and inside is a stunning solitaire with an infinity platinum band.

"Stunning," I breathe.

I look up at him and he's nervous, waiting for me to say more.

"It's the prettiest ring I've ever seen."

He lowers his head and reaches over to take my hand. "I did this backward. I should've waited on the ring until after I'd asked your blessing, but...I saw that ring and just went for it!" He laughs and pats my hand and my eyes well up. "Hence the call!" His shoulders shake and I laugh too because I've never seen him so flustered.

"Mum will totally say yes, and of course, you have my blessing! You coming into our lives was the highlight of my senior year and every year since. It feels like we've loved you forever." I wipe the tears from my cheek and beam. "This will be the best wedding ever."

His eyes are misty as he looks at me. "Thank you, Mira. It means the world to me to know you're happy about this. You and Vanessa are a package deal and I love you so much. I hope you know that."

I lean across the table and hug him, crying into his neck. I cry so hard that eventually he pulls away.

"Hey, are you sure you're okay?" he asks, reaching for the box of tissues.

"I'm so happy about this. Really, I am." I hiccup and then laugh at myself. "You know, I've always thought I was pretty well-adjusted...not having a dad around and all that. I wonder if maybe I'm not so much..." I blow into the tissue. "I think I might have to deal with that pretty soon." I sigh. "But you..." My lip wobbles again. "You have never failed to make me feel valued and loved. Like a real dad should."

"Loving you and your mother are the easiest things I've ever done," he says.

I THINK about Dave's words all the way to the restaurant. I didn't want to infringe on their romantic dinner, but Dave insisted that I be a part of it, so I'm in the back seat half-listening to their conversation up front.

What if loving someone really is as easy as this?

I know it didn't come to my mum easily. She grieved over my dad for years, both while they were together and after he left. It certainly didn't come easily for my dad, who'd been able to walk away from us and never look back. Jaxson and I have skirted around each other for years, too afraid to love at the same time...out of sync. Miles—I don't know if he feels anything like love for me, but he has felt more for me than I feel for him since we met in high school. Why is it easy for some and not for others?

Charles and Anne are already at our table, no sign of Jaxson. I feel like I'm an outsider looking in—not because anyone leaves me out or makes me feel that way, but because I have a hard time shutting off all the thoughts. It's like I'm closing in on something important but haven't figured out what it is yet. I try to shake it for now, especially when I realize the moment is here. Dave is asking Mum to marry him.

She whimpers when she sees him get down on one knee and everyone in the restaurant turns to watch. She's shaking and saying, "Yes!" before he fully says the words. We all laugh and clap when he slides the ring on her finger and kisses her.

"Did all of you know this was happening tonight?" Mum says, wiping her tears with her napkin.

"No idea," Anne says, practically jumping out of her seat.

"Only Mira." Dave winks at me.

I reach across the table and put my hand on theirs. "I'm so happy."

JAXSON TEXTS before I get into bed.

Congratulations! I heard Dave is in for the long haul.

Me: It was pretty great—he got down on one knee and everything. I think we might have a wedding around Christmas.

No need to wait when you know what you want.

I set my phone on the nightstand. Everything Jaxson says lately feels like it has a double meaning, and I'm exhausted trying to keep up with him. I look at my phone and pick it back up.

Me: I'm afraid I won't be able to hang out this weekend. Mum wants me to go dress shopping with her. Between work and school, weekends are going to be insane until January.

Okay.

Can I watch Winston while you shop?

Me: That would be great actually.

What time can I pick him up?

Me: I'm leaving early, but he'll be okay here until you're ready to get him.

He types and the dots go away. That repeats for a few minutes.

Okay.

―――

MUM WANTS to have breakfast at The Cottage on Fay Avenue and lay out the plans for the day. Anne and Liesl show up at the house at seven thirty with Jaxson on their tails, looking very well-rested despite the hour.

He kisses Mum on each cheek, congratulating her, and then turns and does the same to me.

"You're looking lovely this morning, Bells," he says sweetly.

"As are you," I say with a little curtsy.

He lifts a brow and then scowls when Winston growls at him. "It's too early in the day for that," he says, laughing.

I hand Winston to him and my puppy looks betrayed. "I'll be home soon," I whisper in Winston's ear, kissing his face.

"I'm totally envying a dog right now...didn't know that was possible," Jaxson says.

The ladies laugh and I flush. I haven't seen him since we kissed and it's hard to look at him without thinking of that.

"All right, we better head out," I say in a singsong voice, backing away from Jaxson so I can breathe.

He holds Winston up to his face and they are a picture I will not be able to get out of my head. "We'll be waiting," he says.

———

LIESL PULLS out a wedding binder three inches thick at breakfast. She is not messing around. She's mapped out the order of the shops we need to try and even has pictures of dresses she thinks will be perfect on my mum.

"Did you just have this on hand or—?"

"I didn't sleep after she told me the news last night," Liesl beams, "and I had the notebook, so I just started filling it up."

"Impressive."

"Well, we don't have a lot of time." She looks at Mum. "Are you serious about a Christmas wedding?"

"If you think we can pull it off."

"You'll most likely have to wear either a sample gown or something ready-to-wear, but there are lovely options out there...especially at these places." She taps her finger on two of the shops.

"It's my second wedding and the next massive affair we have should be Mira's wedding."

They all look at me and smile and I yelp.

"I can't even keep a boyfriend!"

Anne and Mum exchange looks.

"What?" I ask.

"Oh, I just have a heartsick boy at my house, that's all." Anne laughs. "Don't worry," she holds her hand up when she sees my face fall, "I think it's good for him. Lord knows he put you through the wringer in high school. Just...don't make him wait *too* long, eh?"

WHEN WE GET HOME, Jaxson is in my room looking miserable. "He's hidden under the bed all day. I can't get him to come out. He hates me."

"He'll come around," I tell him.

When Winston hears my voice, he runs out and twirls madly around my feet. I bend down and he licks my face, beside himself with excitement.

I laugh and try to pet his wiggling body. Looking up at Jaxson, grinning, I pause when he looks heartbroken.

"Not a single thing has worked on our list. Are we cursed, Bells?"

31

PAST

2014

Have you ever wondered why some lips completely draw you in and other equally nice lips just don't have that same magnetic quality? I've wondered about it a lot, D.

MILES PULLED AWAY. "Did you feel anything?" He smiled.

I laughed and took his hand. "My heart did speed up," I tell him. "It was nice. I'm sorry I'm such a mess."

"Can't blame a guy for trying," he said.

"Thank you for saving the night."

"Anytime, Mira."

―――

IT WAS after midnight when he showed up and I was ready for him.

"Don't bother coming up," I called down from my window.

"Please, Bells, let me explain. *Please.*"

I groaned, angry with myself for always caving with him but unable to stop myself from lifting the window further and letting him in.

"I'm so sorry," was the first thing out of his mouth when he stepped in my bedroom. "I'm sorry I left—I came looking for you and you were gone."

I scowled at him and turned away. He stopped me with his hand and I looked at him over my shoulder.

"I waited a long time, Jaxson. You didn't come looking soon enough."

"Things have been over between Heather and me, but tonight I finished it for good. I think her pride was bruised, seeing me kiss you like that, but it's over, Mira. I felt like I at least owed her a conversation."

"That's fair. As far as owing me—you don't. I have no idea what we are." My voice rose and I clamped a hand over my mouth and then whispered, "But you asked me to go with you tonight and then abandoned me there. Miles brought me home. He's the one who kissed me good night. It's been a long night and I just want—"

"—*He* kissed you?" He was in my face in seconds, cheeks pink.

"No. You don't get to be jealous, Jaxson. Don't you dare."

His eyes softened and he looked at the floor. "Have I missed my chance with you, Bells? Is he who you want?"

"You want a chance with me? How would I know that? When we kissed before, you still went right back to Heather. Tonight you kissed me and ran after Heather. I don't think I'm the one you should be asking. What do *you* want, Jaxson?"

"I want *you*. I've always wanted you." He sat on my bed and put his head in his hands.

"What?"

His eyes were anguished when he looked up. "I thought I had time…and I just keep blowing it. I got distracted by other things, but I always knew you were the one I wanted to spend forever with." He stood up and put his hand on my arm, his thumb brushing circles across my skin. "We're still so young, you know? There have been times I've questioned if those things I felt as a kid in Holmes Chapel were for life, but every time I've seen your face, deep down, I've known. Even when we weren't talking and you wouldn't look at me in the halls at school, I hoped and prayed it was only a matter of time before we were together."

I swallowed the lump in my throat.

"My mum and Charles have put the fear of God in me about not sullying your reputation…or pressuring you to be with me before you're ready. And I won't," he rushed to add. "I swear I would never do that. Just please tell me I'm right and that you feel the same too."

"I don't know what to say," I whispered. "Shock," I added.

"I love you, Bells." He leaned his head on mine, his hand winding through my hair. "I've never said that to anyone but you…"

I touched his cheek and down his neck, sniffling. "I love you too."

"God, those are the best words I've ever heard you say," he whispered.

His lips landed on mine in a rush, crashing into me as if he wanted to crawl into my skin and live there. I felt completely his, from the top of my head to the tingling tips of my toes.

"You're not running this time?" I asked when he kissed along my jawline and planted small kisses around my mouth before consuming me again.

He hummed his answer.

I floated to the sky and didn't come back to Earth until he pulled away and stared at me, chest heaving. *What was that?* I stared at his lips in fascination, awed that they were capable of evoking such things in me.

"This has been the best, worst, best night," he said.

I smiled. "That describes it perfectly."

"This—kissing you, finally saying how I feel and hearing you say it back—it's a thousand times better than any time I've played it out in my head," he whispered, placing one more kiss on my nose.

I grinned, amazed that he'd been imagining the same things I had.

"I better go. Can I see you tomorrow?"

"Will things really be the same between us tomorrow? I'm afraid if you leave, it'll all go back to the way it was," I admitted.

He took both of my hands in his. "Things can't go backward. Okay? We won't let anyone or anything come between us, including you or me." He kissed both of my hands. "Deal?"

"Deal."

―――

THE SCHOOL WAS abuzz on Monday when Jaxson and I walked from the parking lot into the school, hand in hand. We'd spent the weekend in my room, kissing and watching movies, or kissing at the beach, or kissing in his room. It was my new favorite thing to do: kissing Jaxson.

I didn't see Heather, but her rhyming name posse covered the glares on her behalf. Giselle stared so hard I never saw her blink. Danielle's eyes were going to get stuck if she rolled them back any further. Raquel huffed and turned away like the sight of us was too disgusting for words...and then I saw Miles and the hurt in his eyes, and I felt terrible.

"I need to talk to Miles," I told Jaxson.

He squeezed my hand and let it go, nodding at Miles as he went to his locker.

"Hey," I said.

"Hey." Miles shut his locker and looked at me out of the corner of his eye.

"We...worked things out. He explained what happened and...it's good between us," I fumbled around with my words but eventually got it out.

He shifted his books around and spoke to them more than me. "I'm glad you got what you wanted."

"Thanks, Miles. I-I'm sorry."

"Please don't be sorry for being happy. If you're ever *not* happy, then you can think of me with regret." He grinned then and I knew we'd be okay.

WHEN I GOT HOME from school, Mum was home early and looked like she had a secret she was dying to spill.

"So...how are things going?" she said, kissing my cheek.

"Really good..." I looked at her suspiciously. "Oh! I forgot to tell you—that interview happened...a reporter came over and asked all about Tyra's Closet. They're doing an article for the paper and mentioning it on CBS or something..." I grinned. "So that's cool, right?"

"Wonderful. So...cool," she said. She looked at me and made a face. "Ugh, out with it already. What's going on with you and Jaxson? You've been floating around here for days, making googly eyes at one another, and haven't given me *any* details."

I smiled and ducked my head, looking at her under lowered lids.

"Oh my," she said. "Out with it."

"It's going really well," I said. "He told me he loves me!" I fell into the chair at the table, feeling faint just *thinking* about him saying it.

"And you're just now telling me this?" she yelled. She sat across from me. "Tell me everything and then we're going to the clinic."

"What? Why?" I frowned.

"To get you on the pill, dear girl. I love you and Jaxson, but I do not need grandbabies yet."

I flushed and got up, avoiding looking at her while I got water for us. "We're not having sex!"

"Not yet, but if he's telling you he loves you already, that's not far behind." She looked at me sternly. "Don't let him rush you."

I groaned but agreed to get on the pill, mainly to get her to stop talking. And then I told her everything—well, almost everything—leaving out the parts about Heather, and how he snuck into my window...so the bare minimum/best parts.

32

PAST

CHRISTMASTIME 2014

If you had eyes, you'd think I look different, Dear D. I'm sure of it. I'm in a constant swoony state. It would be embarrassing if I weren't so HAPPY.

I'D NEVER BEEN MORE grateful for my mum's pushiness. I'd been on the pill for nearly a month and things had been steadily heating up between Jaxson and me. Understatement. I *burned* for him. We were together every day after his basketball practice and he snuck through my window almost every night. Our parents were usually home by six and that left a window of time when we had the house to ourselves.

Today we were at his house and to his credit, he had gone excruciatingly slow with me...I was ready for him to speed things up already...

We were on his bed and he leaned over me, the lower half of his body safely on the bed instead of where I wanted him. His head fell between my breasts and he inhaled, as if intoxicated. He kissed the narrow valley, his tongue flicking the edge of my breasts and I groaned, arching into his mouth.

"You're killing every ounce of willpower I have left," he whispered, and the air on the places he'd licked chilled.

"I'm tired of willpower," I said, pulling him by the belt loops until he settled on top of me. My head fell back, eyes closed, as I enjoyed how delicious his weight felt on me. My hips lifted of their own will to find friction and I was momentarily satisfied when his breath caught and he pressed into me.

"Mira," he warned.

"More," I whispered.

"Are you sure?"

"I'm positive."

His hand reached out to rub my nipple over my shirt and I licked my lips, opening my eyes so I didn't miss anything. My V-neck was low but not quite low enough. He moved my shirt to the side and bit his lip when he saw the bra I was wearing. A sheer lace demi bra with an underwire that propped me up to my best advantage—I'd bought it recently, in hopes that he'd see it.

"Mira," he sighed reverently. "Is it okay to say out loud that your breasts are the most spectacular pieces of art I've ever seen?"

I giggled.

"Seriously though. God, Bells." He leaned down and kissed each one and then shifted the material of my bra to the side, his gaze questioning to see if it was okay. When he saw what he wanted, he leaned down and sucked on one side and then the other until I was squirming beneath him.

I loved the feel of his skin on mine and wished our clothes were gone so I could feel the rest of him. Just when I thought I'd go crazy if I didn't get *more*, he shifted slightly and lined up in the perfect spot on top of me.

"Mmm," I moaned.

His arms were tense as he stayed still for a moment.

When he thrust into me, I didn't care anymore that we were still fully clothed. My mouth fell open and I chased the feel of him until we were both panting hard.

"I don't want to hurt you," he said.

"You're not." I felt crazed. I would've done anything and everything right then, but he was determined to take his time.

He pulled away and unbuttoned the top of my jeans. Just enough to get his hand between my jeans and underwear. When his finger started circling over me, rubbing faster and faster in a spot that made me lose my mind—how did he do that?—my eyes rolled back in my head and I whimpered, my insides convulsing to his touch.

"Jaxson," I whispered, my head rolling side to side.

"Does that feel good?"

"So...good," I shuddered. "So good."

He leaned down and kissed my eyelids and then my mouth, claiming my lips as his fingers stilled over me.

I felt like I was in a stupor, but I pulled away when he seemed to be slowing down. "I want to make you feel good," I told him, reaching up to unbutton his pants.

"You do. I loved that," he said. He put his hand on top of mine, stopping me.

"I'm on the pill, you know."

His pupils dilated and he exhaled a ragged breath. "No, I didn't, but good to know." He grinned. "I thought I had semi-decent self-control. Watching you just now, I barely managed to keep it together," he said, laughing. "But damn, you're determined to kill me." He kissed me, three pecks; his full lips like velvety pillows. He nestled back on top of me and I was immediately back in a frenzy. "I've only ever used a condom and Coach has us get tested regularly for a variety of things, not just ST—...well, anyway, I'm clean," he said. "But there's no need to rush...I'm not going anywhere."

He closed his eyes, trying to stay still, but I felt every inch of him, hard and pulsing between us. I giggled and his eyes flew open. "Sorry. I just remembered overhearing your mum talk about how well-endowed you were as a baby. You were the talk of the hospital apparently."

He groaned but then burrowed his head in my neck and we laughed our heads off.

"Well, what do you think? You believe her?" he asked, trying to catch his breath.

"I'll have to see it to be sure," I said, wiping my eyes.

"Hello?" Anne called.

The sound of her walking up the stairs launched us into fast forward; Jaxson jumped off of me, and I flew across the room, heart in overdrive. I picked up my backpack and grabbed a notebook.

"Hey! In here," Jaxson said weakly, turning around in a circle and then reaching for a pillow to hide behind. He put a book on top of the pillow to look like he was studying.

I cackled in the corner and he glared at me just as his mother opened the door. She smiled at Jaxson and then saw me. She beamed and then her eyes narrowed on me and then back on Jaxson.

"Well..." she said, clearing her throat. "Good to see you both. Getting any homework done?" She bit the inside of her lip and looked like she was trying not to laugh.

"Oh...we're coming along," Jaxson said. He lifted his head and rolled his eyes. "I mean, you know...almost done. Getting there."

"Very well," she said. "Maybe you should work at the dining room table where you can spread everything out." She gave a pointed look to Jaxson and he nodded.

"Sure."

When she closed the door behind her, I leaned over, clutching my stomach. "You are so obvious! *Coming along?*" When I looked up at him, I started laughing again. He looked mortified.

"Me?" He pointed at me. "Take a look in the mirror."

"What?" I stood up and made my way to the mirror. "*No,*" I said in horror.

He snorted and came to stand behind me, his arms circling around my waist. "Oh yes. Yes, yes, *yes,*" he mimicked the way I had sounded not even ten minutes ago and my cheeks heated.

I tried to smooth my hair down, but for not actually having had sex, I had the most perfect sex hair *ever.*

ON CHRISTMAS EVE, or maybe actually the wee hours of Christmas, Jaxson sneaked into my bedroom and crawled into bed with me, as he did most nights. We'd been steadily skating around the boundaries he seemed to have set. We'd done a lot in my inexperienced opinion, but to my growing agitation, we were always clothed from the waist down. He still made me feel so good every time he touched me and I thought I made him feel good too, but I was losing my mind. Being with him was all I thought about. And the suspense of there still being *more*...I was ready. More than ready.

I hadn't pushed it, but this time when he crawled into bed with me, I had a surprise for him. I was completely naked.

He stiffened when he wrapped his arms around me. My

laugh tinkled in the room, sounding loud in the stillness.

"What is this?" He nestled his nose in my neck, and I felt his smile on my skin.

"Merry Christmas," I whispered, turning to face him.

"Best Christmas present I've ever been given," he whispered, his fingers sliding down my chest and getting distracted there.

"Thank you for giving me time," I put my hands in his hair and kissed him, "but I don't want to wait anymore."

"Are you sure? I promise you I'm happy—"

I put my fingers to his lips and nodded. The night-light in my room was there for his sake so he could find his way to me in the dark each night. I was glad of the light now—there was just enough glow to see his smile and the contours of his body as he pulled the back of his shirt over his head. My hands roamed across his chest as he took his pants off and then pulled the covers back, letting the light shine across my body.

The way his eyes appraised my body emboldened me. He drank me in and I felt heated from the inside.

"If this is a dream, don't wake me up," he said. "You're so beautiful...so perfect in every way."

His eyes scanned me up and down one more time before he reached out and touched my bare skin; that alone made me lightheaded. I pulled his briefs down and finally put my hands on his velvety skin.

"Your mother was right."

I heard his quick intake of breath and smiled.

"I don't want to talk about my mother. Never. Just no. Not another word about her tonight."

I giggled.

"I wish we didn't have to be so quiet," he whispered. "I want to hear every little sound you make..." He leaned down and kissed a trail down my stomach. "I want to make you scream my name..."

My entire body flushed with his words. He went lower and lower with his kisses, doing things with his tongue and his fingers that I'd never imagined, and I lit up like a never-ending sparkler.

By the time he lifted his head and crawled up my body, I was limp with pleasure. Sated. Nothing could be better than what he'd just given me. But he settled his body on top of mine and when I felt him between my legs, I woke up, every part of me coming back to life.

"I'm nervous," he whispered.

"I'm not," I told him. And it was the truth. I trusted him. I loved him. How many could say that about their first time?

He entered me slowly and I was still so wet from before that it felt tight, but a good kind of tight. When it got a little uncomfortable, he stayed still and whispered, "Kiss me." He kissed me like he'd never kissed me before. I couldn't stand to stay still another second. He kissed me until I thought our bodies melded into one and I could feel every thought and desire he had. The deeper our kiss went, the deeper he delved inside...until he was all the way in and this was really happening.

When he pulled back and dipped back in, sliding more easily in and out of me, he put his hands on my cheeks and looked into my eyes.

"I love you," he whispered.

"I love you."

Something changed with our words; a sudden urgency. He slipped his fingers between us, touching me, and I sank into bliss. He swallowed my sounds with his kiss and I did the same for him when he lost control seconds later. It was the most complete I'd ever felt.

33

PRESENT
DECEMBER 2019

I think maybe I need to go live with the nuns and only eat small portions of meat and potatoes...maybe a Popsicle every now and then.
Somewhere shaded and quiet and drama/risk-free.
Sincerely, Sister Hart

WITH THE WEDDING planning taking every spare moment between school and work, I've hardly seen Jaxson. Oh, and I've been avoiding him. So there's that.

I've had a plan cooking in my mind for over a month now, and despite my mum and Dave and Liesl trying to talk me out of it, they've settled into supporting my decision. For now, anyway. The wedding has been the perfect distraction.

The week of the wedding, I'm off for winter break and just getting home from running an errand for Mum. I'm not even out of the car yet, when the hair on the back of my neck rises. Jaxson. I sigh. *Will I always be this connected to him? It has to go away eventually, right?*

I've felt his hurt emanating from every text and every phone call, but he's accepted all the excuses I've fed him. He looks pissed now though. I shut my car door and lift a hand to wave.

"How much longer can you avoid me?" he says, stalking toward me.

"I've been busy," I tell him.

"I could be helping you with wedding shit...or with Winston...why are you cutting me off?"

I walk toward the house and he follows me, opening the door and holding it for me while I set the bags down. Winston comes flying down the stairs to greet me and growls when he sees Jaxson.

"Yeah, I don't really like you very much right now either," Jaxson tells him.

I open the back door for Winston to go out, and Jaxson and I stand on the deck watching him run around the yard.

"Give me thirty minutes? There's this new pie place I've been wanting to try," Jaxson says, his brows relaxing as he tries to smile.

I feel guilty about the way I've avoided him, so I nod. "Okay."

"Really?" He perks up. "Okay."

Ten minutes later, we're in Jaxson's car. It's a short drive, so he's parking before our silence becomes too awkward.

The pies look delicious and the restaurant is bustling with customers. We sit in a corner booth and study the menu.

"I haven't had peanut butter in a while," I tell him. "And only in *very* small doses...like one night months and *months* ago."

"Who are you?" he asks.

"I know. I have to fit into a goddess dress for this wedding, so I can't believe I agreed to this. Look at this pie." I point to a chocolate peanut butter pie and hum. "Yep, that's what I'm getting."

He orders a slice of Dutch apple pie and we wait, looking shyly at one another.

"Thanks for coming with me. You'll be fine in the dress, I promise."

I lift my eyebrows. "To God's ears, as your nana would say."

He smiles. "To God's ears."

Our pie comes and they're both works of art. I'm tempted to take a picture but don't want to be that girl. Not when Jaxson is watching me so intently.

We both take bites of our pie and sound orgasmic as we inhale them. He tries a bite of mine and I try a bite of his.

"Oh, yeah, you always order better than I do," he says. "And I'm scared to even say it, but…finally, we can sort of check it off of our list…I mean, if we eat it every day starting today." He grins. He points at what's left of mine. "That's going to be my new craving."

I can hardly get the pie in my mouth fast enough. It's the perfect explosion of flavors.

"I don't even care if I don't fit into the dress after this," I say, scratching my neck. "This was such a good idea. Thank you. I'm glad you made me come." I laugh and he does too, the air between us lighter with our sugar highs.

"So is everything pretty much ready for the wedding?" he asks.

"Yeah, the hard part is done, and the fun starts the day after tomorrow. We're doing a spa day at the salon, the day after that the rehearsal dinner, and then the wedding!" I rub at my neck and scratch my arm.

His eyes widen when he looks at my neck. "Mira, are you okay? You're...really..." He grabs my hand and holds my arm out. "What's going on?"

I have little welts all over my skin. "Is this on my neck too?" I lift my shirt a little and look at my stomach. Hives are covering my skin.

"We should get you to the hospital. *Are you allergic to peanut butter?* How can that happen?" He sounds panicked and is already standing up and throwing money on the table.

By the time we pull into the hospital parking lot and Jaxson leaves the car with the valet, every part of my body itches. I'm swollen and miserable. My eyes are starting to feel weird and my mouth...

We go to the desk to check in and one of the nurses—Nan—takes me to an exam room right away, with Jaxson on our heels answering all the questions I don't respond to fast enough. I clutch my chest.

"It feels tight," I whisper.

Dr. Nigel comes into the room, looks at my chart, and goes on a tangent about a shot. I don't really register her words. The grief on Jaxson's face distracts me.

"I'm okay," I tell him. "Don't worry."

He looks so sad I can't stand it. Nan gives me an epinephrine shot and I can breathe a little easier, but the hives don't go away. A while later, she gives me another shot and I feel more of an improvement with that one, but she still sets me up with an IV and runs antihistamines through it. Jaxson scoots up to the bed when Nan leaves the room to let Dr. Nigel know about my progress. He holds my hand, careful to only touch my palm and not the top of my hand that still has welts.

"Are you feeling any different?" he asks.

"It's easing," I say as Nan walks in. "I'm breathing better. Less itchy. But sleepy."

"I should let your mum know—she'll kill me that I haven't already told her," he says.

"We're going to monitor you for a few more hours," Nan says. "If we don't see more improvement, we'll keep you overnight."

I nod, too sleepy to protest. *I don't have time to be in the hospital* goes through my mind right before I fall asleep.

I WAKE up a few hours later. Jaxson is still sitting there and my mum is beside him.

"Oh, honey, are you okay?" Mum asks, hovering.

"I feel much better."

"You look much better," Jaxson says. "God, you scared me to death."

"I'm fine. See? Good as new." I hold up my arm and although there's still a scattering of hives, there are far less.

He looks at my mother. "She didn't see herself," he says. He opens his phone and shows me a picture. My face is unrecognizable.

I gasp. "Do I still look like that?" I clutch my face, looking at my mum. "The wedding!"

"We are not going to worry about the wedding," Mum says. "The swelling has gone down considerably, but if you don't feel up to it on Saturday, we'll push it back. No big deal."

"Uh, no way. We have worked too hard on this wedding for it to be thwarted by a little allergic reaction."

"You could've died, Bells," Jaxson says.

"No..." I scoff at him. "It wasn't *that*—"

"Yes, you could've," he interrupts. "They gave you another shot while you were sleeping and are waiting for a room upstairs to open up to monitor you throughout the night."

I groan. "I can't miss our spa day!" I look tearfully at Mum, whose eyes are full too.

"I'm just so grateful Jaxson got you to the hospital on time," she says, putting her arm around him and squeezing. "Thank you, love."

She's never called me "love" a day in my life, but she bestows it on him like she's always said it. I restrain the eye roll and look on, smiling...because I'm grateful too that he acted so quickly. If it had been up to me, I'd have gone home and wondered why I couldn't breathe very well...

"We'll bring the spa to you if we have to," she says to me.

I DO STAY THE NIGHT, but I feel a thousand times better the next day. I think it was a waste of time, but I guess I was in worse shape than I realized when I came in. I feel bad for putting a damper on the wedding festivities.

I'm expecting my mother to pick me up and then I'm hoping we'll go straight to the salon, but Jaxson is the one who walks in while the new nurse on duty is walking me through my release papers. He listens intently to her instructions.

"You'll have to carry this everywhere." She holds up an Epipen. "A reaction like yours...you'll have to *stay away* from peanuts from now on. If you feel any tingling or get the beginnings of the hives like you had this time, use this and then come into the ER right away. Okay?"

"But I love peanut butter so much," I lament.

"So many do, but it doesn't love them back," she says briskly.

She's a size nothing, so I have a feeling she's never loved peanut butter and doesn't know what she's missing. It's a bitter thought, but one that I'm feeling with all my heart...*no peanut butter?*

"What could happen if she doesn't have the Epipen or doesn't do it in time?" he asks.

The nurse shrugs. "She could die," she says to him. "It's very imperative that you and everyone in your life take this seriously." She points to me and starts gathering her things to leave.

Well, thank you for your charming bedside manner. I don't speak because I'm afraid of what will come out.

Jaxson glares after her and takes me by the hand. "I've been researching this all night. We can figure out places to go...I've got a list of things you wouldn't think of that have peanuts...all that. It's going to be okay."

His face is flushed as the words rush out of his mouth. *God, I love him. Whoa. Hold up. No. Rewind.*

"Did you even sleep?" I ask, looking everywhere but directly at him.

"No, but I can sleep when I'm dead, right?"

"I hate that saying."

"I'm surprised you don't hate me at this point," he says quietly.

I turn to him. "What? Why?"

He reaches out and smooths the crease between my brows and swallows hard before answering. "I don't know, Mira. I think it's safe to say that I need to put the list to rest once and for all. Maybe you're right. Maybe we should only be friends. I don't want to put you at risk for any more disasters..." He attempts a smile, but it's more of a grimace.

A lump grows in my throat and I nod, attempting a smile myself. It hurts way more than a smile should. "Friends."

34

PAST

BEGINNING OF MAY 2015

Just when I think I have a few things figured out, everything comes crashing down, Diary.
Is it me? Don't answer that.

"NO, DON'T GO." Jaxson's arms were wrapped around my waist, pulling my back to his chest.

I groaned but had to laugh when he nuzzled into my neck. "Stop! It's already so hard to leave you."

"So don't leave. Don't you think our parents have guessed by now that we're sleeping together? Your mum got you on the pill...mine keeps stressing the importance of safety ad nauseam. Let's have a little talk with them." He rolled on top of me and I sighed.

I never got tired of this.

He kissed me and we got distracted for another twenty minutes before I tried to leave again.

"We are not talking to our parents. Can you imagine

how painful that would be?" I put on my clothes and walked over to grab my backpack.

"But I'll be away at school soon. I don't want to miss out on any time with you."

I looked up. "You're serious?"

He nodded then bit his lip. "I need to talk to you about something else. I got us a hotel for the night of your prom... can you work that out with your mum?" He grinned but looked nervous.

"I'll figure it out." I smiled, walking over to sit by him on the bed. Junior Prom was two weeks away and Senior Prom was the upcoming weekend...four days away. I had two gorgeous dresses hanging in my closet.

"About my prom. Uh, Heather reminded me yesterday that I promised her we'd go to that together..."

I waited for him to finish his sentence because he couldn't possibly be leaving it at that. I was barely okay with them still being friends but hadn't argued the point. He made me feel secure every time we were together.

When he didn't say anything, I lifted my hand, motioning for him to finish. "And?"

"And I think maybe I should at least go pick her up, get pictures with her. Uh...her parents still think...I mean, you know...it made her stepdad leave her alone more thinking that I was still in the picture," he finishes, threading his fingers through mine. "You and I can still be together the rest of the night. I have a hotel booked for us then too..."

My eyes narrowed on him. "Are you serious right now?"

"Derek will be with us most of the time...it's just a few hours and to make things go easier for her at home."

I pulled away from him and stood up. "Cancel the hotel for both nights. We won't be needing that." I hooked my backpack over my arm and walked to the door.

"Bells, wait. Stop. Let's talk about this," he said, getting up. His naked body nearly distracted me into pausing, but I rushed out of the door and down the stairs, not stopping no matter how loud he yelled for me to come back.

I didn't go home right away, but Mum said he'd left a note for me to call on the door when she got home. I also locked my window and ignored all of his attempts to get my attention. Maybe I was being a hothead, but I knew if I said anything to him at all, it'd be irate and I needed to cool down first. If I ever could.

THE NEXT DAY AT SCHOOL, Derek was waiting for me at my locker. Jaxson was nowhere in sight.

"I heard you're not going to prom with Jaxson."

"You heard right."

He leaned against my locker and smiled. "Would you go with me? You can keep an eye on your boy and he can be miserable watching us dance together..."

"That sounds like the worst idea you've ever had and you've had plenty of bad ones."

"I want to go to my Senior Prom with someone I'm friends with...not these dimwits hanging on me all the time."

"You sound like Jaxson's nana." I smiled despite wanting to kick something.

"Yeah, she's mentioned the dimwits a dozen times or two when I'm around." He laughed. "We've always gotten along well, right? I like to think so anyway." He looked sincere when he said that and I softened.

"I suppose I shouldn't waste my dress," I said.

He rolled his eyes. "If that's what it takes to convince

you..." He tapped my locker. "Thanks, Mira. It'll be fun. I promise."

I didn't see Jaxson until the end of the day. He was waiting at my car and holding a bouquet of flowers. I moved past him and opened the door.

"I worked it out with Heather. I'm going by there the night before...take a few pictures then and you and I can have our night...I never wanted to be with anyone but you that night anyway."

I held my hand up. "I'm going with Derek Saturday night."

His nose crinkled in disbelief. "What? Why? Has Heather been right all along? Do you really have a thing for Derek?"

I wanted to punch him in his cute little crinkled nose. "You're making me so angry right now. I don't know what Heather has led you to believe about Derek, but it's all in her head or something she's made up to make me look bad with you. He's my friend. So you and Heather can do your little fake date and keep up the façade. I had no idea you were still pretending to be her boyfriend. What else are you 'pretending' to do with her?"

His eyes widened and he set the flowers on the hood of my car, moving closer to me. "Nothing. I swear it, Bells. I have not touched her since before you and I got together."

"Why should I believe that when you're doing such a good job lying to her parents?" I tried to step further from him, but he caged me in with his hands against the car.

"Do you remember her parents? It's not hard. And I've been with you every spare minute of every day...when would I have time to be with her?"

"Well, you'll have time this Saturday night. Let me go, please. I have to go to work."

"Bells." He grabbed hold of my face and leaned his head against mine. "Let me in tonight. Please."

"I'm on my period and I'll be too tired after work to hang out," I told him.

"We can just sleep," he said.

I shook my head and got in the car when I saw an opening. Before I shut the door, I said, "You and I aren't going to agree on this, so I think it would be best if you do your thing the next few days and I do mine. I don't want to say anything hateful, and I will if I have to talk to you. You're only a senior once; you have the right to spend your prom however you want to. I'm disappointed it won't be with me, but you made your choice."

"But I did choose you," he said, tugging on his hair.

I shook my head, closing the door and driving away from him. I didn't look at him again until right before I turned to leave the parking lot. He was standing in the same spot I'd left him, head bowed, and holding the flowers that must have fallen off of the car when I took off.

MUM HAD a million questions about why I was crying, why Derek was taking me to his prom, where was Jaxson... she tried to demand that I talk to her, but when I wouldn't, she came into my room and shut the door behind her.

Before she could say anything, I held up my hand. "I have to get ready and I really don't want to cry anymore. I just need to get through this night and then we can talk, okay? Please?"

She reluctantly sat on the edge of my bed and nodded, her lip between her teeth. "All right, honey. I'm just sorry you're hurting. It's a helpless feeling not knowing how to make things better."

I patted her hand and turned back around to my mirror. I had my work cut out for me to get rid of the dark circles under my eyes.

———

DEREK and I arrived at the venue about twenty minutes after it started. Both of our mothers had been at the house clicking their cameras like we were celebrities. It was strange doing all of this with Derek when it should've been Jaxson. The pictures would probably give away how vacant I felt, but I tried to plaster on a smile whenever Derek looked at me.

"You look so good, Mira," Derek said for the millionth time.

I was glad that had at least worked on my behalf. My dress deserved good hair and makeup, so I'd tried my best. I wore a pale pink, low-cut flowy gown that sparkled in every light. I'd fallen in love with it and had been so excited for Jaxson to see me in it. Now I just wanted the night to be over.

"Thanks," I told him.

"I'm going to the restroom and then we'll dance, yeah?" he asked.

"Wash your hands."

"Hardy-har," he groaned, but he was smiling as he walked away.

I decided to use the restroom while he was gone and walked down the long hallway. I got a little turned around, so it took longer than I intended. When I came out of the restroom and had turned the corner into another alcove before the hall, Derek fell into step next to me.

He put his hand on my arm and stopped me. "Mira, can I tell you something before we go back inside?"

I looked up at him and he put his hands on my shoulders.

"It really means a lot that you came with me tonight. I know we've had our differences at times, but I've always thought you were the most beautiful girl in the school...and decent, you know?"

I smiled and narrowed my eyes at him. "Have you started drinking already? I thought that started later."

He smirked and shrugged. "Maybe..."

He lowered his head then and his lips were on mine before I could really register what was happening. I was pushing him away when I heard a hiss and looked over to see Heather standing there, looking like she was about to explode.

"It's not enough that you have Jaxson believing you are Little Miss Perfect, but now you have to have Derek too? What is it about you? *I don't get it!*" she yelled. Then she turned to Derek. "And you, all those things you said..." She shook her head and for a second I thought she was about to cry. "I can't believe I fell for it."

I looked between the two of them and the way they were staring each other down. I couldn't believe I'd missed it all this time.

"First of all, I stopped this before it ever fully happened. I don't know *what* you were thinking." I leveled Derek with my rage and he had the decency to look embarrassed. "But the two of you—you've never stopped, have you? Unbelievable." I shook my head, turning and walked away.

I heard Derek calling me. I ignored him, and Heather

nearly knocked me over, sprinting past me. I felt sick to my stomach and went back to the banquet hall to get my things. I needed to figure out a way to get out of there. I walked toward the table that had my wrap and saw Heather talking to Jaxson. The color left his face and he looked around wildly, his shoulders falling when he found me. He stalked toward me, Heather trailing him, and I stood there bracing myself.

"It's time I tell you something," I started when he got within reach. "I should've told you long before now, but I never wanted to hurt you—"

"You were kissing Derek?" he interrupted. "How long has this been going on?"

My mouth opened and I glanced at Heather in time to see her smirk. I stepped forward and put my hands on Jaxson's chest. He backed away and my hands fell to my sides.

"I don't know what Derek thought he was doing just now, but I stopped it. Derek and Heather have been together for a long time...since before the two of you even slept together."

The shock on Jaxson's face shifted as he looked from me to Heather and then behind me to Derek. His chest was rising and falling fast as he tried to grasp what was going on.

"I heard them...at that Christmas party...having sex—"

It was as if I heard it before I felt it...the sound of liquid rushing toward me. And then red punch all over my head, down my face, over the front of my gown. I sputtered and stepped back, trying to hold onto something solid. I backed into Derek and he steadied me. The music kept playing, but all the chatter came to a stop as everyone stopped and watched us.

Jaxson lowered his head and held his hand to his forehead. "Someone tell me what is *happening* right now?" He looked up, his eyes pained as they searched mine.

Heather dropped the pitcher of punch and put her hand on his arm. "She's lying! You know she's lying."

"Derek?" Jaxson said.

"I've *never* slept with Heather," Derek said.

I didn't stick around to hear more lies. If Jaxson believed a word out of their mouths over mine, he deserved the misery.

35

PRESENT
DECEMBER 2019

Too many changes at one time usually make me itchy, but hopefully this time, I'm heading in the right direction...everything UP from here. Please, please, DD, God, the universe, Jesus, and all of the good angels, please make it so.

CHRISTMAS ALWAYS MAKES me think of Tyra and Jaxson. I think he did that on purpose, forcing us to wait until Christmas to have sex for the first time so I'll always think of him on this holiday. Fortunately, now Dave and Mum's wedding will provide new memories too, with it being on Christmas Eve. Still, even as I stand here, proud of how beautiful everything looks and fully in the moment, Jaxson is always part of my thoughts.

I catch myself crying more than once during the ceremony. Jaxson's eyes on me heat my skin, making me feel like I have nowhere to hide. An arch laden down with cream and red flowers surrounds the bride and groom and each row of chairs has a matching bouquet at the aisle. Mum is beaming and looks like a dream by the backdrop of flowers and her true love. I pull the tissue out of my bouquet and dab my eyes once more when I see how Dave looks at her.

And then it's official. They kiss, we cheer, and after taking pictures until we're antsy, we move into the reception area where the guests have already been celebrating.

Jaxson and his band have set up to play later and he's placing his guitar on the stand when I walk in. He looks up as if he knows I've come into the room. He smiles and makes his way over to me.

"Just when I think you can't get any more beautiful," he says, leaning over to kiss me on the cheek.

My heart flutters with his words and the proximity of him, and I try not to sound breathy as I thank him.

"You were right," he says, smiling. "Goddess dress." He tilts his head and lets his eyes linger over my skin. "And you are filling it to goddess perfection."

I flush and duck my head, biting the inside of my cheek. When I meet his eyes again, I whisper, "Thank you."

"How are you feeling?"

"Still fine. Very few hives left." I smile. "I'm excited to hear you guys play."

"I'm only bummed I won't get to dance with you," he says.

"Ah...we're doomed for dances, right?" I try to sound lighthearted, but the pain that flashes over his eyes makes me regret my words. *No, I don't regret it*, I tell myself. I need to hold onto some of the residual anger from our past in order to follow through with my plan.

With it being my mum's day, I didn't even try to talk her out of Jaxson sitting at our table. Anne and Charles are there too, and Liesl and her girlfriend Sarah, so as we sit down, I'm hopeful that they can help be a distraction.

"You still haven't told him?" Liesl says under her breath when she sits next to me.

I turn to see if he's heard her, but he's on the other side of me, taking a sip of the ice water.

"No," I say firmly and give her my fiercest look.

Her brow lifts and she shakes her head. "I hope you know what you're doing," she mouths.

I try to enjoy my meal but just pick at it. My meal had to be prepared differently than everyone else's and it's bland. It'll take time to adjust. Hopefully my new way of eating won't be as daunting as it feels now. Jaxson is supposed to eat quickly so he can be onstage when Mum is ready to start the dancing. I look down and realize he's eating the same thing I am.

"Why did you get this meal? The others look so much better," I say.

He grins like he has a secret and tilts his head. "Maybe I was hoping for a kiss."

I just stare at him and then shake my head. "Jaxson, you need to give this up. Okay? I'm just not there right now."

"Does that mean you think you will be eventually?" He leans closer to me and I nearly sink into his neck and take a long sniff. He smells so good and I know his arms would wrap me up and hold me tight.

I turn away from him...into a safer proximity. "I think you should move on."

"Why don't I believe you?" he asks, his breath on my ear making me shiver.

"Jaxson, I believe it's time for you to start playing," Anne says.

We both look at her and she smiles apologetically.

"This conversation isn't over," he says, kissing my cheek and heading to the stage.

———

THE BAND SINGS a mixture of covers and songs Jaxson has written. He's in his element when he's lost in the song, eyes closed; the emotion in his vocals is devastating in all the right ways. I can't believe he's so good.

I dance with Dave and Charles and then end up dancing near Liesl, Sarah, and Maddie the rest of the night. Gemma comes and dances with us when she's not with her boyfriend. We laugh maniacally at Charles' awful dance moves, and I watch Jaxson in all of the other moments, grateful that I get this time to stare at him without him noticing every embarrassing second.

When he sings the line: *I can't believe I let you walk away*...I stop dancing and stare at him. His eyes are wide open now and he sings the next words to me.

I didn't know you meant forever
We spent a lifetime chasing firefly dreams
Now it seems you have forgotten

BLUE-EYED SHADOW
   Black-haired beauty
   Remember me
   Come home

LIESL CLUTCHES MY ARM MID-CHORUS. "This song is about you, isn't it?"

"Mm-hmm," Maddie answers. "It sure is. And he is screwing you so hard in his mind right now," she adds.

"Maddie!" I smack her arm and look around to make sure Gemma or Anne aren't close enough to hear. Fortunately, they're both across the room.

"Well, he is." She laughs. "I think you should make it a reality tonight." Her eyes widen and she flutters her eyelashes, while I groan. "Give him something to remember you by," she says, her face falling. "There's time, right?" She puts her head on my shoulder. "Are you sure about this?" she asks.

"I'm sure," I tell her. *I am. I think I am. I hope I am.*

I STAY FOR ANOTHER HOUR, dancing until my feet hurt. Right before I go, during one of Jaxson's epic guitar solos, I go up to the stage and yell, "This is what you need to be doing for the rest of your life, Jaxson Marshall!"

He looks surprised and then happier than I've ever seen him. The light radiates off of his face as he sings his heart out.

I back away, content.

I find Dave and Mum and hug them both at the same time.

"We'll call you when we get to Hawaii. And you call us too, okay? We need to know you're safe," Mum says.

"I will. I'll be safe," I tell her. "Have the best time. Take tons of pictures."

Dave kisses my cheek and steps back. "Love you, Mira. Thank you for making this such a special day for us."

"You are worth it," I say, grasping his hand.

Mum hugs me tighter then, her eyes filling. "I love you, Mira. I just want you to be okay. You'll let me know, right?"

"I love you, and I'll be okay, I promise."

She nods and Dave hands her his handkerchief. She dabs her eyes and takes a shaky breath.

I look at Jaxson one more time and walk out into the crisp December air. An Uber is waiting for me.

"The airport, huh?" the driver says. "Where you headed?"

"Home."

36

PAST

2015

Sometimes it doesn't change a thing to be right.

WHEN I GOT HOME EARLIER than expected, I wasn't surprised to find an empty house. Mum and Anne were probably hanging out, drinking wine, and lamenting over the fact that their kids couldn't seem to get it together. Wherever she was, it was a relief that she didn't have to see me in that state; my ruined dress and equally ruined heart would devastate her.

I put my dress in a garbage bag and got in the shower, crying as I scrubbed the red food dye off of my skin. What Heather had done was inexcusable, but I couldn't say it surprised me that she was capable of that...or that Derek had lied to Jaxson—they'd been doing that for years, why did I think they'd come clean now? But Jaxson...his distrust and the way he'd believed them over me...I didn't know if I'd ever get over that, not to mention the fact that he didn't jump to my defense when she ruined my dress and embarrassed me in front of everyone. It felt like middle school all over again, only much worse since I'd shared my heart and my body with him.

I crawled into bed before midnight, unable to get Jaxson's look of rage out of my mind, and cried myself to sleep. I was in the middle of a dream when the window opening startled me and I sat up, turning on the light. The clock said 2:14 a.m. and Jaxson was crawling in my window.

He stumbled into the room, bumping into my lamp and righting it with exaggerated slowness that I'd only seen on drunk people. I'd never seen him drunk though. One word out of his mouth and I knew he was.

"Spill," he said, flinging his arm out.

"What?"

"Spill! What made you feel like you had to lie to me about Heather and Derek? Haven't I—"

I got up on my knees and held my hand out. "Stop right there. You can't honestly believe I'm lying...why do you think she tried to keep me from talking? They've both been lying to you for years. I'd hoped it ended a long time ago, but tonight confirmed that I was wrong."

He stepped closer and my hand dropped to my side. "*She* was wrong to humiliate you like that. I told her so."

I rolled my eyes. "Too little, too late."

He nodded like he agreed and sat down on the bed, tossing his phone next to us as he took my hand. "I don't want to fight with you. Derek and Heather—they're my friends—but you're the one I love," he slurred. "More than anything." He lowered his head and shook it and when he looked at me again, my heart fell.

"Jaxson, what—?"

"I'm just sorry. That's all," he said. "None of this

would've happened if we'd gone together tonight, the way we were supposed to."

His phone beeped and I looked down.

Heather's face and boobs popped up on the screen, and if that wasn't enough, the text she left...

Still coming over tonight?

I saw red.

I held the phone up to him and his face lost all color. His eyes were despondent when he finally looked at me. Ashamed.

"What did you do?" I asked, my voice as dead as I felt inside.

He put his hand on my cheek and I shook it off.

"I came over here instead," he said.

"But you almost went to her."

"I almost went to her," he repeated after me, nodding. He stood up and paced in front of my bed. "You kissed Derek tonight. I've been so pissed at you!" he yelled.

"Keep your voice down!" I hissed. "For the last time, I did not kiss Derek. He tried to kiss me and I stopped him. When have I ever lied to you? I am not the one in the wrong here! And if you thinking I kissed him could make you turn around and think about sleeping with Heather so soon, we're nothing."

"That's not true. We are not nothing." His words were still slurring and it made him sound ridiculous.

"Get out," I told him. "And don't come back. Go be with Heather. I'm tired of watching you walk away from me."

"I don't want her-Heather," he stuttered. "I wa—"

"Get out," I whispered, which seemed to shout louder than a tantrum.

He heard me and deflated. "We'll talk in the morning. I love you, Mira."

I shook my head. "I won't want to talk in the morning either."

"This whole night was just a big misunderstanding," he said, going to my window. "You'll see."

———

I BEGAN LOCKING MY WINDOW.

My mum was furious when she found out what had happened and gave Jaxson a piece of her mind when he came over, begging to talk to me. She wanted to demand that Heather pay for my dress, but I told her how awful her stepdad was and that I didn't want to cause trouble for her, in spite of how she'd treated me.

"That girl is good," Mum said. "She can act like the devil and everyone still walks on eggshells around her! I'm not even sure I believe she's got it so bad at home. There have been so many lies that point back to her lying tongue."

I remembered how her stepdad had made my skin crawl and wasn't so sure, but I knew she had wrecked my life one too many times and I wasn't going to watch her do it again.

I ended up not going to my own prom, the tradition forever ruined for me. Jaxson came over that night and I leaned out of the window instead of ignoring him.

"Please let me come up," he said.

"Do you still believe I'm lying about Derek and Heather?" I asked.

"They swear up and down they've never slept together." He gave the trunk of the tree a slight kick. "I've asked around. No one has seen them together but you. If I say I believe you, will you let me come up and let us fix this?" He looked up and put his hands together, like he was pleading.

"No, don't bother," I told him, shutting my window.

I WAS TEMPTED to go see him the night before he left for Boston. Mum even tried to make me go to the get-together Anne and Charles were throwing for him.

"He feels really bad about the way everything ended," Mum said. "I don't think he'll be home until winter break..."

"I just can't, Mum. It's too painful. And if I have to see Heather gloating around him, I'll die."

"Anne mentioned she hasn't seen her or Derek much lately at all...specifically Heather."

"You go. Tell him I wish him a very successful first year of college. He can go sleep with all the girls and get me all the way out of his system..."

"Mirabelle!" she said, horrified.

I shrugged. "This is why I can't go. I'll be hateful and ruin the night."

She put her arm around me. "I'm so sorry, honey. I can stay home with you."

"No, go. I'm going to take a bath and go to bed early."

"If you're sure. There are leftovers in the fridge. Eat something. You're getting too thin."

I DIDN'T HEAR from Jaxson once he left for college... maybe he was mad that I hadn't come to his party, or maybe he'd finally given up. I was actually glad I didn't have to constantly wonder if I was going to run into him at the beach or the grocery store...or crawling in through my window. But then late on Halloween night, he called.

I don't know why I picked up—chalk it up to a lonely week with too much homework and nowhere I wanted to be on Halloween. I was already in bed and it wasn't even midnight.

I said hello and then waited.

There was a long pause and he finally said, "Mira? Is this really you?"

It sounded like he was in a crowded room, maybe a party. I heard people yelling in the background and the sickening sound of girls laughing nearby. I clutched my stomach, feeling a sharp pain, and I pulled the blankets up to my chin.

"Yeah. It's me."

"I'm drunk," he said. He laughed and I didn't know if the people in the background were laughing at him or something else.

"I hope you're being smart," I said. "And safe. You are, right?"

"I never drink and drive and I'm practicing safe sex, yes, thank you for reminding me, *Mirabelle*." He laughed again.

The tears were instant. "Okay, good to know. Bye, Jaxson."

"Wait, Bells, I-I'm sorry. I shouldn't have said that..."

But I hung up before he could drive the knife in further.

———

IT WAS on a Saturday in December...Mum and I were Christmas shopping. She had been seeing this guy, Dave, for a few weeks and already liked him so much. I'd met him and had to admit, he seemed pretty great. She didn't know whether she should buy him a present or if it was too soon.

"What if you get him something and if he gives *you* something, you'll have it ready just in case?" I suggest.

"What if he gets me something fabulous like jewelry and I've bought him a mug?"

We giggled over that and weren't paying attention when we went down the wrong aisle and ended up in the baby section of Nordstrom.

"Well, I hope you're not trying to tell me something," I said and we laughed harder.

The girl in front of us turned around to see who was making all the commotion and Mum and I stopped in our tracks.

It was Heather, hair dirty and not dyed platinum blond like it had been all through high school. But what stood out the most was that she was hugely pregnant.

She stared at me and then waddled away as fast as she could.

Mum clutched my arm and looked at me. I shook and her hands steadied me.

"Do you think—?" I whispered.

"No, no. Can't be his." She shook her head, but I could see the concern in her eyes. "She would've been flinging it in your face before now if that were the case."

A few torturous days after that, I knew Jaxson was in town when I got home from work and there was a note from him on the front door.

I'm so sorry. You were right. And I've been the worst kind of asshole.

Anne told Mum later that Derek had finally admitted Heather was having his baby and that he'd been sleeping with Heather off and on since they were fifteen.

"But she always wanted Jaxson," Mum said. "Derek told Jaxson he thought she'd wanted to sleep with Jaxson once more at prom to make him think it was his. Sounds like Derek is finally done with her too, but he's going to make sure he's a good dad."

I tried to work up the energy to care, but it was too late to even feel justified. I knew Jaxson must be hurt and that was unfortunate, but I didn't feel the need to go tell him I forgave him when I didn't know if I ever could, and he didn't feel the need to try to talk to me the rest of the time he was home.

I heard from him every birthday, either a text or a voice mail, but other than that, he was silent. It's hard to believe, but it was years before I saw him again.

37

PRESENT

SEPT 2020

I'm touching up on my British ways. It's like putting on a familiar sweater and putting my hands in the pockets to find a favorite smooth stone from the beach.
It's part of me.

LIFE IN HOLMES CHAPEL is quieter than I remembered, but I love it. I feel grounded in a way I haven't since living here as a girl. I miss California...with everything in me. It still feels like home too, but I needed to step away and figure out who I really want to be.

I completed my year at the university nearby and it feels great to be done. I used my dad's address to qualify for home student fees. Things with my dad haven't changed overnight and still aren't perfect, but he was happy to pretend I lived with him...only wishing I would make it legit. He's different now. Humbled. Kinder. I've been getting to know him again, and day by day, I feel the bitterness slowly leaving my system. But no, I won't be moving into his house. That would be taking it too far. I'm enjoying my freedom too much.

I work at a small salon in town and for the last three months I've been doing makeup for weddings. I miss having Liesl with me at every wedding, but it's been good practice to do it on my own.

Winston and I live in a cute little first-floor, one-bedroom corner flat. It's nothing fancy, and I don't have much to fill it up, but I like the simplicity of only having the bare necessities. What I'm lacking in furniture, I'm making up for with plants. My first month after moving here, I was homesick and depressed over how dreary everything was in the winter, so I bought a plant, and it turns out I have a way with them. When Mum and Dave came to visit me in the spring, they were shocked and maybe somewhat worried. We FaceTime every other day and I think Mum is finally relaxing over the fact that her baby is across the globe.

I haven't heard from Jaxson. At all.

The guilt eats away at me some days—that I left without saying goodbye, that I didn't try to give us a fair chance—but most of the time, I attempt to put him out of my mind and just *be*. I didn't know how much healing I needed to do until I had this time of quiet, but also time with my dad...it's been eye-opening. A conversation during a lunch date with Dad a few days ago sort of knocked me over the head, and I'm beginning to realize why it's been so important for me to be here.

"I talked to your mum the other day," he said.

"I didn't know you and Mum talk," I looked at him, shocked.

"Since you've been here, we have," he said. "And, uh, she wanted to know if I thought you were still running from your feelings for Jaxson. I told her you haven't said a word about that boy. I didn't know he was still in the picture."

"I don't want to talk about him with you, Dad."

"Well, why not?" he demanded, his bushy eyebrows distracting me.

"I'm sure you'll make me feel ridiculous for being upset over the things he's done...and well, maybe I left before he could leave me. I'm always the one who gets left, you know? You left. Jaxson left. Tyra left. Jaxson left again. I don't think my heart is up to being abandoned another time."

Dad ran a hand over his beard and looked distraught. "Mirabelle...I'm sorry for what I've done to you and your mum. The hurt I've caused by not being a part of your life...I don't deserve your love, I really don't. But Jaxson...well, I don't know what he's done to you, but your mum seems to believe he's a good person and that he's in love with you." He stopped and let that sink in, and when he seemed assured I'd heard him, he continued. "Don't put my sins on his head. If that's what you've been doing, you're hurting yourself and him too...and you're missing out on something lasting."

I've been thinking about it for days. Shocked that it took my dad to help me see the truth. Wondering if I've been a fool.

I'm pretty sure I have been.

———

TWO WEEKS PASS and I feel like I'm coming down with something. I feel sluggish, no energy whatsoever. I can't pinpoint any certain thing that feels *terrible* necessarily; I just don't feel *right*. Dad keeps checking on me and says I have a case of the mopes.

"Or maybe it's lovesickness?" He wiggles his eyebrows, but to my utter humiliation, I burst into tears.

He tries to get me to talk, but I can't. It's like the distance between Jaxson and me has suddenly caught up with my heart and my brain isn't overriding it anymore. I miss him with a desolation and longing that feels like a starvation that is never fed. My entire body hurts with the missing.

Once Saturday hits, I shower and then get back into my pajamas, letting my hair air dry while Winston and I play fetch. Winston goes flying after the ball, picks it up with his teeth, and then drops it, growling at the door.

"What is it, boy? I didn't hear anything…"

He runs to the sound, still growling, so I stumble over him to get to the peephole and open the door to show him that no one is there. But he sniffs something and when I lean down, I see a CD in a slim, clear case with no writing on it.

I poke my head out further but don't see anyone.

"Creepy, but you were right. I'm glad we've got your ears," I tell Winston, scratching his neck.

I grab my laptop—the only thing I have that will play a CD—and I pop it in.

I recognize the sound of the band immediately and when I hear Jaxson's voice, my throat constricts. I put my face in my hands and weep when I hear the words.

WE SAID *we would do it all,*
With a list and promises
We said time would not conquer us…
We'd always be the two of us,
Knowing and known,
And always home
To each other

. . .

WE TRAVELED FAR *and wide*
   And sometimes pride got in the way
   Even when I lost myself,
   You gave me another chance
   I wish I could go back again,
   Tell the kid to man up then.
   (I'd give anything to go back again)

IT WAS THERE ALL *the time,*
   A love so pure, and so alive,
   Went to hell and still survived
   5,331 Miles

I GRAB a sweater before the song has finished playing and rush out of my flat, Winston's ears flapping as he runs next to me. I open the door to my building and Jaxson is there in the parking lot, leaning against a car.

He doesn't smile when he sees me. He looks like a tragic figure, devastatingly handsome and stoic; he puts his hands in his pockets and watches me get closer and closer.

When I've almost reached him, the car next to him starts and I gasp. It's my dad. He smirks and gives me a brisk wave before backing up, not waiting around to see what happens.

I stop when my feet bump into Jaxson's. He reaches out and wipes a tear from my cheek.

"Jaxson." It comes out as a sob, and I lean my head onto his chest.

His arms circle around me, making me instantly feel better. *Home.* One of his hands moves to my hair and he gives it a soft tug, forcing me to look up at him.

"I don't care where we are. I just want to be where you are," he says. "Do you believe me yet? And does it matter?"

Tears fall down both of my cheeks and his thumbs catch them. "It matters," I tell him. "It means everything."

"You say the word and I will move heaven and earth to be with you. Nothing will come between us."

And this time, for maybe the first time since my tenth birthday, I believe him.

"I'm done running," I say.

His mouth crashes into mine, claiming what I've held back from him for so long.

"Come inside," I whisper against his lips.

———

WE BARELY MAKE it inside my flat before I'm climbing him like a tree. He lifts me the rest of the way, wrapping my legs around his waist and propping me against the back of the door, kissing me hard.

"I love you," he whispers against my lips when we come up for air.

He moves down the hall and into my room, tossing me on the bed like I weigh nothing. I grin when he pulls my pajama pants down.

"Still feeling Christmas-y, huh?" he teases, throwing my reindeer pants behind his shoulder.

I tug on his shirt and lift it over his head. "Later, I will be embarrassed about how awful I looked when you saw me again for the first time in so long, but right now, let's get naked."

"You could never look awful, but I agree...we should get naked." His teeth look stark white against his skin and he is out of his pants in seconds flat.

I reach up and pull his boxer briefs down, eyes widening at the sight of him.

He groans, leaning over me. "You're making me crazy, looking at me like that. Let me see you." He pulls my shirt over my head and pulls his lower lip between his teeth when he sees I'm not wearing a bra. "I can't believe this is happening," he says, leaning down to take my nipple between his teeth. "Definitely feels real..." He tugs it back, looking at me when he does and I arch into him. "Oh, I can't wait," he whispers.

He moves his fingers between my legs and works his way in and out of me, the sound of my excitement making me flush. I close my eyes and when he pulls his fingers out, just as I'm about to lose it, I moan. He drives into me, filling me with one long push, and I pulse around him, throwing my head back and crying out his name.

He looks beautiful and tormented, a fine sheen of sweat on his forehead, but he thrusts into me with a singular focus, starting an agonizing pace where he pulls out and then hits every nerve ending when he drags himself back in.

I can't think straight. It feels like heaven. "Faster," I cry.

He goes faster and faster, until I feel like I might pass out, it's so good. Just when I think I can't take another second of hanging over the edge, we both explode and the feeling eclipses all rational thought.

While he's still inside of me, both of us still feeling the gentle waves of our connection, I realize that if I want it—this all-encompassing love for the rest of my life—all I have to do is take the leap and let the miles of hurt and bitterness and pain dissolve once and for all. This feeling of utter fullness, being filled up by him in every possible way, can be mine if I will only let him in.

38

PRESENT

JULY 2021

Can we really have it all? What do you think, DD? I think I'm going to do my best to find out. I'm sure we'll even have some surprises along the way.
XO, Mira

THE PAST TEN months have flown by.

Jaxson and his band have created quite the stir in England; their indie single of "5,331 Miles" is being played on every college radio station and it's gotten the attention of a reputable label in L.A. Charles has finally accepted that besides me, music is what makes Jaxson happiest, and if things don't soar with a music career, he always has a place in Charles' company.

Tonight we've been talking about buying airline tickets to finally return to California for good, but Jaxson distracts me by pulling me into bed. He isn't happy unless I yell his name at least twice in the heat of the moment, and this time he goes for three.

"What's gotten into you?" I laugh when he collapses next to me, both of us panting hard.

"Maybe we should give it another try..." he says, rolling over to face me.

"Give what another try?"

"The list. I've been thinking...we were trying to do all of those things when we weren't together." He leans in and kisses me until I'm ready to crawl on top of him and see if we can go for round four or five. "Maybe that's why it never worked."

"Hmm. I don't know. I'm a little scared to see what else could go wrong."

He reaches over to pet Winston and smiles. "I think we've gotten through the worst, don't you? Even Winston has finally warmed up to me. How about we give Paris another try?"

I smile and kiss him back...and end up crawling on top of him before we buy the tickets to Paris.

When the day comes and we're finally on the plane, I smile again thinking of that night. We're about to land in Paris and I've gotten over my jitters. I'll miss that little flat in Holmes Chapel, but I'm ready for whatever adventure is next.

Liesl has been after me to come home and help her with all the celebrity weddings she's been working. I've flown back to do a few of them with her and the potential is huge.

Winston is sleeping in a soft carrier under the seat in front of me and Jaxson has been a bit preoccupied on the flight. Neither of us are great flyers after our emergency landing. I usually take something to knock me out and would have this time if the flight weren't so short.

"Are you sure you're okay?" I ask for the second time in an hour.

He leans over until his nose touches mine. "I'm great."

That's all he says and I decide to believe him and let it go.

I always breathe much easier when I'm on the ground and Jaxson does too, his earlier pensiveness dissolving once we land. We check into Hôtel de Crillon, one of the few hotels in Paris to allow dogs, and I think the staff might treat Winston even better than us. After we get him settled into the room, we go sightseeing and stop at two different cafes, getting wine and fresh bread and cheeses at both. It's so good and we eat so much, we don't really need dinner after that. We're buzzed and slightly giddy when we fall into bed that night, and with the starry night twinkling into our room, we worship each other until the sun comes up.

"Today was perfect...I think it's safe to say the curse has lifted," Jaxson whispers, kissing me one more time before we fall asleep.

ON OUR LAST DAY, we sleep in, order room service, and take Winston for a walk. After he's worn out, we take him back to the hotel and go to the Eiffel Tower. It is beautiful, day or night, and from every angle. We ride the lift on the way up and it's worth waiting with the crowd to experience it.

When we get off the lift and see the panoramic view, Jaxson turns to me and kisses me, our hair whipping around in the breeze. I'm so overwhelmed that we're here and together and happy.

"It's better than I expected," I whisper. "This view. You and me. My heart...you make my heart pound like this every day," I tell him, placing his hand over my racing heart.

Jaxson gets choked up, and I tease him as we walk the 704 steps down the Eiffel Tower.

"Paris suits you," I tell him. "I like sentimental Jaxson."

He smirks but doesn't say anything. He still looks like he might cry.

We go back to the hotel to shower and change for dinner. We haven't dressed up the whole trip, and I'm a little surprised to see Jaxson in a suit when I step out of the bathroom in only my underwear but full hair and makeup done.

"Oh, look at you," I say, grinning. "Do we really need to go anywhere? Let's just stay here and look at you in your suit."

"Had I known that's all it took to make you happy…" He laughs.

I pull a short red cocktail dress out of my suitcase and wave it in front of him. His mouth drops like I knew it would.

"I did bring a little something you might like. We'll see." I shrug.

"Here, let me just take this from you for a moment," he says, taking the dress and carefully draping it across a chair. "Bend over," he says, giving my back a little nudge and then dipping his fingers inside me. "I'll see if I can ruin you without letting a hair go out of place." He pulls a curl. "Although I do love it messy."

"You better not," I threaten, but I don't mean it. I don't care what he does, I just want him to keep on doing it.

AFTER A DELICIOUS MEAL at La Fontaine de Mars, the sun is just beginning to fade and as we walk near the

Eiffel Tower, the sky turns the most beautiful ombre, starting with blue at the top and fading into shades of pink. I turn in a circle, admiring the colorful sky juxtaposed with the Tower. When I turn back around to face Jaxson, he's down on one knee, holding a box.

"I want to make your heart pound out of your chest for the rest of your life," he says, looking up at me, eyes glistening with the light of the Tower and unshed tears. "You are my forever. You always will be. I knew it as a kid, and I know it more than ever as a man. Will you marry me, Bells?"

He opens the box and I gasp, tears rushing to my eyes.

"You're really doing this?" I whisper.

He nods, grinning up at me. "I want to wake up and fall asleep next to you...and do nothing and everything with you for the rest of my life. How would you feel about that?"

I get down on my knees in front of him, whispering, "Yes, yes...yes. You are everything I will always want." I kiss him and can't tell whose tears I feel the most, but I put his hand on my palpitating heart and nod. "Yes."

He slides the ring on my finger and it's then that I look at it for the first time.

"I thought it looked like royalty. Like you," he says.

I stand up, unable to sit still any longer, and he follows, looking concerned.

"We can get something else if it's not you," he says.

I sniffle and then lean my head over on his chest and bawl. "I'm just so happy!" I cry.

He laughs. "Me too. Bells? Don't be mad, but look up and say, 'I love Jaxson.'"

I lift my head and a cameraman is clicking away, his long lens out even though he's very close to us.

"Has he been here the whole time?" I ask.

"Yeah," Jaxson says, biting his lip. "I knew our mums would never forgive me if I didn't make sure it was captured on camera."

I start laughing and can't stop. We get up and run, stopping to kiss and smile for the camera. It's easy to forget he's there; we're too caught up in the moment to mind an audience.

THE NIGHT BEFORE THE WEDDING, the wine is flowing and we're eating a delicious meal at The Marine Room. Overlooking the water is a glorious sunset and my stomach hasn't stopped buzzing all week. I can't believe I'm marrying Jaxson. It still feels surreal.

Our parents are having a little too much fun sharing stories about us. Anne leans in and looks at my mum, who seems to know what Anne is thinking because she cackles.

"I do miss the footage of Jaxson sneaking into her room every night though," Anne says, and our mums wheeze they laugh so hard.

I clutch Jaxson's hand. "*No*. What footage?"

"You really thought we didn't know?" Mum says. "Remember the year that awful thing happened with the spray paint...Charles put cameras in?"

Charles and Dave both grin like we're the only ones out of the loop.

"You all watched?" I put my head in my hands, my face crimson. "How could I forget?"

"I only heard about it," Dave says, like that makes everything better. "Good stuff."

"The times Jaxson ran out still pulling up his pants when he heard me coming," Mum says and they start another fit of laughter. "I had the timing down to a science." She wipes her eyes. "Oh lord. We had such fun with that. It made for the best weekly viewing," she barely gets out.

"Oh, you guys are just...too...much," I say with a straight face, but it's all over when I look at Jaxson.

"I told you they knew," he says, as his laugh bursts out. "And speaking of the cameras, did you ever find out who did the spray paint?"

"Ugh. I always knew who did that, but it's ancient history...and not going to be part of this night," I tell him, kissing his cheek.

"Tomorrow night will be even better when you're my wife," he says, kissing the top of my hand.

Our mums sigh and he shakes his head, smiling. "They're going to be psychotic if we ever have kids."

I laugh and dig into my cheesecake.

WE GET MARRIED on the beach behind Jaxson's house. Our mums haven't stopped smiling since we came home. When we told them we were engaged, they wailed and laughed and then got straight to planning the wedding. We've had to keep pulling the reins along the way, but once they realized we really wanted something intimate, they dove into that plan wholeheartedly. The only people watching us say "I do" are our parents, stepdads, Gemma, Nana, Maddie, Liesl, and the guys from the band. Winston is also right there, sitting at my feet and looking remarkably calm.

As I say my vows, I get choked up midway through. "I vow to love you even when you're not so fun...which seems impossible because you make even the most mundane thing in the world seem exciting and brand new. Even nearly crashing in a plane...not that I want to try that again, but everything with you is an experience. I'm ready to try the dolphins again. I'm ready to try all of it with you...maybe not peanut butter but everything else. Specifically number eleven..."

Jaxson chuckles and just as quickly sobers, seeing the serious expression on my face. Mum had our list printed on cute cardstock for bookmarks as a wedding favor, so everyone else will eventually know what I mean if they don't already.

"Wait a minute. Are you saying—?" he asks.

I nod and his head falls back when he laughs. He dips me back and kisses me hard while everyone applauds.

The minister clears his throat and Jaxson reluctantly sets me upright again so we can be pronounced as husband and wife.

We've always excelled at doing things out of order.

The End

Read a FREE BONUS novella—*Miles Ahead*—
about Miles!
https://dl.bookfunnel.com/6dxeoohpc3

ACKNOWLEDGMENTS

I started 5,331 Miles back in 2015 and posted the first four chapters on Wattpad...then moved on to other books. I eventually continued writing for my newsletter and I'm so glad I did. Your input was so fun! Thanks to all of you who asked me to go back to this book. I should've done it sooner because I had so much fun writing it! And update...after I published it and had to start saying it out loud more, I realized how hard 5,331 Miles was to say every time. Ha. *Miles Apart* is what it should have been all along.

Thank you, Christine Estevez, who has hashed EVERYTHING out with me more hours than I can count. This story is better, thanks to you! I'm better, thanks to you. Thank you for the edits, for the shoulder to lean on...I'm so grateful for you.

Thank you, Erica Russikoff, for your eye in looking over this book! I love hearing your thoughts and value every chance I get to work with you.

Thank you, Darla Williams, for your exceptional beta skills. The timeline would be a mess without you. I thought of you every time I typed "Dear D"...

Which leads me to The Vault—thanks, Darla and Priscilla Perez, for being the Vault where I can just be ME. I love y'all. We know.

Thank you, Blade, for my beautiful cover. You're my favorite.

Thank you, Christine Bowden, for being my always

encourager. You make me cry on the regular with your incredible love and kindness. I can't believe we live a world apart and I still feel like you're right here with me always. I love you so.

Thank you to my beloveds: Tosha Khoury, Ashleigh Still, and Courtney Nuness... TAWC. You are my rocks and I'm so glad we're in each other's lives. There's more love than I can say.

Thank you, Staci Frenes. I wish we lived close enough to go to lunch AT LEAST once a week. Love you so much.

Thank you, Dawnita Kiefer, for never giving up on this story.

Thank you, Steve and Jill Erickson, for the steady, loving presence you are in our family. I love you both dearly. And thank you for selling my books at Spoils of Wear!

Thank you, Tarryn Fisher—for so many things—but when it comes to books, thank you for believing in my work from day one. It's an honor to write books with you and it's an honor to call you my family. I love you.

To my dad. I still get hives when I think of you reading my books, you little sneaky critter! I love you so much.

Thank you to the rest of my family and friends who pour into my life with love and prayers and kindness. Grace Place, I'm grateful in particular for you. Savita Naik, I love you. Kell Donaldson, so much love for you. I could go on and on. Claire Contreras...our voxes are life. Sidney Parker, love you. Maria Milano, that goes for you too.

To Nate, Greyley, and Indigo, my everythings. Thank you for cheering me on, even when it means far-off eyes and a spacey wife and mama. You're the best part of me. I love you.

Thank you to the Asters. You have a special place in my heart, always.

A very special thank you to Winston...#SirWinstonofInver...the only true part of this story. You have made my life a thousand times better. Thanks to Underdog Rescue for getting him and so many others out of these horrific puppy mills.

Thank you, Nina Grinstead, for giving this book a new and improved life. So happy to have you in my life!

Thank you, Laura Pavlov and Catherine Cowles, for being my constants. Love you!

Last but certainly not least, thank you to all of the bloggers who signed up to read this book and all those who didn't but have read my work in the past. I'm so grateful for every review and for all your help! And thank you to every author who has been warm and welcoming...for those of you who have been on my podcast, Living in the Pages, or who have shared cover reveals and thoughts about my books—so grateful for every one of you!

XO,
Willow

ABOUT THE AUTHOR

Willow Aster is a USA Today Bestselling author and lover of anything book-related. She lives in St. Paul, MN with her husband, kids, rescue dog, and grandcat.

For ARCs, please join my master list: https://bit.ly/3CMKz5y

For behind-the-scenes of my books and freebies every month, sign up for my newsletter: http://www.willowaster.com/newsletter

www.willowaster.com

ALSO BY WILLOW ASTER

Standalones
True Love Story

Fade to Red

In the Fields

Maybe Maby (also available on all retailer sites)

Lilith (also available on all retailer sites)

Miles Apart (also available on all retailer sites)

Falling in Eden

Standalones with Interconnected Characters
Summertime

Autumn Nights

Landmark Mountain Series
Unforgettable

Someday

Irresistible

Falling

Stay

Kingdoms of Sin Series
Downfall

Exposed

Ruin

Pride

The End of Men Series with Tarryn Fisher

Folsom

Jackal

The G.D. Taylors Series with Laura Pavlov

Wanted Wed or Alive

The Bold and the Bullheaded

Another Motherfaker

Don't Cry Over Spilled MILF

Friends with Benefactors

FOLLOW ME

JOIN MY MASTER LIST...
https://bit.ly/3CMKz5y

Website willowaster.com
Newsletter willowaster.com
Facebook @willowasterauthor
Instagram @willowaster
Amazon @willowaster
Bookbub @willow-aster
TikTok @willowaster1
Goodreads @willow_aster
Asters group @Astersgroup
Pinterest@willowaster

Printed in Dunstable, United Kingdom